Romeo Blue

by **PHOEBE STONE**

SCHOLASTIC INC.

For Ethan with boundless love.

Arthur A. Levine Books hardcover edition designed by Whitney Lyle, published by Arthur A. Levine Books, an imprint of Scholastic Inc., June 2013.

This book is a work of fiction. Names, characters, places, and incidents are either the product of the author's imagination or are used fictitiously, and any resemblance to actual persons, living or dead, business establishments, events, or locales is entirely coincidental.

ISBN 978-0-545-44361-6

12 11 10 9 8 7 6 5 4 3 2 1   15 16 17 18 19 20/0

Printed in the U.S.A. 40
First printing 2015

Book design by Whitney Lyle

Every effort has been made to locate the copyright owners of previously published materials: "Lily Marlene"; "Stormy Weather" by Ethel Waters

Derek and I were heading towards an old house with a dark granite facade, tucked among a group of pine trees on a knoll above the ocean. As we got nearer, the house looked a bit like a large, angry cat sitting up at the top of the ridge, not wanting to be disturbed. There was something straightaway about that house I recognized, as if I had seen it before. But I hadn't. It was the first time I had been here.

"Derek, wait. You're going too fast," I called out. He was the long-legged quick one and I was still smaller and younger by a year. I was quite anxious to catch up actually, but I didn't suppose I ever would. No matter how hard I tried, I would always be a year younger than Derek.

He seemed a bit moody today, but I rather liked moody. It could be quite dashing when hovering over someone like Derek. I would have followed Derek to the edge of the world, if he had wanted me to. And then perhaps we would have had to hold hands because it must be quite windy at the edge of the world.

At the top of the path, we came to the front of the shuttered-up, unwelcoming house. We stopped at the door and Derek pulled the cord that rang a bell. There was a tilting marble statue of an angel near the path, but then the wind came along in a fierce way and knocked the angel over, right in front of our eyes. It soon lay in the wet autumn leaves and rain, staring up at the clouds.

Derek pulled the cord again and through the glass I could see a blurry shadow coming towards us. The door opened. "Oh, Derek," Mr. Fitzwilliam kind of shouted out into the rainy wind. "Hang on to your hats. The wind will steal them if it can. If it can, it will steal your scarves. I've seen scarves carried away in the wind to who knows where. . . . Aha, I see my angel has fallen over again. No bother. I'll get it later. Come in quickly. You must be Flissy B. Bathburn?"

"Yes, most of the time," I said, "though I used to be Felicity, actually."

"Well, either way, do come in and hang on to everything," Mr. Fitzwilliam said in a growling, shouting, windy kind of way. "I have lost too many hats to who knows where."

We stepped into the dark, gloomy hallway. I started writing a letter in my head to Winnie and Danny immediately. I was always writing to my mum and to my dad, but they never answered me because they were missing or lost somewhere in Europe. I couldn't mail any of my letters to them because I didn't know where they were.

Dear Winnie and Danny,
    Today we've come to see Mr. Fitzwilliam. He's helping Derek with something. Derek hasn't told

me what. Mr. Fitzwilliam's house could use a bit of
freshening up. He has statues in his hallway.
   Love,
   Your Fliss

We went down that very long hallway with all those brooding statues staring off towards the darkness. We finally came out into the drawing room and there was a fire going in a great black marble fireplace, one of those kind that look rather like a big, glowing mouth that could easily swallow you up. But I was relieved to see it, as I was quite chilled from our walk along the coast.

"Please do sit down," Mr. Fitzwilliam said. "Feel free to look around. You know this house was designed by a famous architect in the last century." He watched us both carefully as he spoke. "Yes, the day he died, the design for this house was sitting on his desk. But unfortunately for all, someone broke in and stole the papers the moment he died. Was the architect murdered? Why would someone steal plans for a house? Those questions were never answered. However, after things settled down, the plans showed up at auction and my grandfather was able to purchase them and he built this house. I guess I'm a bad grandson, after all the trouble he went to, I am thinking of selling the place. Would you care for some tea?"

"Lovely high ceilings," I said. "If you were very tall, you'd feel quite comfortable in here." It sounded as if I *wasn't* comfortable in the house, which I hadn't meant to say. But to be quite honest, I did feel a bit uneasy. Perhaps it was the sad story of the poor architect who died or was murdered. Or the way Mr. Fitzwilliam kept an eye on me as if I were a hat that was about to get blown away to who knows where.

We sat at a little table and Mr. Fitzwilliam brought out a pot of tea, saying, "Oh well, I heard you were English and that you'd been dropped off, so to speak, by your parents to stay with your American grandmother up the road. Oh, and I know how the British like their tea!" He poured the tea and I stirred in some sugar. He seemed to have a whole sugar bowl of it. We hardly ever saw that much sugar these days because it was rationed now.

"Oh yes, I know all about you. Derek's told me. He talks about you quite a lot, actually. But I don't suppose he's told you anything about me. Has he?" He was trying to smile but he had a naturally glowering kind of face that didn't take on a smile very well. When he did manage one, it was a bit craggy and fierce looking.

"Have you told me anything about Mr. Fitzwilliam, Derek?" I said, scrunching up my nose, trying to think. "Did you, and I forgot?"

"Well, no matter," said Mr. Fitzwilliam. "The truth is, I've been helping old Derek here. Helping him with something important. He's trying to locate someone."

"What sort of a someone?" I said, taking a careful bite of a smooshy chocolate biscuit.

"Fliss," said Derek, "Mr. Fitzwilliam has been trying to help me locate, um, my father. My real father."

I felt a bit tippy for a moment, as if the floor were slanting downhill suddenly. "Oh, Derek, shouldn't you ask first at home? It might upset everyone," I said.

"Really? I don't see any reason for a foster boy not to search for his real father. And that's just what we're working on, isn't it, Derek? It takes time. We're doing our best, Flissy. Am I right about your nickname?" said Mr. Fitzwilliam, frowning at his housekeeper, who stood suddenly in the doorway. He shook his head at her quietly. She was staring at me. I think she was deaf, because Mr. Fitzwilliam used sign language to tell her something. Then she quickly turned and left the room.

Perhaps it was because the wind picked up from the south suddenly and started rattling and battling against the far windows, making great washes of rain stream all over the glass, but I began to feel just a bit more uneasy. One of my feet was ever so cold and the other one was quite toasty, and whenever that happened, it meant I was feeling nervous about something.

Mr. Fitzwilliam sat back and eyed me. "So your mother is away, I hear."

"Yes," I said. "Far away."

"But where?" said Mr. Fitzwilliam. "Have you any notion about it at all?"

"Not at all," I said, looking down.

"I find myself fascinated by your mother. What's her name?"

"Winnie," I said.

"Yes, I'm fascinated by Winnie. I understand she is very beautiful and yet I'm curious about someone who could leave her child on the coast of Maine and go back into the war in Europe, and for what reason?"

"Well, I couldn't say, really. I think she went back because she loves roses and she wanted to be in London when they bloom," I said. Then I rolled my eyes round the room, wondering how my answer had fared. Had it fallen on its face or had it slipped along unnoticed?

"Ah, of course. I should have thought of that. Roses, yes. Well, I hear she's magnificent," he whispered.

"From whom?" I said. I often liked to use the word *whom* in its proper place. But whenever I used it, Derek always went to pieces laughing over it.

"Oh, I hear things. People saying this and people saying that. Take another cookie. You too, Derek," he said. "I hope you will tell me more about your mother. I do know she mails things to the Bathburn house. I hear she's as lovely as a butterfly. Just as pretty and delicate as a swallowtail. I have more cookies and lots of time. I'm very interested."

"Derek, we might be too busy to sit and talk. Perhaps we should head back before it storms," I said, frowning and trying to smile at the same time.

"You know, I tend to be good at finding people. You see, here I have located an address for Derek's birth father. When a person has been living with a family, without official records, it isn't always easy. But I followed a lead and have come up with this." And he pulled a piece of paper from a little side pocket and he waved it in the air like a flag. "He's only given us a hotel address, the Eastland Park Hotel in Portland. I took the liberty of mailing him your address too. So one of you will have to get in touch. Perhaps you will be the one to reach out first, Derek." Then he dropped the paper on the little table in front of Derek.

Derek flopped back on the sofa and I thought he suddenly seemed quite pale round the edges. He looked down at the paper and then he closed his eyes.

"Oh, but, Derek," I said, leaving my teacup on the table and going to sit beside him, "don't you think we ought to ask The Gram and Uncle Gideon first, I mean . . ." I took the opportunity to touch Derek's hand, not the one that got paralyzed by polio when he was sick last year, but the other perfectly good one. I squeezed it gently and I meant for that squeeze to tell him that we ought not to be talking about any of this. But Derek didn't seem to hear me. He had gone all silent, like a cabinet with its doors closed and locked.

"This is a wonderful opportunity, Derek. One that may not come along again," said Mr. Fitzwilliam a few moments later. "And in the meantime, if you've finished your tea, come into my garden room at the back. In his day, my grandfather called it a conservatory, but we're modern folks now, aren't we? To us, it's a garden room. Felicity Bathburn Budwig will like this, won't she, Derek? And as we walk together toward our garden room, perhaps we could have a little chat and you could tell me when and if your mother ever comes to visit. I adore butterflies."

My head started to spin. I looked up at the ceiling, where a carved figure seemed to be swimming among birds in the plaster.

Derek patted my back in a chummy way that made me feel a bit better. "Oh, Fliss, you'll like the garden room. It's full of butterflies. Mr. Fitzwilliam hatches them from cocoons. They live in there. That's what I wanted to show you. That's why I brought you here."

"But, Derek," I said, "weren't we supposed to hang these posters downtown? Didn't the air-raid warden ask us to do that for him?" I unrolled one of the posters and showed it to Mr. Fitzwilliam and Derek. It pictured a great multicolored battleship sinking in waves and underneath were the words LOOSE LIPS SINK SHIPS.

"Lovely artwork and a most important message," said Mr. Fitzwilliam, walking away.

Derek then pulled me along as Mr. Fitzwilliam beckoned us from the end of a dark hallway. I looked back at the table and saw that the crumpled piece of paper was gone. Derek must have put it in his pocket. I had hoped he would leave it here and forget the whole matter.

We followed Mr. Fitzwilliam into the garden room, which proved to be all glass. There were green trees and flowering plants in that room, just as if we were outside on a summer day. And this was late September 1942, on the cold, windy, rainy coast of Maine. Among all the flowers and trees, there were hundreds of butterflies, all different sizes and shapes. They floated over my head and brushed against my hair, beautiful blue ones and tiny yellow ones and stunning black-and-orange monarchs. I thought for a moment about my mum, Winnie, somewhere in France. I felt quite nervous because I knew very well I wasn't supposed to talk about the work my mum had been doing. I knew the code name she used. It fluttered now across my mind.

★ *Two* ★

On the way home I decided Derek's mood matched the autumn sea. Both were rough and shadowy, verging on stormy. We didn't walk home along the water because the south wind was even more fierce down there on the rocks and it would have been like walking against a wall of wind. Up here on the road, we were closer to the tumbling clouds and the gray, stirred-up sky.

"Derek," I said as we passed the old White Whale Inn with its long, lonely porches, "perhaps we should not go back there to Mr. Fitzwilliam's house. How did he go about finding your father? And wouldn't it upset everyone at home if they knew?" I was walking backwards, all of me pushing against the wet wind.

"Never mind," said Derek, looking up at the sky, letting the rain hit his cheeks. "It's my business, that's all. Mr. Fitzwilliam feels that it's my choice and it is. Perhaps *they* don't have to know."

Derek smashed his foot down in the center of a puddle in front of us. Then he kicked at the air.

"I don't think I like Mr. Fitzwilliam," I said. "He seems a bit nosy."

We were getting closer to the Bathburn house, my grandmother's house. I could see it rising up from the rocky point. It was brown and sober looking with all of its many roofs and gables. As we drew closer I could hear music. Uncle Gideon was playing the piano. Whenever he played, it seemed to thunder out to the whole world.

Just as we neared the garden gate we passed a group of American soldiers in training. They were jogging along the road in khaki pants and white undershirts, which we called vests in England. I felt dreadfully sorry for them as it was quite rainy and wet. Derek said there was a training camp nearby and we often saw soldiers in town, because America had joined the war ten months ago. That was the war that I thought I had left behind in England when my mum, Winnie, and my dad, Danny, brought me here last year for safekeeping.

"Well, Mr. Fitzwilliam was helping me. It was *his* idea. At first I was unsure, but now I think it might be something I *should* do," Derek said, opening the back door at my grandmother's house. He had such brown eyes and they seemed almost black at this moment, with extra shadows stirring round in them. We stepped into the house, headed towards the kitchen. Piano music rippled down the hall and through the air.

On the metal, enamel-topped table in the kitchen were two sandwiches sitting on a blue willow plate. The plate had a funny crack along the rim and I was thinking it looked like a strange little smile. And then I noticed leaning against the plate was a letter, an envelope addressed to Derek Blakely. Most people did not know that Derek's true, *real* last name was Blakely. Everybody thought it was Bathburn. We didn't ever talk much about it and so it was very strange to see that name. I wasn't sure that I had read the words properly and so I looked closer. The upper left corner said it was from Edmund Blakely.

Derek grabbed the letter. He held it against his body so I couldn't check to make sure that I hadn't mixed up the whole thing. And I have been known to mix things up, to think I'm dreadfully right when I'm dreadfully wrong. "Oh, Derek," I said, jumping up and down. "Do let me see what you've got." But he held the letter high. It was very silly of me to leap and grab, but I kept on trying. And then Derek turned round and drummed down the hall and pounded up the stairs and went in his room and slammed the door.

I sat alone at the blue metal kitchen table listening to the music, which seemed to get in under the wallpaper, to get in behind the wooden cabinets, even to get in under the soft linoleum. I felt for one moment a pang of regret about boxing up my old, stuffed, British bear, Wink. I had wrapped him in soft tissue paper and I had put him in a box under my bed. I hadn't mailed him away to my friend in England yet because Uncle Gideon suggested I save it till things quieted down on the sea. "You don't want Wink to end up at the bottom of the ocean, do you? Mail vessels are prime targets these days, Fliss." So Wink was still waiting patiently under my bed in his box for the seas to quiet down, for the world to quiet down. I thought about getting him out but then I reminded myself that I was twelve years old now and girls of that age never get out their old bears and start hauling them about again. And so I let Wink rest and I let Derek stew and I hoped soon enough he would come to a full boil and let me see that letter.

★ Three ★

I stayed there at that kitchen table for a long time for me, because normally, even though I was twelve, I still liked to hop about and leap from chairs to sofas just for the lark of it. I liked to see if I could jump from rug to rug without ever touching the wood floor. I did once make it from one end of the house to the other, but Derek said it didn't count because I pushed a rag rug all the way down the hall to the kitchen.

I had a lot on my mind recently. And I knew what Derek was going through. So much had happened in the last year concerning *my* father. After being here in Maine for nine months, I found out that, even though I had only met him recently, Uncle Gideon was my real father. My mum Winnie had been married to him thirteen years ago and that's when I was conceived. Everyone was mad at my mum now because she had broken Gideon's heart by leaving him then and marrying his brother, Danny, instead. After I was born, Winnie and Danny had raised me in England until the war came. Then they brought me here and left me, without explaining much of anything.

I hadn't quite become accustomed to the whole thing yet. Gideon wasn't exactly my uncle anymore but he didn't exactly feel like my father either. I still called him

Uncle Gideon. I needed to find a new name for him that seemed right. What should I call him? Papa? That sounded very old-fashioned or French. Isn't that what Sara Crewe called her father in *A Little Princess*? Pa sounded very American but more like what a cowboy child would call his cowboy father. Like, "Pa, should I saddle up your horse so you can race those other ranchers to the canyon?" Perhaps a different name every day would do, until suddenly one would just feel right and would stick like spaghetti when you threw it against the wall to see if it was done.

So far I felt very awkward about calling my new father anything at all. And I tried to avoid it. Gideon said I could call him "Thing-a-ma-bobby," if I wanted to, or even "What-cha-ma-call-it." He said he didn't mind at all. Any name would do. But my mum Winnie would not have liked me calling my sort-of dad "What-cha-ma-call-it."

But then, I wasn't sure at all when I might see Winnie and Danny again. I missed them terribly and sometimes I would sit at the window and simply wait for them. I had been sitting at that window for almost a year and a half.

That was something I was always trying *not* to think about and so I took a nice bite of a very lovely strawberry jam sandwich. And just as I did, Gideon poked his head through the kitchen doorway. "Hello and good afternoon, Fliss," he said. "It's your what-cha-ma-call-it here.

Haven't forgotten me, have you? Haven't come up with a name for me yet, have you? You know it doesn't really matter. Even Thing-a-ma-jig would be just fine."

"Oh, hello," I said, leaving off his name all together. "It's *you*!"

"I put a letter for Derek on the table here a while ago. It arrived this morning while you were out putting up posters. Fliss, the letter appeared to be from a relative of Derek's, oddly enough. Derek doesn't exactly have any relatives and, um . . . well, do you know who the letter is from? Has he read it?"

"Oh," I said, and the posters we hadn't hung yet swirled in front of my eyes for a moment. CARELESS TALK COSTS LIVES. DON'T SAY WHAT YOU KNOW. YOU NEVER KNOW WHO . . . WHO . . . WHO . . . That poster showed an owl in a tree and a battlefield in the background. It floated up in my mind now.

"These posters," the air-raid warden had said to Derek and me, "are to inform people not to talk too much about the things they know, things like where a husband or brother or father might be stationed, or what his squadron is doing, or even what boats you might have seen passing along the horizon. There are people sending information back to the Nazis. They sell the information you know. This is war and every family has their secrets that must be kept." He had then handed me a pile of rolled-up posters.

Gideon was looking at me rather sadly just now,

watching my face as if I were a book with very small type he was trying to read.

"Well, yes, um, the letter did appear to be from his, um, father, I think. But I am not sure. Perhaps Derek won't answer it," I said.

Gideon looked startled and then his eyebrows seemed to slip down to his chin. He sort of stumbled to a chair and sagged into it.

We sat there together as if we were on the shore in an early morning fog, a fog so thick, we were unable to see anything, not even each other. Finally, I said, "But it's quite nice for Derek, really. He didn't seem to have a father before and now he might. I imagine his papa will only pop in and say hello and then leave."

"Oh yes. No. Of course," said Gideon. "But this is very serious. His father could take Derek away from us if he . . ." And then he didn't finish his sentence, and Gideon always finished his sentences. After all, he was a sixth-grade teacher called Mr. Bathtub at the John E. Babbington Elementary School. It was usually his students who stopped in midsentence, saying things like *um* and *uh* and *er.*

It was the same way with Aunt Miami. She was ironing in the laundry room. I was in there knocking about while she sprinkled water over linen napkins. Then she bundled them up and piled them all wet at the end of the ironing board. Soon enough she unbundled them and began ironing each lace-trimmed napkin. I loved the smell of the steam and the hissing sound of the iron as it went over the damp cloth.

"Mr. Henley will be here in a little while," she said and her lilac-colored eyes looked a bit dreamy. Aunt Miami always called our postman Mr. Henley when she talked about him, but she called him Bob when she saw him in person. He'd recently been taking her "out to the movies," as they say here in Bottlebay, Maine.

"Ah, Henley," said Gideon, suddenly appearing again in the doorway, swinging his arms about. "Has he popped the question yet?"

Gideon was always asking that and I sort of guessed what question he hoped Mr. Henley would pop.

"Derek's gotten a letter, you know," said Gideon, looking at the floor. "It's from his father."

"What?" said Aunt Miami. I could tell she was quite shaken because she left the iron on the damp cloth a bit too long, leaving a brown, burned shape of an iron on it. It looked like a dark ship crossing the surface of the napkin.

I thought for a moment about all the ships crossing back and forth over the dangerous ocean, the British ships and the American ships and the Nazi ships, and all of the submarines and the U-boats moving deep in the darkness, unseen, unheard. Why oh why had Mr. Fitzwilliam been nosing about? Why did he ask all those questions? Why hadn't he left well enough alone?

Four

One summer when I was nine, before the war, Winnie and Danny and I left London to go on holiday for the summer. We moved to a cottage near the sea in Selsey, West Sussex. It was the only house we ever had. There, I used to walk down the block to the sea. But the seawall bothered me. It had recently been rebuilt. A little girl named Dimples told me the seawall had been washed away a few years ago by huge waves. She said lots of people were carried off into the swell and were washed up dead on the shingles later.

Dimples would have made a lovely, sad-looking stone statue. She had such big eyes and she was very interested in tragedy. I didn't know what a swell was, even though I was older than Dimples by quite a few years. *Swell* was what Danny said when he thought something was lovely. "Now, that would be swell," he'd say, my Danny. It sounded very American, very posh to me and to Dimples.

In thinking back now, our cottage in Selsey had a visitor one day, a woman with a knitting bag. She came to chat with my Winnie. I was sent out to the garden to follow our gardener about. Before I left the room, though, I glanced back and saw that the woman was knitting already. Her needles were working on a muffler and she had just begun to add a butterfly to it. It looked like a swallowtail butterfly, made of black-and-yellow wool. "There are swallowtails and clouded yellows in your garden today, Winnie," said the woman. "What do you think?"

"Hmm, perhaps that would do very well as a name for our circuit. I'll ask the others," said Winnie.

The war hadn't started in England yet but on the wireless they said that Czechoslovakia had gone under and drowned in a sea of Nazi soldiers and tanks and bombers. The word *drowned* made me think of our sea-wall. In Selsey, Winnie and Danny were already starting their secret work.

Five

At dinner that night, Derek was still unwilling to say a word about the letter from his father. His mouth was sewn shut, just like my old bear Wink's mouth. Derek was making an interesting arrangement with his fork, knife, spoon, and napkin on the table, not answering anyone.

"Derek? Would you tell us about your letter?" said my father, Gideon.

It was still raining outside in a long-stretching autumn kind of way, pulling at everything, leaves and the last of the flowers. The blackout curtains were drawn, so I could only hear the rain needling the windows.

We were having boiled potatoes and The Gram's home-canned green beans. Both of them came from our garden. The potatoes had just been dug up. Soon enough, the government had announced, all sorts of things besides sugar might have to be rationed, things like meat and cheese and butter and oil and even bicycles and typewriters and shoes! I had been through all that in England. We got these little ration books full of ration stamps. The stamps allowed you to buy a little bit of meat once a week, mostly just enough to make a soup. I used to wait in a ration line at the butcher's shop in London with Winnie, hoping to get some meat. But usually by the time our turn came round, the meat was sold out and the butcher would look at us in a sad sort of way and say, "Carry on, then."

Tonight, Uncle Gideon looked very worried about Derek's dad and this unexpected letter that seemed to have fallen out of the sky. "Derek, can I see the letter?" he said again, pinching the bridge of his nose and frowning.

"Well," said Aunt Miami, glancing quickly at Mr. Henley, who was having dinner with us, "instead of pouting and looking glum, I think we should dance."

"Not while we're eating, dear," said The Gram.

"Well, we don't have to dance, but we can certainly put a record on the Victrola," Auntie said, getting up and going to the brown wooden record player. "I don't want Bob to think we're the gloomy set around here."

She put on the 78 called "I Think of You." It was everybody's favorite in the Bathburn house. It was known to wedge Derek out of all sorts of dark moods because he loved the tune.

When the clouds roll by
and the moon drifts through
When the haze is high
I think of you.
I think of you.

When the mist is sheer
and the shadows too
When the moon is spare
I think of you.
I think of you.

Gideon looked even more anxious now. That song made him remember my mum, Winnie. Even though his brother, Danny, stole Winnie away thirteen years ago — Gideon still loved her.

When the night birds cry
and the swallows too
When west winds sigh
I think of you.
I think of you.

"This is a grave matter, Derek. We would like to know what's going on," Gideon said, nodding at Derek with a bit of melancholy.

But Derek didn't look up. Then the 78 came to the end of the song and the needle of the Victrola was scratching softly against the center of the record in a rhythmical way, reminding me of a nagging thought that I wished would just go away.

"Derek, dear," said The Gram, looking straight at him. "We've all been at sixes and sevens here, especially Gideon. Are you ready to tell us what the letter said?"

Derek continued to stare at his plate. There was one last green bean lying there. It was turned down, like a frowning mouth.

"Sometimes when I read my poetry aloud, I know what I want to change or add to the poem. Sometimes reading aloud helps find an answer," said Mr. Henley.

"Oh, Bob, what a lovely thing to say," said Auntie. And she and Mr. Henley began staring into each other's eyes.

Derek slowly reached in his shirt pocket. He laid a folded piece of paper on the table. He lifted his one useless arm and dropped it on a corner of the paper to hold it down. With his good hand he then unfolded the letter and read in a low, quiet voice:

"Dear Derek,

I just landed in Portland. I am a merchant seaman on the USS Washington *anchored out in the bay. I'm on shore leave for a while. I've been walking around the streets thinking about you and finally after all these time hoping to see you. May I come over just for an afternoon? We have so much to talk about.*

With love,

Your father, Edmund Blakely."

"Hmm, after all *these* time?" said Gideon. "Your dad seems to be a bit, um, sloppy."

"It's just a letter, a slipup. Who cares," said Derek.

"No, no, it's fine," said Gideon. "I was just noticing that . . ."

"Gideon, hush," said The Gram. "Must you always be a teacher?"

"Oh, Derek," I said. "Will you see your father? Will he be coming here?"

"What are his intentions?" said Aunt Miami. She was holding Mr. Henley's hand under the table. I saw it only because I happened to be under the table myself for one minute, fetching two wandering green beans that had rolled off my plate by mistake.

"I don't know what his intentions are," said Derek. "But I think I am grown up enough now to make this decision for myself."

"Well," said Aunt Miami. "You could write him and tell him you are indisposed and far too busy. He's waited twelve years to see you. Tell him you need some time now and lots of it. Then toss away his letter and let him get back on his ship, the USS *Thanks a Lot for Nothing, Pal.*"

The Gram and Mr. Henley began clapping and cheering. Aunt Miami stood up and took a bow.

"Okay. Perhaps. Yeah, you're right," said Derek, folding the letter back into his pocket. "I'll write and say no. Sorry. Too late."

"There you go, good boy." said The Gram, putting her arm round Derek. "And now let's hope he leaves us alone!"

Uncle Gideon put a piece of driftwood into the wood-stove. He left the door open and stared at the fire that seemed then to sizzle and spark and leap about, like a caged tiger. Outside, curtains of rain swept against the windows. I could hear the anxious ocean breaking on the rocks below. And I stared at the large oil painting, above the sideboard, of the old sea captain who once lived in this house, who once built this house. Captain A. E. Bathburn, 1854.

★ *Six* ★

Unfortunately, at school in Bottlebay, Maine, there was to be an autumn dance for teens at the end of October. I was only twelve and would not be admitted. Derek had been practicing waltz steps and swing steps in the parlor. Before the letter came, I had been helping him get his steps right. "How am I doing?" I had said to him a few weeks ago as we made a last twirl to a song called "When I'm Not with You."

Derek had looked down at me. He smiled and he said, "You're the cat's pajamas, Fliss." Ever since he had entered eighth grade, Derek loved slang. And I did too. I was awfully curious about *the cat's pajamas*. I pictured a cat wearing flannels covered with cowgirl hats and stars. I hoped it was a good thing to be *the cat's pajamas*.

I was thinking about that when the phone rang, which was a rarity at the Bathburn house. I knew Gideon used to ring up Washington when we were out. The whole family knew all about Gideon's work — not his work at school as a teacher but his secret work with Mr. Donovan in Washington. It was the same kind of work Winnie and Danny did. Every time the phone rang I thought of them, because they were missing and lost and we hadn't heard from them in months. How I longed for Winnie and

Danny still. How my longing followed me about the way the wind seemed to follow me sometimes.

Usually I had to race with Miami to answer the phone on the landing but she was in the gymnasium upstairs arguing with Uncle Gideon while he stood on his head. "Well," Uncle Gideon was saying, "Henley should pop the question now so we can have the wedding before Christmas, when I have to go overseas."

I would have rushed to the phone but now I stood frozen in the hall, frozen hearing those words, *when I have to go overseas.* I was frozen, suddenly thinking of Captain Bathburn's ship in 1855, which finally came home, finally sailed over the horizon and into port. It was pure white, they said, frozen solid. The masts and sails all covered in ice. It was like a ghost ship, arriving eight weeks late in the middle of winter. But it had made it, with Captain A. E. Bathburn and half of his crew still alive and on board.

Two things were happening at once now. Gideon was going overseas at Christmastime? At *Christmas*? And the phone was ringing.

I finally picked up the receiver. "Hello," I said.

"Oh, Flossie, it's Brie. Derek's cousin Brie," the voice said.

"Well, actually, I'm your cousin too," I said. "And my name is Flissy, not Flossie."

"Oh, I never thought of you that way. I mean as a cousin. I guess because of your accent and you being so foreign and everything. *Flossie* is cute, don't you think? Is Derek there? I'm inviting him to the autumn dance."

I held the receiver in my hand. It was very heavy and instead of answering Brie, I kind of dropped it on the small table and went off to find Derek.

I passed Aunt Miami on the stairs as she rushed by, her silky chiffon skirt fluttering past me in a whirlwind. "Gideon will be going overseas right before Christmas. Mother! Where's The Gram?" she said and she seemed to swirl and dissolve in soft silk and tears.

"And Brie's inviting Derek to the dance. She's just rung up," I called.

Aunt Miami didn't answer. She seemed to lift up and disappear down the hall, past moving curtains and fluted shadows, past paintings of Captain A. E. Bathburn's staring daughters. Then I heard her crying in the kitchen and The Gram too.

I went on up to fetch Derek from his room. He was studying a map of Europe in there, looking at France. I opened the door. "Gideon's going to Europe before Christmas," he said without turning round.

"But that's where the war is," I said. "Why would he go there now? I've been in the midst of that, Derek. It's dreadful. Everyone at school thinks we're not very safe here in Maine either, because of the coast. We don't even know what's lurking in the waters. The Bagley family moved back to Illinois because they thought the coast was too dangerous. Oh, Derek, everything is changing. I don't want Uncle Gideon to go. Must he? And I don't want you to go away with your father either or even talk to him. None of the others want you to answer him."

"I don't know what they're worried about," he said. "But whatever I decide, it's up to me now. I don't want them to know any more about it. Okay?"

"Brie is on the phone, Derek. She wants to talk to you."

"Oh well, that's peachy keen," said Derek, dropping his pencil and turning round.

Then I got rather bold in a British sort of way and I said quite sadly, "Derek, is Brie the cat's pajamas as well?"

"Oh, Brie, she's the dog's necktie!" Derek said and he smiled that smile that sent me spinning out over the ocean like a piping plover or a bufflehead or a lost and diving common goldeneye.

Seven

I cried that night alone in my widow's peak room at the top of the house, with the widow's walk outside it and the terrible gray ocean beyond and all round me. That little walk was built so that Captain A. E. Bathburn's wife could look out and wait for her husband's ship to come over the horizon. And that fall it didn't. And it didn't and it didn't and it didn't and winter came and the snow roared at these windows and she waited and she waited.

I cried for three reasons that night. The first was for un–Uncle Gideon, my newfound father whom I had grown to love during these many months in America. The second tears were for Derek, because his father had returned, changing everything here forever. And the third tears were for myself, because Derek was going to the dance with Cousin Brie. Those tears were the most raw. I wasn't at all a pair of cat's pajamas anymore. I was a pair of plain gray flannels with ugly buttons down the front.

That night, the wind and rain came in under the window ledges into my room, and when I woke up in the morning, my pillow was damp. When Gideon found out, he said, "Fliss, we'll have to get you out of that room for winter. The windows have gotten worse and you're just too exposed to the sky and the sea up there." Well, I had always liked Miami's large, airy room anyway.

And so it was that I packed my yellow suitcase and Uncle Gideon shut up the tower room. "Leaving Wink up here, are you? Too old for Wink now, I imagine," he said to me as he turned the key to lock the door. "Well, you'll outgrow us all, I suppose, soon enough. Yes, soon enough."

"Oh," I said. "I don't need an old bear anymore. I'll be sending him off to England soon."

"It's a shame you and Derek are in such a hurry to grow up and throw away old friends," said Gideon. "Well, bears like the cold and I suppose he'll be hibernating anyway." He looked at me then with a good-bye kind of look in his eyes that reminded me a tiny bit of Wink for just a moment and then I did feel a little tug in my heart.

That night I moved downstairs to Auntie Miami's room, which was quite grand. She had a lovely canopy bed that they said had once belonged to Captain A. E. Bathburn and his wife, Ada. And there were great, long windows to the sea and soft hooked rugs on the floor, covered in wild roses and trumpet lilies. (The Gram had hooked them all.) I had a little bed at the far end of the room. It had a bedspread with a cat on it but the cat was not wearing a pair of fancy pajamas.

It was nice because Auntie and I could lie in the darkness and talk. That very first night we did. Uncle

Gideon popped in with a cup of Ovaltine for me. He wanted to say good night. He sat on the edge of my bed with the hot chocolaty drink steaming up between us, looking at me as if I were a new kind of seashell he'd just found on the shore. "I was visiting Derek a moment ago, and I think he's going to listen to us, so there's no need to worry. And I won't be leaving for several months. That's ages away." Then he frowned in the almost darkness and said, "It's for Winnie, you know, and Danny." And he didn't say anything else and I understood what he meant and in my heart I felt proud and sad and nervous.

Later I heard his Victrola in his room playing jazzy songs again. One of them was "I Think of You." And I knew he was thinking of Winnie, dreaming of her, reaching out to her as she floated near him, with her beautiful, dark eyes, reaching out to her as she floated away into his brother's arms.

Eight

When I came downstairs the next day, Derek's face was bright, like a fire in a fireplace, and yet hidden at the same time, like a fire in a closed-up stove. There was no one about. The Bathburn house was empty except for the two of us sitting at the card table in the parlor.

"This is to be a secret, Fliss," said Derek, looking over at me, "but I am going to write to my father. I'm going to invite him over when everyone's out next week."

"But, Derek," I said, "I don't think Gideon will like that. Nor will The Gram. They don't like people coming to the house. And they're so upset about this. They don't want to lose you, Derek, because you were not adopted officially."

"Never mind about all that," said Derek. "My father *will* be coming over. Let's write a letter to him now."

I do love writing letters and straight off I suggested he say, *"Dearest Papa, how long it has been since we've strolled down the avenue of life."*

But Derek said, "No, I'd rather just say, *Hello, would you like to come for lunch on the point in Bottlebay? Thursday at noon?"*

"For lunch?" I said.

"Yes," said Derek. "We don't drink tea like you do over there. He'd probably rather have that swell new instant coffee called Nescafé. Everybody loves it."

Derek looked pleased as he signed the letter and handed it to me. I stuffed it in an envelope and addressed it, though I did not want to. Still, I bent towards Derek and his wishes.

We gave the letter to Mr. Henley when he popped round with his mail pouch slung over his shoulder. We were standing on the little porch outside the kitchen. Mr. Henley smiled and looked up at the house, hoping to see Auntie at the window.

Then Derek said to him, "Are you driving into Portland later today and could we possibly go along?"

I loved being *we* with Derek. I suddenly felt like the cat's pajamas again. Like fancy silk pajamas, pajamas with pizzazz, as they say here.

"Yes, *we* should very much like to go along," I said, jumping up a step and then down a step and back up a step again.

As soon as I could, I whispered to Derek, "Why are we going to Portland?"

I didn't really get an answer from Derek until later when we were in Mr. Henley's car, riding along in the rain. More gray, gloomy autumn rain. We drove along the rocky coast with the ocean below us cloaked in mist and drifting fog.

Mr. Henley was breezy at the wheel. He loved his car. And so did Aunt Miami. They were always putting on fancy "duds," as Derek would say, and driving to Portland to the Rotary Club dances just for the fun of it.

"I shouldn't be driving at all now because rubber tires wear out and you can't get new ones these days. The rubber is all being used by the government for the war. And you know gas is going to be rationed soon but because I am a mailman, I'll have a C sticker and I will get more ration tickets for gas than some," said Mr. Henley, smiling. Then he began to recite some of his poems. He was a poet and getting better and better with every poem, Auntie said. But no publishers ever liked them. He could never even get his poems accepted by a magazine.

Mr. Henley was coming into his third verse of his third poem when I whispered again to Derek, "Why are we going to Portland?"

"Because I want to see my father before he sees me," Derek said.

"Oh," I whispered. But my heart dropped and sank, like a small pebble tossed into the sea.

"Have you heard the poem about Portland and the harbor there, by Henry Wadsworth Longfellow?" said Mr. Henley. "He grew up in Portland, you know."

I remember the black wharves and the slips,
And the sea-tides tossing free;

And Spanish sailors with bearded lips,
And the beauty and the mystery of the ships,
And the magic of the sea.

"Oh, that's lovely," I said and then I whispered to Derek, "You mean we are going to the Eastland Park Hotel?"

"Yup," said Derek.

We passed a jeep carrying a naval officer going the other way out along the peninsula to the point. He was probably headed to the Coast Guard station out there. The Coast Guard had started patrolling the beach below us. They were also seen along the rocky cliffs to the north of our house along the coast, especially at the cliff walk where Mr. Fitzwilliam lived. They were looking and watching for Nazi submarines. We saw them ourselves sometimes when the U-boats rose almost to the surface. They needed oxygen to run their engines to recharge their batteries. I'd seen once the gray top of a U-boat sticking up out of the water but I was all alone that day. I had tried to call the Coast Guard but I couldn't get through. I didn't get a chance to tell Uncle Gideon about it until later that day. Usually he reported the whereabouts of a sub immediately. It was never in the papers, any of this. It was something that we didn't talk about. I think the government didn't want the people along the coast to know. But we knew. If you lived with the Bathburns, you knew.

"We're almost to Portland now," said Mr. Henley. "I'll leave you at Monument Square. And we can meet back there. But first I have to drop a package off at the dock."

Soon we were passing the piers and wharves of Portland harbor. A huge cargo ship was docked along a wharf. And as we drove by, sailors and navy men and dockworkers carrying their lunch pails walked past us.

Mr. Henley delivered his package and then we climbed the hill, the car sputtering along. As we rose higher, the rain stopped and it felt like we were riding to the top of the sky, like we might lift up and fly away into the clouds. Then we would be able to see the harbor below and the bay and to imagine, beyond that, the ocean and all the capes and points and islands farther out.

At Monument Square, Derek got out of the car and looked back in at Mr. Henley. "We'll see you here in one hour. Thanks." He patted the top of the car just like Uncle Gideon always did and then he took my hand. Yes, Derek took my hand. He didn't know it but suddenly I *was* flying over Portland. His hand felt warm and strong.

"Portland is peachy keen," I said.

"You're on the right trolley there," Derek said, looking up at the tall buildings. Then, as if a cloud scattered a shadow across his face, he looked down. "We have to find the Eastland Park Hotel now, Fliss. We haven't got a lot of time."

But Derek and I were holding hands! I could feel his fingers entwined with mine. Brie was a million miles away.

We walked farther up the hill, past fancy department stores and ornate banks. Benoit and Company had American flags in every window and painted words on the building: FOR VICTORY BUY WAR STAMPS AND BONDS.

Most of the women and teenage girls passing us on the street were wearing cute little felt hats with veils, while all I had on was an orange woolen beret I had knitted myself. I buttoned up my jacket and held on tighter to Derek's hand.

Derek looked wondrous against the city sky. We walked all the way up Congress Street and turned down High Street. There sat the Eastland Park Hotel with its grand-looking entrance. Derek froze on the steps and dropped my hand. He looked up at the tall building and he wouldn't move.

There were quite a few sailors and naval officers on the steps. And there was a poster on a stand by the doors. It showed the ballroom inside the hotel filled to the brim with sailors and soldiers and girls dancing to a big band. The poster said, FRIDAY NIGHT COUNT BASIE PLAYS AT THE EASTLAND. BRING YOUR GAL TO BEBOP, JITTERBUG, AND SWING. I remembered for a moment that Derek and Brie were going to the autumn dance together.

"Come on," said Derek suddenly. "Let's go in. We have to be quick and quiet and calm. Okay?"

We walked in the doors and found twisted painted columns and arched doorways on all sides. There were steps up to the grand mezzanine, with plush rugs and soft-looking sofas and bright-colored Spanish tiles on the walls near the wooden front desk. "What a swanky place," said Derek, rolling his eyes across the room.

"Your father must be dreadfully rich," I said. I was hoping Derek would reach for my hand again, but he didn't. Instead, he crossed the polished marble floor to the desk. There were hundreds of wooden cubbyholes for keys and messages and letters for the guests.

"Hello," said Derek to the hotel manager. "We're here to see one of your guests, my father, Edmund Blakely. Is he in?" Derek seemed to exaggerate the word *father*.

"I'm sorry to say he's not," said the manager. "Mr. Blakely only stayed one night with us last week and left. He does pick up his messages occasionally. Perhaps you'd like to leave him one."

Derek backed up, shaking his head, and then he trailed away. I followed him.

We walked to the edge of the dining room and peeked in. On all the walls there were Egyptian murals, as if the dining room were in an Egyptian tomb. It was dimly lit and full of tables and every one of them was taken. There seemed to be naval officers and sailors and welders and ironworkers from the shipyard having lunch. We were told the government put up shipyard workers here. They said all the rooms in Portland were occupied because shipyard workers from across the country were brought here to build the new Liberty ships for the war. I was feeling proud and pleased to see them all. But then, in the far corner, I spotted someone.

"Derek," I said. "Do you see that fellow who has turned away from us now? Isn't that Mr. Fitzwilliam having lunch over there?"

"What?" said Derek. "Yes, it does look like Fitzwilliam."

There was also a fellow who appeared to be lunching with Mr. Fitzwilliam, or rather just leaving him, putting his share of the bill on the table. Quarters and nickels spilled out and rolled onto the floor. "I'd like to get a photo of the parade," he called out to Mr. Fitzwilliam as he crossed the room and walked past us.

He took some photographs of the lobby. He dropped some newspapers on the tiled floor. He leaned over and picked them up, then pushed out the main doors. We went towards the glass double doors too. There was a small parade going down the street outside. There were several marching bands and soldiers carrying banners that read, SUPPORT YOUR COUNTRY AND YOUR SOLDIERS. BUY WAR BONDS NOW. It was too bad about the rain. It had started again. Umbrellas lined the street.

We were just going to go out the doors ourselves when we realized that the man had also dropped an envelope, a letter not yet mailed. It was lying there in the corner on the tiled floor near the exit.

Derek picked up the envelope. It was stamped and addressed to Louise Mack in Cape Elizabeth. "What should we do with this?" he said, handing me the envelope.

"I don't know," I said. Derek took my wrist then and sort of pulled me out through the doors on to the sidewalk. Sailors playing trumpets were pounding by. We could hear flutes scaling high notes and people cheering and clapping. We looked for the man who had dropped the envelope but it was quite crowded in spite of the rain and we didn't see him.

We wove through flocks of people and umbrellas and then, because it was getting late, we headed back towards Monument Square to meet Mr. Henley. We had decided now to mail the letter for the man. But before we did, Derek became a bit curious and worked the seal open without damaging anything. Then of course we decided not to bother to mail it because the paper inside was completely blank.

"She mails things to the house, doesn't she, your mother? I hear she's as lovely as a butterfly," Mr. Fitzwilliam had said. *"Just as pretty and delicate as a swallowtail."*

★ *Nine* ★

The ride home in the dark would have been cozy but there was something looming in the stormy air. Bob Henley had offered a ride to a coastie who needed to be dropped off at the top of our peninsula. I had learned that a coastie was one of the Coast Guards who patrolled the shoreline and bluffs here. He was rather a rough fellow as all the coasties were. It was still raining, that dark, misty kind of rain and our windscreen wipers were slowly dragging back and forth over the glass. They only went as fast as we were traveling and we were moving slowly because it was hard to see with our dimmed headlights.

"Well," said the coastie. "Come to find out, a freighter blew up a few miles out from Bailey Island two days ago. They're saying it was a faulty boiler that exploded but I have my doubts. They never want to admit foul play. They don't want to scare folks."

Derek and I were sitting in the dark, listening. My hand and his were so near each other on the seat, so close, almost touching. Perhaps his hand was tingling and longing to be held like mine was. Perhaps. I wasn't sure. Derek's face looked serious and pale, the way it always did when he was thinking.

We were both wondering why Mr. Fitzwilliam had been at that hotel. Perhaps it had been a coincidence. The memory of him seemed now, in the wet, lonely night, to be floating in front of us in a shadowy, gloomy way. It was curious too that the letter we picked up had been blank. Why had the man sealed up a blank letter? The car sputtered and stalled and finally stopped at the edge of the road and we let the coastie out. He disappeared into the rainy night with a flashlight in his hand. Like our headlights, it had a piece of red cellophane over it to keep the light low.

When we finally got home it was rather late and The Gram was cross with us. Where had we been? Why did we go? Derek slipped away, leaving me to make up some story about writing a report for school on Henry Wadsworth Longfellow. I said I thought Henry Wadsworth Longfellow had a jolly nice name. "I especially like the *Wadsworth* part, don't you? And do you think he would still have been a famous poet if his last name had been *Shortfellow* instead of *Longfellow*?" I said. I tried to recite the poem Mr. Henley had told us, but I got the black wharves and Spanish sailors and the ships all mixed up and The Gram frowned.

Then I tried offering to play Parcheesi with The Gram and Uncle Gideon. That seemed to work, but the whole time they played, Uncle Gideon and The Gram were speaking German.

All the Bathburns were dreadfully good at languages. Even The Gram. Like Uncle Gideon, she spoke French and German. "Without a trace of an accent," Aunt Miami told me once. It was another Bathburn trait, like winning at Parcheesi every single time. They had been speaking German quite a bit in the last few days and The Gram had been testing Uncle Gideon and hovering over his every German word.

★ Ten ★

The sun was shining quite brightly on the morning Derek's dad was to visit. Derek had been awfully clever in picking the time and day for all this. The Gram and Auntie had gone to the greengrocer's for shopping. Uncle Gideon had been fetched by the music teacher, Miss Elkin, in a car. She was terribly pleased to have Mr. Bathtub in her car. There was a large cello in its dark case sitting up in the backseat. As they drove off the cello looked a bit like a somber, unwilling passenger to me.

Derek had everything arranged and insisted before I was allowed to remain at the house that I keep his father's visit a secret. "Fliss, like I said, this is my business. I want the visit to be nice. Will you bring the sandwiches and coffee on a tray? Will you also answer the door and escort my father in? I'll be sitting in the living room, reading."

"Very well," I said. I went into the kitchen to check what we had for food. Just then I heard a knock at the back door. When I looked outside, someone was holding up a sign that said, BOTTLEBAY SALVAGE SCRAP DRIVE. Then a face peeked round the sign. As soon as I saw that pointed nose, I knew it was Stu Barker, Derek's friend. I had to go and fetch all the flattened tins and bottles and a jar of bacon fat we had collected above the cooker. Everybody also saved their worn tires and even their old rubber galoshes and handed them in. It was all to help the war. Stu Barker waved and carried everything off in a red wagon.

Afterwards, I peeked in at Derek in the parlor. He was lounging in a chair, swinging his legs back and forth in a nervous sort of way. I looked at the clock. It was a quarter to twelve. I put on a white apron and I wished I had one of those very keen white maid's hats. I tried to frown and look terribly serious like a maid or a cook or a housekeeper. Then I went back and looked through the cupboards for something to serve. I finally came up with peanut butter, lettuce, and mayonnaise sandwiches, a great Bathburn favorite. I had never had such a thing in England. (We used to have tomato sandwiches in London before the war, bread and butter and a slice of tomato. It was scrumptious with tea.) I decided to be awfully posh and I tried to cut the crusts off the bread. But the knife wasn't sharp enough, so I ruined one of the sandwiches. I whistled a lovely tune to cheer myself up about that and I decided to eat the sandwich since it looked so pitiful all cut up and crooked.

Then the doorbell rang in the front. Derek ran into the hall. "Fliss," he called, "he's here! Open it. No, don't. What if he doesn't like me?"

"Oh, Derek, he will," I said.

"What if I don't like him?" he said.

"You will. He's your father; of course you'll like him. You'll just naturally have things in common. You'll see." But then I felt a tug of something. Something I couldn't quite identify. It was like looking at a blurry photograph and trying to guess what was in the blur.

"Go on, then," he said, turning back into the parlor. "Answer the door."

As it happened a great gust of wind came up from the north and a window upstairs slammed shut on its own. I stopped cold in the hallway. It sounded like a gunshot, shattering everything. Then the house was silent. I went towards the front door and turned the handle.

"Good afternoon," said Derek's father. He had a likable, relaxed, and easy air about him and he looked quite comfortable in his hat and necktie. "I am to meet a Derek Blakely for lunch?" He smiled at me with a mixture of happiness and regret.

"Oh yes, of course," I said. "Please follow me." Then I opened the door of the parlor and said, "Derek, there's a gentleman here to see you."

"My son!" said Mr. Blakely, going towards Derek with open arms. "This is indeed a great moment."

"I shall bring the sandwiches shortly," I said and though I didn't want to, I backed up and left the room and closed the double doors as Derek and his dad embraced.

Eleven

When you live among a family of secret agents, you know much more than you should. You try to not hear or see things, but the truth is, everything is laid out before you and in that way you too are a kind of agent. The next day a very large package for Uncle Gideon arrived from Mr. Donovan's office in Washington. I had to carry it upstairs, though it was quite heavy. I went down the hall with it and knocked on the door of Uncle Gideon's private, off-limits study.

"Well done, Fliss," said Uncle Gideon, opening the door. "That package is almost bigger than you and you managed it just like a pro!" I handed him the box and then he said, "I shall miss you, Fliss, when I'm away." He sort of stumbled over his feet and almost fell. Then he backed up and said, "You won't forget your old what-cha-ma-call-it, will you?" He took my hand and squeezed it.

I looked up at him for a moment but then it felt like my eyes might be getting tearful, so I decided to study my shoes. That's a clever British trick I learned. If you look down at your shoes, it completely fools everyone. No one will ever suspect that you are about to cry. Then my what-cha-ma-call-it carried the package into the study and closed the door behind him.

I went on down the hall to Auntie's room. She was sitting on her bed, putting nail varnish on her toenails. "Flissy, sweetest," she said, smiling, "want me to paint your toenails with nail polish?"

"Oh yes, I would," I said, looking out her long windows at the ocean. The water was all foamy and white and full of worry and wonderment, the waves slapping back and forth in the autumn air. The big, dark rocks along the shore looked almost like large animals crouching, ready to leap into the water. In the daytime they looked like dogs. At night they looked like dark whales.

"Do you like the color of this nail polish? It's called Pink Passion. Would you like some Pink Passion on your toenails?" said Aunt Miami. I thought of my mum Winnie. Perhaps she would not approve. How far away Winnie seemed now, as if she were only made of filmy, threadbare memory. My longing for her was so constant that I had grown accustomed to it, the way you become accustomed to the constant hum and rhythm of the sea.

I sat down on the edge of the bed and Aunt Miami painted my toenails.

"Derek says Brie is hotsy totsy. Do you think there's a chance I could be hotsy totsy, I mean, now that my toenails are Passion Pink?" I said.

"Oh dear," said Auntie, looking into my face, reading it like it was one of those painted portraits of Captain

Bathburn's daughters. "Oh dear. I see, you're quite gone on Derek, aren't you?"

"Yes, rather," I said.

"I can understand why. He's a darling, handsome boy. We love him so much, Flissy. We couldn't bear to lose him. I am so glad he decided to tell that father of his to shove off."

"Yes," I said and I looked away. I am quite sorry to say that I was a bit clever about changing the subject then. I added, "You're rather gone on Mr. Henley, aren't you?"

"Yes, oh yes, Bobby is wonderful," said Aunt Miami and then she got up and spun round the room. I hadn't heard Mr. Henley called Bobby before.

"Do you love Bobby desperately?" I said. "Has he popped the question yet?"

"Oh, you've picked that up from Gideon. He's an awful tease. Don't you go and become a tease like him," said Auntie.

"What will you wear when you go out dancing with Bobby?" I said. "Do you like taffeta or silk? Do you think if I had a lovely new frock that Derek would forget about Brie? Derek has told me he thinks I should buy some new 'duds.' Do you think new duds would make me a bit more hotsy totsy?"

"Flissy McBee, I think you and I should go shopping for a new dress for you before they ration clothes. Before you know it we will have to have tickets to take a breath of air! It's time you had a brand-new store-bought dress anyway."

I smiled and then I skipped round the room a bit and went out into the hall. I skipped up and down along the stair rails, looking at my Pink Passion toes. I paused for a moment. The study door was slightly ajar. I could hear Uncle Gideon in the kitchen below, with The Gram. I pushed the door a little wider open. There I could see the large empty box sitting on the desk, and hanging beside it on a hook on the wall was a wool soldier's uniform. That must have been what was in the package. It was quite clearly a German officer's uniform because it had fancy gold trim on the shoulders and a red armband with a Nazi swastika on the sleeve.

★ *Twelve* ★

The next morning the air had a soft, forgiving feel. It was a warm autumn day and for some reason that made me remember spring in England. In London we usually had crocuses in our little walled-in garden. I can remember their brilliant purple color against the brown, newly melted earth. I don't suppose a bomber flying over England ever thought about a bed of crocuses finally coming to life and blooming after a whole winter of darkness and waiting.

Uncle Gideon was out on the porch with his morning coffee, looking at the sea. I went out and stood with him. He was very quiet, which for him was unusual. After a while he pulled on my braid and said, "What do you call this in Britain? Isn't it a *plait*? Have I got that right, Fliss?"

Then he made a whistling sound and within minutes Sir William Percy was flying towards the porch, squawking all the way. He was a bit of a baby, that seagull, I thought. Uncle Gideon had made a proper pet of him, feeding him all the time and he had named him after a teacher he had at Oxford, in England. The Gram had been cross about it at first, saying we would soon be inviting huge packs of seagulls, but in the end she too fed Sir William Percy. He had sweet, red-rimmed eyes and he talked and cried, and usually every morning he was waiting for his breakfast on the porch railing.

"When you're overseas," I said, "who will feed Sir William?"

"Oh, Fliss, I should love so much not to go, to stay here, and be your father." He looked over at me and then he looked down in a shy way. "About Sir William Percy, I'll be counting on you," Uncle Gideon said and then he was silent again.

I couldn't think of an answer, so I grabbed on to the weather, the way people do when there are no other words in sight. "Is it going to rain or will the wind blow or will it be sunny today? I don't know." And I rhymed the words by mistake. I wanted to say that I would miss him terribly, but somehow those words hadn't appeared as I had hoped they would.

We just stood there until finally Gideon said, "By the way, Fliss, Miami says you received a telephone call yesterday from a Mr. Fitzwilliam. You should call him back. I've left his number on the table on the landing. And if you don't mind, may I ask what this is about?"

"Oh, it was nothing. It was about those posters we put up all over town," I said, and I gave Sir William the last of my toast.

Later, during the afternoon, in the dining room, I put a 78 record on the Victrola. I was waiting for Derek, who was late for dance practice. The record was playing the song "When I'm Not with You."

When I'm not with you
the sky's no longer blue.

I was sitting at the table alone, listening to the music. All the somber daughters of Captain A. E. Bathburn watched me from their painted gold frames. They thought I was a dreadful sneak for not telling Uncle Gideon about Derek's father and his visit. Most British children are proper and honest. Perhaps I wasn't British anymore. Perhaps I'd turned into a dreadful "dual citizen," who had no country and no manners. Still, I loved Derek and I wanted to be loyal to him. If he wished to keep his father's visit a secret, then I should stand by him, even if it did make me into a dreadful beast of a child.

As I sat there, I was wondering about a lot of things, but most especially why Mr. Fitzwilliam had rung *me* up. I did not want to speak to him. I would never tell him anything about my mum Winnie. I would certainly never tell him that her code name was Butterfly, but he seemed to know that already, didn't he?

When I'm not with you
the sky's no longer blue.
When you're not with me
the stars fall in the sea.
When I see you not
the clouds pile up and plot.
The wind kicks up a knot
when I'm not with you.

★ *Thirteen* ★

When Derek finally walked into the dining room that evening, he seemed quite happy, really. He looked like he had just removed a dark, heavy blackout curtain that had been hanging over him, shutting out all the light. Ever since April, the government had announced that we were to cover our windows and all light from our houses at dusk with blackout curtains so enemy submarines could not see our coastline or our ships leaving the harbor at night. Some people were lazy down the road and painted their windows black so they didn't have to bother to close blackout curtains every evening. But I shouldn't like to live in a black room.

Aunt Miami was in the dining room now, folding napkins. As Derek walked in, Uncle Gideon did too and he grabbed Auntie and they started swinging and dancing round the room.

"Mr. Henley," I called out, pretending he had walked into the house, "someone's nabbed off with your dance partner!"

"'Nabbed off,' Fliss? I see you are still English all the way down to your wellies. Well, Bob'd better step up and pop that question. Miami's dance card is filling up fast."

"Oh, stop it," said Auntie, pushing Uncle Gideon away. Then she went off to the parlor and threw herself on the sofa and soon he followed and they both sat there talking. I heard Uncle Gideon say, "Miami, what have you decided to do? Are you going to do volunteer work? We must all pull together."

"Mrs. Boxman is urging me about the USO. Gideon, you do so much. You put me to shame." Then they went on murmuring and laughing.

Derek was sitting *on* the dining room table in a very casual, daring kind of way. I don't think The Gram would have approved, but she was upstairs, cutting out tiny quilt pieces for her new quilt. "I'm so happy to finally have a dad," Derek whispered, swinging his legs back and forth. "They can't know, but it felt fine, really fine. I've never had a dad before."

"It's quite nice, isn't it?" I said, pulling at Derek's good arm, as if to remind him we were to start dance practice.

"Knowing you, I'm surprised you didn't listen in at the door when he was here last week."

"Oh, I did, a bit, though I didn't intend to. I hope you'll forgive me. He's quite charming, your father, isn't he."

"Would you expect less?" Derek said, smiling down at me.

Still, that dark photograph of doubt blurred before my eyes.

On the gramophone, or phonograph, as they say here, the song "When I'm Not with You" was playing again, over and over. Oh, when I was with Derek, the moon seemed to sail so lightly in the sky. Dancing to the music and looking out the window at the evening sea, my head felt like it was fainting. Can your head faint while your arms and legs and feet stay normal? If so, my head fainted away. I did care for Derek, swimmingly so, and the music made it stronger and the dance coming up with Brie made it all the more maddening.

"In fact, Fliss," said Derek, "my true father coming here has really changed everything. You are right. He was nice. Very nice. I feel like I understand now who I am. It's good to have at least part of a father in my life. Not everybody can be lucky and have two fathers, like *some* people I know." He looked at me again as we danced and I felt a chill wash over me because somehow something didn't seem quite right.

★ Fourteen ★

"Hey, what's buzzin', cousin?" Derek was saying on the telephone, the next day after school. I was sitting on the steps below. I am sorry to report I was listening, trying to hear his conversation with Cousin Brie. He was using all sorts of posh slang and he was laughing constantly.

I was very quiet when Derek got off the phone. I didn't answer him when he said, "Brie just told me a story that really snapped my cap."

I turned my head away.

"She lives in Cape Elizabeth, you know. Something happened there last week."

I was still silent, studying the wall next to me. Not that it was at all interesting. It was a very dull portion of the plaster, with no visible cracks or bumps that looked like a face or a rabbit or anything like that.

"It was touch and go," said Derek. "Fliss? Are you there? Can you hear me?"

I suddenly felt itchy all over. I was itchy, itchy, itchy, and dying to ask Derek what he meant. I tried to stay angry and silent. I held on to my anger as tightly as I could, but soon it floated away like a great balloon and I couldn't keep myself from jumping up, turning round, and saying, "Cape Elizabeth? What is it, Derek? What happened?"

"A German woman living down the street from Brie was just arrested. She had come to live in Cape Elizabeth on the seashore two years before the war. Brie said she had been living there quietly, not mixing much with the town."

"Really," I said. "What happened?" Derek went on to say that the German woman hung her laundry on a clothesline every day. But then it seemed someone noticed she was hanging her white shirts and red shirts and yellow shirts sometimes upside down, sometimes right side up. They were always hung in a planned order. It began to appear that the order and the color of the shirts had a meaning, a kind of code for the U-boats lurking under the water not far away. Since she lived right on the coast, her laundry drying on the line was a way to send messages, to alert the U-boats of cargo ships passing Cape Elizabeth.

Then those U-boats could follow the ships farther out to sea and when they were alone, the U-boats could torpedo the ships, blow them up, send them to the bottom. Those wolf packs had been sinking so many ships off the east coast recently. The newspapers were full of reports about it. Perhaps that Nazi washerwoman was to blame for some of it. But the FBI had caught her. They also found a wireless transmitter in her house.

"Oh, Derek, is that a coincidence?" I said and I

remembered the blank letter written to a woman in Cape Elizabeth. Derek shrugged his shoulders.

"But still, I suppose you enjoyed your conversation with Brie?"

"It was great to hear from her," said Derek.

"Yes, how lovely," I said in my best British accent. It was changing a little and getting rusty. I had thrown out so many British ways of saying things that I often forgot what some of those phrases meant. The dance at the end of October still hung over me like a shadow and every time I turned round, Brie seemed to be in the air. Now she was ringing Derek up more and more. I walked into the dining room and sat down and looked at the portrait of Ella Bathburn, Captain Bathburn's middle daughter. I knew very little about her life. Had she sat at this very table almost one hundred years ago, her heart full of sadness, like mine?

"You're a bit off today," said Derek, following me into the dining room and looking at me, with all those daring freckles tossed across his face. "But come on, Fliss," he said. "Cheer up. You've got a letter!"

"You're making a game of me," I said.

"No, Fliss, here it is. A letter for you," he said.

I got awfully excited as I'm mad keen on letters and I am always hoping for one from Winnie and Danny. Winnie. My mum. I could see her now, driving away with Danny in the little sports car after they left me here, her veil on her hat blowing in the wind. Danny waving.

Naturally, I rather tore the envelope to pieces. The letter inside proved to be from Mr. Henley. With his note he included a poem he had just written about the sea. He wrote poetry all the time and he got so many rejection slips from magazines that he had made a whole scrapbook of them. But he kept on writing his poems anyway. And they were growing more lovely, really. The letter said:

Dear Flissy,
  Will you meet me at the library in Bottlebay
tomorrow at three thirty? I have something to
show you.
    Yours,
    Bob Henley

I put the letter in my pocket and went out on the porch. I wondered what Mr. Henley wanted to talk about. I wondered too why Brie was calling Derek so much. I wondered as well about the Nazi laundress, hanging her plain, colored shirts in different ways every morning. Yes, the war had a hidden side in which secret agents moved about in darkness, changing the course of the war with simple tools like a laundry basket and clothes-pegs and a long, cotton rope.

★ Fifteen ★

At nearly three thirty, after school, I walked back into town by myself. I felt a little lonely as I moved quietly through the fog. I could hear a foghorn repeating its call over and over again, mixed with a distant bell clanging somewhere offshore. Seagulls followed me and seemed to dive in and out of the murkiness.

I first came upon the harbor full of lobster boats and sailboats wrapped in blankets of mist, their masts and sails shrouded in wispiness and clouds. The fog too poured through the narrow streets of Bottlebay. It floated and twisted into cracks and crevices, like white smoke. I wondered if I would ever see clearly the shapes of things as they were forming round me. Everything seemed hidden, as if in a dream.

The town was quite empty, which gave me a shivery feeling. The lights from the shops and houses glowed a soft yellow in the dampness of the afternoon. I walked up the narrow winding streets to the central part of town and found the library sitting up on a rise, with four large white columns at the front.

I opened the door and went into the warm, cheerful room, full of library tables, each with a green lamp on a small brass stand. All round the tables were walls of shelved books. Mr. Henley was sitting at a large oak desk in a corner. He waved. "Flissy McBee," he whispered. "Good to see you! Thanks for meeting me. Let's step back into the stacks, where we can talk." We spotted two tall stools under a large oval window, and after struggling a bit, I found myself perched on the top of one.

"You have something on your mind, then," I said.

"Yes," said Mr. Henley, reaching in his pocket. Now he had a small red leather box in the palm of his hand. He held it out to me. "Open it," he said. His face was all tingly with nervousness and excitement.

I took the box carefully and opened the lid. Inside was a delicate little ring propped up in velvet. The gold band was thin and fragile. The ring had little red rubies and pearls round a miniature portrait of a young woman painted on a tiny dome of porcelain.

"Doesn't the woman in the little painting remind you of your beautiful aunt?" said Mr. Henley. He looked pleased and shining, the way postmen often do when they know they have something nice in their mailbag for you.

"Yes," I said, "she does."

"Do you think Miami will like it?" he said with his eyes all lit up softly, like the lamps on the library tables.

"I shouldn't wonder," I said. "It's lovely."

"It's an antique," he said. "It's from 1750. It's a family ring. I needed to show it to you. Do you think it makes a good" — he paused — "a good" — he paused again — "a good engagement ring?"

"Oh!" I said. "Oh my. Oh yes. Uncle Gideon will be terribly pleased. I mean, oops, I mean, Auntie will be pleased, of course. An engagement ring! It's a smashing good idea. Perfect!"

"Really? I mean, do you think she'd rather have a more traditional ring? I mean, are you sure?" Mr. Henley looked quite wobbly and ruffled in a cheerful sort of way, tipping about on his tall stool. "Flissy," he said, "could you by chance find out for me what kind of rings your aunt likes? I mean, how does she feel about antique rings? Can you let me know as soon as possible? Everything shall be on hold until I hear from you."

I felt quite fond of Mr. Henley as we left the library. He trusted me and he loved my aunt so very much. "You sent me your new poem and I read it," I said. "And I thought it was wonderful."

"Oh, thank you," he said. He smiled at me in a happy, wistful way. "You liked it. I'm very glad to hear that. Well then, it doesn't matter if I never get published as long as my friends read my poems." Then Mr. Henley headed off down Vine Street. He turned and waved to me in his chipper postman sort of way and the fog seemed to wrap its long, smoky arms all round him and draw him away into the whiteness.

Sixteen

Yes, when you live among a family of intelligence agents, everything is hazy and yet a word or a picture can come up out of that haze in spite of itself and can hang before your eyes at night when you should be sleeping. The blank letter to a woman in Cape Elizabeth seemed to swirl before my eyes. Why would someone stamp and address an envelope with a blank piece of paper in it?

I also knew I had to ask Auntie about her favorite type of ring and I didn't know how to begin. I didn't want to give away Mr. Henley's surprise. It made me feel awfully nervous and important at the same time. I wondered if other children, age twelve, had any of the same problems I had. I rather guessed not. I wondered too if any other children had a mother and father missing in France. It was hard to even say those words. Were they missing or were they just out of contact? We hadn't had a coded letter from them for almost a year. The Gram kept telling me they had gone underground. It made me think of rabbits or foxes or groundhogs, but not people, not parents. Parents didn't go underground. Oh, how I missed my mother especially. To want your mother as I did was like living with a river that ran under everything that happened. That river flowed on behind everything, with its ice-cold, freezing, uncaring waters. And soon my new father was going off to the war as well. Were there other children out there, beyond our blackout curtains, beyond our wind and salt spray, beyond our point and peninsula, who felt as I did?

"Auntie," I said into the darkness of our bedroom, guessing she hadn't fallen asleep yet either. "What do you think of *old* things?"

"Well, like this house, you mean?" she said from across the room, in her bed.

"Well, yes, sort of," I said.

"Oh, I would like to give this house a big face-lift. I should like to steam off all the old wallpaper and put up something with some pizzazz, like big, bright daisies in the dining room. Now, how would you feel getting up in the morning to big, bright daisies?"

"I rather like the house the way it is," I said. "I like Captain Bathburn's daughters."

"I think they are a dreary bunch, clutching their whalebone combs," she said.

"But I like the whalebone dominoes in the parlor, carved by one of the shipmates of Captain Bathburn on his voyage to India. Don't you? Mr. Bathtub told us in class that Captain Bathburn's cargo, on the way to India in 1855, was ice. Ice! Great blocks of it wrapped in sawdust and hay, stored down in the hold. That way, after three months, the ice only melted a little bit. Ice was like gold in India. It fetched huge prices. After all, they couldn't keep iceboxes there without ships bringing ice to them from places with winter and icy rivers like we have here in Maine."

"Flissy, you are a card. You're always running around like a little ladybug all wound up, even when going to sleep at night. When do you slow down, sweetest?" said Aunt Miami.

"Um, well, if you don't like old houses, is there anything old you do like?" I said.

"Hmmm, I like The Gram," said Auntie.

I felt a bit discouraged after that and so I changed the subject. "Auntie," I said quietly, "have you ever seen a letter arriving with an address and a stamp and simply nothing on the letter?"

"Well, either the person forgot to write something or they've used invisible ink, which is a subject Gideon would know all about. Speaking of my brother Gideon, you know, I think he rather enjoys intrigue and danger as much as Danny. I wish he'd get on with it and forget Winnie. Sorry, sweetest. I know you adore Winnie and I'm sure she's lovely. It's just that Gideon is wasting his life pining over a woman who ran off and married his brother."

"How do you make invisible ink visible?" I said.

"Oh, I think there are several different kinds that respond to different things. I believe the Germans are experts at it. Some types of invisible ink must be treated with chemicals, while others can be ironed, I believe."

"You mean, ironed like a pillowcase or a napkin?"
I said.

"Yes," said Auntie, yawning. "Shall we go to sleep,
sweetest? Oh, little ladybug, with all your questions.
Flissy McBee, you are such a card."

★ *Seventeen* ★

I wondered if ladybugs went to sleep at night or did they stare at the ceiling for hours as I did. Did little insects go to sleep? I knew they drank water because I had seen them at our birdbath, perching delicately on the edge, leaning over to drink. Being restless tonight was not my fault. The sea was quite rambunctious and noisy and I couldn't wait to tell Derek about invisible ink. I wanted to write a letter to Winnie and Danny with invisible ink. I could say anything I pleased because most people knew nothing about invisible ink. But Winnie and Danny would know. The letter would say, completely invisibly:

> *Dear Winnie and Danny,*
>   *I have grown weary of missing you. Every night I still cry for you. Do you hear me when I cry? And do you know that I truly love Derek Blakely? It's rather painful and seems to get worse every day. We are practicing dancing together and we are getting to be very good. Even Gideon says so. He called Derek "a good hoofer." I wish you could see us. I shall wait for you forever. I shall never stop waiting. Please be safe and if you did go underground, I hope you will soon surface. And*

*when you do, I shall finally stop longing and smile
gladly again.*

    Love,

    Your Felicity, waiting. Waiting.

I didn't say a word about Brie and the dance coming up. It was such a lovely letter without it, all invisible the way it was. I wrote to all sorts of people in my mind that night with invisible ink. And in the morning, I am afraid to say that I was bit cross. I hardly slept at all and I was late getting downstairs for breakfast. I missed helping Uncle Gideon feed Sir William Percy. That seagull had been trained to sit on Uncle Gideon's knee and squawk. It was quite my favorite way to start out the morning, but today everyone was ready to leave when I finally got downstairs.

Mr. Bathtub had on his macintosh and Derek was all set for school, wearing a little cap with a bill that his father had given him.

Mr. Bathtub did say, "Is that a new hat, Derek?"

And Derek said, "Not really, I just haven't worn it before." Of course in my loyalty to Derek, I would never say a word. If he needed to see his father in peace, then I would stand by him.

I had to eat cold toast in the car and I didn't have a chance to tell Derek about invisible ink on the way to school because Mr. Bathtub was driving. He was singing a song called "Lily Marlene," which he said was a favorite among the German soldiers.

"Outside the barracks by the corner light,
I'll always stand and wait for you at night.
We will create a world for two.
I'll wait for you the whole night through,
For you, Lily Marlene,
For you, Lily Marlene."

"That's a very pretty song, isn't it?" I said.

"Yes, it is," said Gideon. "Soldiers on both sides suffer. They are cold. They're hungry. They all want to go home. War is a terrible thing."

"When we are marching in the mud and cold
And when my pack seems more than I can hold,
My love for you renews my might,
I'm warm again, my pack is light.
It's you, Lily Marlene,
It's you, Lily Marlene."

Then my father sang the song in German. Looking out the window as we drove along the road to school, I felt a strange worry ripple through me. We passed the salt marshes and I saw a last great blue heron and flocks of gathering ducks preparing to set off on long journeys. Autumn was slowly opening up like a great papery orange flower and I marveled at it, in spite of the darkness that seemed to loom at the edge of my vision.

★ Eighteen ★

Gideon took me and Derek to the movies on that Saturday and so we did not have a chance to iron the letter. At the intermission we saw Bugs Bunny cartoons. (After that my father did a great imitation of Bugs Bunny chewing his carrot and saying, "Eh, what's up, doc?" Later at school the first graders adored it and flocked round him as he chewed his invisible carrot.)

We also saw a newsreel about Eleanor Roosevelt and her trip to Great Britain to visit Prime Minister Churchill. The newsreel showed her visiting the American soldiers stationed there too. I heard she said that our soldiers had blisters from tight cotton socks and that they needed nice wool socks.

All through the end of the movie I was feeling antsy and itchy. I was hoping we would have a chance to go into the laundry room later at home and do some ironing. Just to try it. Just to see. And, in fact, when we got home, The Gram and Auntie had gone off in a carpool to visit Miss Elkin. My father went on one of his long walks, leaving Derek and me alone in the house.

"Perhaps now is a good time to see if we can iron that letter," I said.

Derek nodded at me. I jumped up and we headed for the little laundry room next to the larder and kitchen.

The room still smelled of fresh, damp, ironed sheets and pillowcases because Aunt Miami had been in there working earlier. There was a lovely, white, lacy cotton nightdress hanging on the wall. It had been Ella Bathburn's. Her name was written under the collar. Auntie had washed and ironed the nightdress carefully. And she told me she planned to wear it on her wedding night. I had been quite relieved, actually. That proved to me Miami did like old things after all and I had already reported my findings to Mr. Henley, who had turned lobster red in the cheeks and smiled.

Now I plugged in the small, heavy iron with its black-and-white argyle cloth cord. And Derek got out the envelope addressed to Louise Mack, Cape Elizabeth, Maine. Inside was the blank piece of paper. "Fliss, you really know your onions," Derek said, looking at me in a close sort of way as we waited for the iron to heat up.

We soon placed the hot iron on the corner of the paper. We moved it across the page carefully. A strange chemical smell filled the air and then we pulled the iron back. Soon, in the heat, faint, blocky letters began to appear on the page. A few letters didn't come in at all but we were able to make out the sentence. It read, *The Gray Moth will have an identifying mark on his forehead.*

★ Nineteen ★

Everything now was troubling. Nothing seemed as it truly was. The days that followed were sunny and airy but I had something new gnawing at me, something new fluttering and dodging in front of me. It was the Gray Moth. It fluttered here and it fluttered there in my mind, always casting a dark, winged shadow.

"Derek, shouldn't we tell Gideon about this?" I whispered as we passed in the hallway upstairs.

"No," said Derek, "because then he'll want to know where we found it and he'll have to know I was at my father's hotel. And then he'll find out I've seen my dad and I don't want that yet. Please?"

"Can't we just show him the letter and say we found it somewhere else?" I said.

"No. Then we'll get tripped up and have to say really where we found it. No," Derek started to shout. He slammed the door to his room. Then he opened the door and softened his voice. "Please, Fliss," he called.

I was on my way to the attic with a box of empty canning jars. Once there, I sat on a broken rocker. I wanted to be alone. I stared at an old papier-mâché jack-o'-lantern. It had a terrible grinning smile and it seemed to leer and glow in orange from the dark shelf where it sat.

Halloween was in eleven days, but it had been canceled this year in Bottlebay because of the war. Unfortunately the autumn dance that night was still being held. Yes, I was being pulled by so many things suddenly and I didn't know what to do.

Still, normal life seemed to go on. We were asked recently not to use our car very much because petrol was needed for the war. There was a little bus that came round every morning now, which we rode to school, and that meant getting up sometimes before daylight. Mr. Bathtub rode the bus with us and Miss Elkin got on a few stops after ours. She always wanted to sit with Mr. Bathtub but he was dreadfully popular with all the students and she never seemed to get a chance. Right away Mr. Bathtub had the whole bus singing funny army songs.

> The biscuits in the army they say are mighty fine.
> One fell off of the table and killed a pal of mine.
> Oh I don't want no more of army life.
> Gee but I wanna go home!

A lot of the children happily sang along and forgot, during those rides, that their fathers and older brothers had been drafted or enlisted and would soon have to go to war.

My father was in contact with Mr. Donovan in Washington by telephone, though they often spoke in odd ways, saying things like, "The orange isn't ripe yet, but perhaps the apples are." I wasn't really supposed to know about this and yet I heard a sentence here and a word there. But my father trusted me about this, and that only made me feel more torn about Derek and his wishes. It seemed fitting that one morning I found a butterfly on the porch floor that had been battered by the wind, its wings torn and full of holes.

Derek and I spent many hours talking about the invisible-ink message and wondering if Mr. Fitzwilliam could be the Gray Moth. We went round one afternoon to his great, dark house to have a look in his windows but he wasn't about and his deaf housekeeper came out to the garden and threw her arms into the wind, telling us with gestures and expressions that Mr. Fitzwilliam was gone. Gone.

One day Aunt Miami and I rode bicycles into town and Auntie bought me a lovely green-and-red plaid taffeta frock. Oh, it was a smashing dress. We left the store and I was carrying it in a shopping bag when Auntie said, "Sweetest, little ladybug dearest, would you do me a favor and run this letter up to the post office and drop it in the slot? If you see Bobby, don't say a word about it, will you?"

"But, Auntie, what is the letter about?" I said. We were headed towards the soda fountain where Auntie had promised me an iced tea. I took the letter. It was addressed to an office in New York City.

"Mrs. Boxman has been urging me," said Miami. "She feels I have talent and that I should be helping with the war like the rest of my family. I'm applying for a job as an actress with this USO traveling theater. It will be to entertain the troops. Mrs. Boxman knows the director."

"Oh," I said. "Would you be going to New York City, then?"

"Maybe, if the theater accepts me," she said.

"But maybe you won't be accepted. It's possible, isn't it?" I said.

"Felicity Budwig Bathburn, how can you say that? I must do some work for the war. Everyone is doing something and all I'm good for is acting. I want to help. I just can't sit by and watch."

"But what about Bobby Henley?" I said. "You can't just go off and leave him. His heart will break. You said you loved him. You told me so."

"Oh, sweetest," said Auntie. "I do love him very much. That's why I don't want him to know yet. I so much don't want to upset him. He's in the reserves, Flissy. Every day, I worry that he's been called up and soon I'm afraid he will be. If I have something to keep me busy, I'll manage. And I must do my part as a Bathburn, you know. Bobby and I will have our whole lives to spend together after the war."

I walked down Main Street, feeling quite mixed up, really. I didn't want Auntie to go away. The only good part might be that I could sleep in her big canopy bed while she was gone. But I didn't want her to go! I wanted her to stay here and accept the beautiful ring Mr. Henley had for her.

At the post office I looked at the letter in my hand. I was thinking that I could easily tear it in two right then and toss it into the dustbin and be done with it. I stood in the lobby of the post office for the longest time and then I dropped the letter in the proper slot and off it went to New York City.

★ Twenty ★

The dress was even more smashing when I brought it home. I loved Auntie for buying it for me. I tried it on in her room. As I stood before the long oval mirror at her dressing table, The Gram came in. She wanted to look at the seams and the fancy metal zipper up the back. "Well, it's pretty, but frivolous, Flissy B. Bathburn. I could have sewn you a much sturdier dress. You'll freeze to death when you wear it this winter. I don't know what Miami was thinking. That girl has her head in the clouds. She should have bought you a winter corduroy."

"But it's lovely, isn't it?" I said, spinning round. Derek poked his head in the doorway and the oddest thing of all was that he blushed. It was a slow blush that started at his neck and crawled all the way up to the top of his forehead. Soon he looked like a red jellyfish. Then he hurried off down the hall, singing quite loudly.

Uncle Gideon came in next with Aunt Miami. He sat in the soft, pink stuffed chair in the corner, smiling at me. "Oh, Fliss," he said, "you'll be all grown up by the time I get back. Don't do it, will you? Stay just like you are right now. Don't change."

At that, Miami jumped up and threw herself on Gideon's lap and kissed his cheek and said, "Oh, Gideon, don't be such a goat."

Yes, the dress was perfect. But I wouldn't be wearing it to the dance because no twelve-year-old had ever been admitted to that dance at Babbington El. And so the dress too had a shadow over it, because Brie and Derek would soon be swinging and bebopping and jitterbugging together, while I would be out here sitting on the porch in the darkness looking up at the stars.

I was thinking about all this when the back doorbell rang. I'm like a horse when I hear a doorbell or telephone ring. I always start racing. I tore downstairs in my new taffeta dress, leaping over everything in my path. I simply adored the swishy sound the taffeta skirt made when I ran.

But when I opened the door, there was Mr. Henley beaming at me. He raised his eyebrows, nodded and then he handed me a letter, looking at me in a very hopeful manner. I'm sorry to report that I smiled back quite cheerfully and grabbed the letter and leapt out of the kitchen like a prima ballerina. I did several unmatched grand jetés in the hallway. I was only stopped from completing another leap because I bumped into Derek, who looked at me in a stunned way. He immediately started singing again quite loudly.

I took the letter into the library, staring at the envelope the whole way. It came from Selsey, West Sussex.

"All the way from England!" said Uncle Gideon, popping into the room and peering at the envelope. "Now, that's amazing. They say mail from England never makes it all the way here. Most of those slow-moving ships get blown up."

"You are quite nosy, actually," I said, holding the letter away from him.

"It takes one to know one, Fliss," said Uncle Gideon, tweaking my nose and smiling. He didn't mind at all when I pushed him away. He just kept humming a tune.

When I opened the letter I saw that the handwriting was extremely messy. The letter read:

Dear Felicity,

It rained here yesterday and I made a fishpond in the mud. We are moving out of our council house. Sheila Wills is in hospital. I shall be going on a boat with other children to stay with Canadians in Quebec. Last week a big silver ball washed up on the shingles at our seashore. It looked like a gigantic Christmas ornament. It was a mine, a bomb that had been dropped off a ship and had made its way to shore. All the children came to have a look, but the bobbies sent us packing. Everyone was scared but me. I didn't give a toss. The man came to defuse it. Then they took it away in a lorry so we did not get to play with the big silver ball.

Well, I didn't know who Sheila Wills was, though I was quite sorry she was in hospital, but I guessed the letter was from Dimples McFarland, even if she forgot to sign her name at the end. Actually, I knew it was from Dimples because of the splotchy ink and the messy handwriting and the drawings of sad little ghosts at the edges of the paper.

I held the letter carefully. It had come all the way from England. My England.

★ Twenty-One ★

Autumn was winding down now. Most of the leaves had turned brown and blown away. The crows at the top of the pines in the woods cawed and cawed. What could they see from their highest perch? I had been here with the Bathburns for a year and a half. I had seen the wild roses and the butterflies come and go along the American sea. And I received no word from Winnie and Danny. But they would not forget me. They would write one day. They would know I was waiting and longing and wondering and worrying.

I worried about other things as well. Now Derek had begun to truly get to know his newfound father. And the more he heard from him, the happier Derek became. His father rang up one day when everyone was out and Derek had a good chat with him. But I still did not feel right about it. Something was nagging and tugging at me. I hadn't always been like this. Wasn't it lovely seeing Derek happy, after all?

Derek planned to invite his father back to the house for lunch again and now he said I could visit with him too. But all this had to be kept a secret still. And I had to promise Derek and I did.

"Fliss," he said as we waited for the small school bus one morning, "I have told my father all about you. He likes you already. He calls you the little general."

"Oh, I wouldn't want to be a general," I said. "I'd rather be a mess cook or something like that because I do not like to shoot at things. And I hate fighting. I even hate to hear birds in the trees squabbling."

The bus then came to a stop in front of us. We hurried aboard. Derek found a seat with his pal Stu Barker. Derek didn't ever mention to Stu any of the things that had happened. I had an idea the various things that had occurred were in some way knitted together. Derek didn't mention anything to anyone, not even to his father. But perhaps we *should* have told Uncle Gideon. Yes, perhaps that was our mistake.

Mr. Bathtub wasn't on the bus this morning. I didn't know how he got to school some days, but he often took long walks in the morning and he was quite busy with preparations for his journey to Europe. I sometimes thought about why he might need a German officer's uniform and why he might need to speak perfect German. And all in all I was nervous and uneasy about everything.

Mr. Bathtub was busy with his sixth-grade classes as well, but very often when he hadn't been on the bus that morning, he would be at school already when we got there, welcoming us, ready to start making jokes and poking fun. "What ho, Fliss!" he would say when I walked down the hall, passing his classroom first thing in the morning with all the others. "Where have you been? I haven't seen you for eight moons and a dog!"

Soon enough, the bus stopped and Miss Elkin got on. I saw her glancing round for Mr. Bathtub and I saw her look disappointed as well. She had her enormous cello in its huge black case with her and she sat with me. Well, it wasn't all peaches and cream because her big cello case poked me a bit in the ribs. We were rattling along the motorway when Miss Elkin finally said, "Felicity, you know how the chaperones at the autumn dance always jump in for a few of the dances, especially the fox-trot?"

"Yes," I said, looking out the window as we passed a new group of winter seabirds flocking over the salt marsh.

"You know the tradition at Babbington El. The chaperones always have as much fun as the kids," said Miss Elkin.

"I've heard all the stories," I said.

Soon Miss Elkin started whispering to me, "I'd really like to ask Mr. Bathtub to be my chaperone partner! You know the tradition at Babbington. Would you mind doing me a tremendous favor and seeing if he's at all interested in the dance? I mean, discreetly. I mean, does he ever do anything like that?"

I didn't answer Miss Elkin right away. I knew Uncle Gideon loved to dance because he and Auntie were always cutting a rug, as Derek called it. But I wasn't sure what to tell Miss Elkin. I began to feel suddenly quite heavy with other people's secrets. Honestly, I did. I did not want to encourage Miss Elkin. I knew Uncle Gideon still loved my mum Winnie, even if he hadn't been with her in thirteen years. He still loved her. I did not think he would ever go to a dance with anyone but Winnie.

★ *Twenty-Two* ★

When I came home from school that afternoon, Mr. Bathtub was in the library, grading papers. He looked over the tops of his reading glasses at me and said, "What ho, Fliss! We meet again! To what do I owe the pleasure?" I leaned against the back of his big green stuffed chair and I tried to think of a way I could ask him about the autumn dance coming up and Miss Elkin. I was also trying to see what paper he was grading. In a very casual way, I tried to peer over his shoulder. The report said across the top of the page, *The Vicious Mighty Shark by Charlie Tabbet.* At school, all of Charlie's reports were about sharks. Mr. Bathtub had given Charlie an A minus. Mr. Bathtub brought sandwiches into school every day for a group of children who didn't have any breakfast or lunch. I think Charlie was one of them.

"What are you reading these days, Fliss?" Mr. Bathtub said to me. "No longer the expert on Frances Hodgson Burnett?"

"I've read *The Secret Garden* eight times and I will *not* be reading it again. I am way too old for that book now," I said.

"I see, that's a shame," he said. "By the way, we're having some visitors this month. Bill Donovan will be here in a few days and he is bringing along a Canadian fellow named Bill Stephenson. They are great friends and we call them Big Bill and Little Bill. Little Bill will be very pleased to meet you."

"Why is Mr. Donovan coming back?" I said, running my foot along the tassels at the bottom of the chair. "Wasn't he here already? Can he tell us where my Winnie and Danny are?"

"Oh, Fliss, can I ask you not to question all this? I know you are a bright girl and you've noticed so much. And I'm very proud of you for that. But for your own sake and for your own safety, please don't poke around. Don't ask any questions." My father put his arm round me as I stood there next to his chair, leaning against him, looking right into his eyes, which seemed to be full of sweetness and sadness again. Right then I should have broken my word to Derek. Right then I should have told him about Mr. Fitzwilliam at the Eastland Park Hotel, snooping round, trying to find out about Derek's dad. I should have told him about the invisible-ink letter. And I should have told him about Derek's father and his visits. Right then I should have spoken.

★ *Twenty-Three* ★

How easy it is to think later, *Oh, what I should have done!* But how hard to think clearly when you are smack in the middle of the soup of your life. Instead of telling my father everything, I skipped towards the kitchen singing a jump-rope song I learned from Dimples.

> *"The man in the moon sang me a tune,*
> *Then he handed out sweets on a silver spoon."*

I finally tossed the invisible jump rope aside and threw myself into a chair at the blue metal table. The Gram was making bread. She was rolling and turning the yeasty, sweet-smelling dough on a breadboard. She let me poke it with my finger and it was soft and springy. Finally, she pulled off a part of it and let me roll it and work it along with her. As we rolled and pushed, I started talking. I was not at all good at being quiet. Ideas inside me were always pushing to pop out. Danny always said so. Winnie always agreed. Words and ideas inside me were just as jumpy as my feet, even though I was twelve years old and should have been by now very proper and grown-up and polite and quiet. "The bread dough feels as though it's alive," I said.

"Well, Flissy, because of the yeast, it is alive in a way," said The Gram. "Until we cook it, of course. We're having some visitors, you know."

"Yes," I said, "I know. But why? Why is Mr. Donovan coming back? Does this have anything to do with my Winnie? And what about the Butterfly Circuit? Isn't that what it's called?"

The Gram dropped the dough on the floured bread-board. She tapped her fingers up and down, leaving white floury fingerprints on the blue metal. "Felicity, your father and I very much would like you to stop poking around. We are living in very dangerous times. We Bathburns are doing the best we can to help fight against the Nazis. Danny, Gideon, myself, and your mother, Winifred. Although I do not like Winifred because of the way she hurt my Gideon, I do admire her for her work. You must protect her by not asking questions." The Gram put her flour-covered hand against my cheek. "We so love having you with us, Flissy McBee. Perhaps you should not be here. Perhaps we are fools to keep you with us at this time. But we have waited so long for you. We have waited and waited and longed to have you with us. And suddenly here you are amidst all this." She hugged me and I could feel her whole being rising and falling against me, crying in a silent, tearless way.

Soon enough, my father came bubbling into the kitchen with a cheerful smile. "What ho, Fliss! Has The Gram fallen into a heap? What shall we do? How about we all go out for dinner tonight? We'll go to the place along the wharf. What's it called, the Boiling Pot? We haven't done anything like that since Fliss has been here. What do you say, old bean?" said Gideon, patting me on the back and then putting his arm round The Gram.

"Oh yes, please!" I said, jumping up and down.

"We'll take the whole clan and we'll even ask Bob Henley along," said Uncle Gideon.

"And what about Miss Elkin?" I said. "I think she would be ever so pleased to be invited as well." Gideon frowned and didn't answer me. He sat down at the blue table and opened the newspaper. He started whistling and turning pages. The Gram and I began tucking the soft, pliable bread dough into buttered baking tins. Soon, five fat little loaves were sitting all ready to be popped into the cooker.

I left the room and went upstairs and when the loaves had baked, the delicious smell drew me back downstairs. I stood in the hallway for a moment and I could hear Gideon talking quietly to The Gram. "I've heard from Donovan, actually. Unfortunately, our sources tell us there's a rather important German agent in the area."

★ Twenty-Four ★

It was as if someone had taken a basket of laundry and dumped it all out into the wind. Shirts and skirts and sheets and towels were let loose, flying every which way. Every idea in the world popped in and out of my mind. Was Mr. Fitzwilliam the Gray Moth? Was that why the man at lunch had planned to mail that letter to Cape Elizabeth? Never before had I ever met anyone who seemed so dark and dangerous as Mr. Fitzwilliam. How long had he been living in that big house on the cliff walk? Not long, I should imagine. Wouldn't we have run into him around town before if he really lived here? And one day recently, though he didn't see me, I spotted him down on the rocks below, staring up at our house, studying it, watching for something. What about that story of the architect who had been murdered? I should have realized right then that there was something wrong. And what had this to do with Derek's father?

Oh, I so hoped Derek would come home soon. We were to begin dance practice at seven and he was already late. I needed to talk to him. I wasn't going to tell Uncle Gideon anything until I had talked with Derek.

I put on a little jacket and went out the back door into the garden. The full moon cast an oddly bright light on the sleeping wild roses. In the fields beyond there were seas of drying goldenrod bending and rustling and glowing yellow with the wind and moon.

Then I saw a shadow of someone up on the road, walking briskly towards the house. It startled me at first but soon I realized it was Derek. I ran up as fast as I could to the road. We stood there in the stark moonlight, our long, pale shadows shimmering on the road before us. "Derek. Oh, Derek. I just heard Gideon say there is a big German agent in the area," I said. "Don't you think we should tell Gideon about your father and Fitzwilliam?"

Suddenly, Derek grabbed me. He wrapped his one good arm round me and he held me really tightly. I was pulled in close against him and I could feel him trembling. He kept on holding me like that and he pushed his face against my cheek. His lips brushed across mine and I felt as if I were swimming in a warm blur. Then he whispered, "Fliss, don't say anything yet. It has nothing to do with my father. We have to figure this out on our own. Don't say anything. I want to get to know my father first. I *need* to get to know him. My father is *my* business. No one else's." Then he let go of me and rushed on into the house, leaving me standing alone in the shadows.

★ Twenty-Five ★

Yes, America was losing many, many ships along the coast. German U-boats were everywhere, lurking, and when supply ships or even convoys went through the eastern waters, U-boats torpedoed and sunk many of them. It was like an epidemic. Gideon was dark and gloomy about this and he had gone off to talk with a friend who was on sub-watching duty up on the hill in a cement tower with open windows all round the top. It was tucked away in the pinewoods but if you looked up at the hill, you could see the eye of the tower poking out of the trees.

It was another one of those windy, rainy days and Derek had built a fire in the fireplace. Everyone was out of the house that day, as planned, and Derek's father had just arrived. He was standing in the hallway with an umbrella that the wind had ripped to shreds and turned inside out. He was quite wet. The water rolled off his macintosh and he stamped his boots. Then he shook off the macintosh and shuddered. "Oh, I'll keep this on," he said, touching his hat. "It loses its form if I take it off when it's wet. It will dry to a perfect shape this way." He smiled at Derek, and Derek looked proud and pleased. Derek's father was happy to see the fire in the fireplace and the two of them settled down together in front of it, like old friends.

I brought in the tea tray. All the while I kept wishing Gideon would suddenly come back and barge in and ease my mind about this. I did not like deceiving him. But there was nothing wrong with a father visiting with his son, was there?

"Well, she is British," Derek was just saying, "and one of my favorite Bathburns, actually."

"Honestly, truly, Derek?" I said, setting the tea tray down. I put the cups out and poured the tea. "I am actually a dual citizen," I added, looking away.

"But this is terrific for you, my son, to have someone your own age here. And to live in this marvelous house. What a view, even with the rain. Do you often see whales and porpoises?"

"All the time," said Derek. "We see all sorts of creatures, even sharks, I think."

"Sharks too! Quite exciting. Is that one there now?" Derek's father pointed out the window.

"Look through these binoculars. It's probably a seal. They love rain," said Derek.

"Oh," he said. "Oh, how do you focus them? Let me see. I guess I need to remove my glasses." He took off his glasses and looked through the binoculars. "Ah yes, I can see the water now. There are certainly plenty of birds floating about." Derek's father put down the binoculars.

"Well, this is a grand place. The water is quite rough out there today!"

"Did we live here by the water when I was a baby?" Derek said then, suddenly. The words came out in a rather awkward way and he seemed startled himself by their sound. Derek's face rather crinkled up, as if someone had just clapped their hands way too close to his ears. "Where was I born?"

"Ah, of course, you would be curious. Do you really want to open this can of . . . this can of . . ."

"Worms," I said.

"Yes, this can of worms," said Derek's father. "Well, perhaps it's time. You know I hadn't wanted to talk about it. Really, I had hoped we could somehow just let it go and start afresh. It's rather sad. Your mother and I were married in Texas. She had the idea that she wanted to marry a cowboy. You were born in that state. I worked on a ranch outside of Austin. I *was* a cowboy but I must confess I wasn't a very good one. I never could lasso a single steer because I couldn't handle a rope. This was because of muscle damage in one of my arms from a childhood injury."

"Oh, but that's like me," said Derek. "My left arm is pretty much paralyzed. I can't use it."

"I am so unhappy to hear this. Ah, but we are father and son, are we not? Parallels, you see," said Derek's dad.

"But how did you come to leave me or whatever it

was?" said Derek, sort of twisting in his chair. "What happened anyway?"

"Well, your mother died. I became deeply depressed. I am sorry to say that I am given to depression. I do hope you have not inherited that! I came to Maine because I lost my job. I really don't like horses anyway."

"But why did you not want me anymore? Why did you leave me here? What happened?" Derek's voice was plaintive and his face was pale. He looked tired suddenly and I barely recognized him for a moment.

"Derek, people's lives are changing. Sometimes there is no use for regretting. We cannot look around. It would be too painful. I cannot talk about it. I do not want to break down and cry. I don't have a handkerchief. Will you excuse me for a moment? Where's your lavatory? I think I've drunk too much tea. And I cannot bear to remember." He laughed and cried in a confusing way and stumbled out of the room, as if the sadness made it hard to walk.

"It's just up the stairs and down the hall on your left," said Derek. And then he propped his chin in his hand and looked down into the depths of the floor.

I was always looking to cheer up Derek, so when his father left the room, I picked up his glasses, which he had left on the table in his confusion and sadness. I put them on and I made a face at Derek.

"Come on, Fliss," he said, "put those down."

"Very well," I said, looking round the room through them. It was really quite strange. I expected them to be blurry because most glasses are fitted with lenses to suit the needs of the owner. But these glasses seemed to have no special lenses. They were clear glass. I had no trouble seeing through them.

I put the glasses back on the table and I looked up at Derek. He was now inspecting the little brochure that came with the box of Lincoln Logs that his father had brought him. "This is a special, complicated set. It's not for little kids, Fliss. It's a teenager's set," said Derek, looking a bit brighter.

"Derek," I said, "perhaps we shouldn't allow your father upstairs. I mean, perhaps Gideon would be upset."

"Oh no, he's family," said Derek. "It's fine. He was so sad. I shouldn't have asked all that. Didn't you see how he almost cried?"

I was wondering why someone would wear a pair of glasses that did not help him see better. I mean, what purpose would those glasses serve? Why wear a pair of clear glasses? I suddenly felt a draft sweep through the room.

Lying in my bed across from Auntie that night, I felt I was drifting in a kind of fearful fog. As Derek had said, why can't a person wear clear glasses if they want to? Why was I being so glum? Why did I want to cast shadows on the best thing that had happened to Derek in years? He said he loved his father. He said he would trust him with anything. Derek and his father had built a wonderful Lincoln Log construction together and then they had gone outside and taken photographs. Derek's father brought out his camera and took a number of pictures of Derek standing by the house, on the porch, in the hallway. Then Derek brought out his Brownie box camera. But his father protested. "No, no, I don't look well in photographs. My nose is swollen from a cold I had. Another day, but not today."

Why was I becoming so fearful? What was it that seemed to be flying over me like a shadow of a bomber moving over a city? I stayed awake for a long time that night, listening to the waves hammering the rocks below. I kept saying over and over to myself, as the waves broke, *I love Derek. I want to be loyal to him. I don't want to hurt him.* Derek had been calling me crazy as a loon recently. Perhaps he was right.

But after visiting, Derek's father had set off down the road on foot, walking into Bottlebay, where he said he had parked his car. As he walked along he was humming a tune. He had given Derek a great hug good-bye and he had taken my hand like a true gentleman and pretended to kiss it in a jokey way. Then he had set off down the road. Only now something came back to me. As I lay here in my bed, the tune Derek's father was humming suddenly played in my mind. How easy it was to miss things, to not notice things when you were smack in the middle of the soup of your life. Yes, he was clearly humming a song I had heard before. It was the German soldiers' song called "Lily Marlene."

Outside the barracks by the corner light,
I'll always stand and wait for you at night.
We will create a world for two.
I'll wait for you the whole night through,
For you, Lily Marlene,
For you, Lily Marlene.

★ *Twenty-Six* ★

I tried to talk to Derek about his father and my fears the next day but he would hear none of it. "But, Derek," I said.

And he said, "No. I don't want you to say anything about my father. He's my father and whoever or whatever he is, I stand by him."

"But, Derek," I kept saying. "Please just think about this."

"Stop worrying," he said. "He's family. He's a photographer, like me. And he's a great photographer."

"No, Derek," I said. "You must stop seeing him. I don't like all this. There's something wrong. Why was he humming that song?"

"You've got rocks in your socks," said Derek. "It's a pretty tune. Even you said so. You've gone nutty, Fliss."

"Well, I haven't gone round the twist yet," I said.

"Yes, you have. That's just it. You have gone round the twist. Or the bend, as normal people say. Let's face it, Fliss, you're just not normal," Derek said. He looked at me with his eyes that had turned fiery like burning coal.

"No. Gideon won't want him in the house here," I said.

"Gideon won't know. He'll never know unless *you* tell him," said Derek.

"Please," I said. "Maybe we should just talk to Gideon first."

At the mention of Gideon, I became quiet in my heart. I knew the dance was fast approaching and I had not asked him if he would like to go as a chaperone. I certainly hadn't mentioned Miss Elkin. He hadn't wanted to take Miss Elkin to the Boiling Pot, so why would he want to go to the dance with her? As The Gram had said, "In case you haven't noticed, Flissy dear, my children live in the clouds. They are not an ordinary breed. And they cannot marry everyday, regular people."

Oh, I felt dreadful on all counts. Everywhere I turned, I felt sorrowful. Poor Miss Elkin. Poor Derek. Poor me! I almost wished I had my old bear, Wink, back. He was always so levelheaded when I was not. He always had that steady smile I could trust, even if it was a sewn-on smile that never changed. I wished then that I wasn't twelve. Twelve-year-olds do not believe in bears and I needed now to believe in something.

Yes, I tried to listen to Derek and forget my fears about his father. I tried to think of other things. But I did not forget about Derek and me on the road that night. How he held me close to him. I wasn't sure if it was just because he was momentarily stirred by the news or if it had meant more to him than that. But the feeling of his cheek against mine followed me everywhere. It brought with it a kind of joyous, tingly feeling, a kind of enormous happiness and that happiness seemed stronger than my fears about Derek's dad. I supposed Derek was right. Perhaps his father was just a character who put words together in a slightly different way and wore clear glasses for the fun of it. The dreamy feeling of Derek holding me seemed to push away everything else. And I walked round the Bathburn house in a haze of mixed-up happiness and anxiousness.

Four days before the dance I opened the icebox door and there was a corsage, sitting in a box on the shelf, a bright purple rose blooming, glowing in an eerie way, with its terrible, fleshy petals like tentacles. Gideon had been to Portland and had bought it for Derek to give to Brie, for the dance. I hated it. Every time I opened the icebox, there it was.

And Auntie and The Gram were cleaning furiously. I had to help. We opened up the two back bedrooms beyond the little gymnasium and we aired out the curtains, fluffed the pillows, and swept the floors. Mr. William Donovan and Mr. William Stephenson were coming to stay with us.

"Two Williams?" I said.

"Yes," said Auntie. "They are big shots from Washington and New York. Mr. Stephenson works for Prime Minister Churchill."

"Well then, we should make autumn bouquets," I

said, "and fill the house with them because I am a great fan of Prime Minister Churchill."

The Gram scrubbed the kitchen floor and we made all sorts of biscuits and pies, even though we had some trouble getting enough sugar and we had to borrow some ration stamps from Miss Elkin.

When I went round to her house to get the tickets, she looked at me in a longing sort of way and said, "Did you ask Mr. Bathtub? Do you think he would want to go with me as a chaperone to the dance?"

"Oh, Miss Elkin," I said. "This may sound odd but you know that Mr. Bathtub still loves my mother, even though he isn't married to her anymore. It's a bit of a mess."

"Oh, Felicity, I was hoping, that's all. You know. It would be nice," she said.

"My aunt says that some people only love one partner in their lives," I said. "She says those people are like Canada geese. They marry for life. If they lose that partner, they won't accept anyone else. They often spend the rest of their lives alone."

Miss Elkin looked suddenly brisk and impatient and she hurried away into her house.

★ Twenty-Seven ★

It was quite festive when our guests arrived. I had gone outside and picked dried flowers and branches of berries and turning hydrangeas for all the rooms. Aunt Miami was dressed up in her rose silk gown and she floated about the house in a swirl of fabric. I put on my new plaid taffeta frock, the one that seemed to make Derek blush and look at the ceiling. (Perhaps the green and red colors bothered him.) It was almost evening when the great dark car pulled up outside. We went out to help Big and Little Bill carry their baggage into the house. They had brought all sorts of things, like a small film projector and briefcases that Mr. Stephenson (Little Bill) wouldn't let anyone carry. We had a lovely dinner in the dining room and we sat there making jokes and laughing.

Mr. Stephenson had sort of a sad face with a little scar by his mouth. He and Big Bill were quite good friends and they both adored Winnie and Danny. As we passed round Auntie's special mashed potato casserole, Big Bill wanted to know about the portraits of Captain Bathburn and his family on all the walls of the dining room.

"Every night, that family watches us having our dinner," I said, taking a great bite of gravy and potato. "I should imagine they must be terribly hungry after all these years."

"Our Flissy is very outspoken," said The Gram. "If you think she's reserved and still very British, well, think again."

"But she's completely quiet when it comes to certain things," said Uncle Gideon in a soft voice.

"That's wonderful," said Little Bill, smiling. "Of course she is."

I looked down at the tablecloth. It was The Gram's very best one. There were angels and lilies and butterflies woven into the creamy white, polished fabric. Butterflies. Yes, I was quiet about everything. Perhaps too quiet. I remembered the hot iron rolling over the invisible ink on the paper, the words, foggy and blurry, coming up out of nowhere. Derek's father too seemed to circle round my thoughts, casting his own moving shadow. As I watched the candles burning in their silver holders, a terrible thought fluttered through my mind. Was Derek's father the Gray Moth?

Just then Derek kicked his foot against mine, saying, "Flissy's a trooper. She knows how to keep a secret." I looked up at him and smiled. Then my eyes fell back to the tablecloth and I counted the butterflies repeated and repeated in the weave of the pattern all across the table.

After dinner Big and Little Bill played a special game of dominoes while Derek and I looked on. They used the old carved whalebone dominoes that had once belonged to Captain A. E. Bathburn. Big and Little Bill took the game terribly seriously and tried to beat and outfox each other every step of the way. Derek and I were sent off to bed before the game was finished and Big Bill and Little Bill were both still gnashing their teeth at each other in a jovial sort of way when I had to say good night. I was sad to go because they had been quite good fun, really, but The Gram was very firm about bedtime and school and all that rot.

"He isn't called Wild Bill for nothing," Mr. Stephenson was just saying as my foot hit the top step. "He's thrown caution to the wind this time. I've got you now, for sure, Wild Bill."

It was hard to sleep with the lights on downstairs, with the laughter and jokes and the sweet tobacco smoke that drifted up the hall. Soon Aunt Miami came in from her date with Bobby Henley. She had gone out after dinner and her skirts rustled in the darkness as she laid her cold, silky coat on the chair next to my bed. It brought with it the smell of the outdoors and the chill of an evening out and all that I was missing as I lay there, pretending to sleep.

Auntie moved round the room in the darkness like a ghost. Finally, I heard her bed sag as she climbed in. All the beds in the house had once belonged to the captain's family. They were called rope beds and they didn't have box springs as modern beds did. Instead, under the mattress there were ropes to hold the mattress up, which you tightened every night with a key that went into a keyhole in the bedpost. You turned the key and the ropes tightened. Uncle Gideon told me that was where the saying *sleep tight* came from. Because it was too dark and Auntie didn't want to wake me, she didn't tighten the ropes as she usually did and so her mattress would slump a bit that night.

Lying there, hearing Uncle Gideon roaring and laughing away, I could tell Little Bill was now beating Big Bill, whose title in Washington was Major General William Donovan. The Gram had got on the side of Big Bill and was offering him advice. But it was no use; Little Bill triumphed. When it was over, they had Nescafé coffee and talked about how the troops overseas loved this new instant coffee and how it was much easier for the army cooks to prepare. I could hear the tinkling sound of coffee cups against china saucers and it was a lovely, cozy noise, one I was used to in England. But then The Gram said, "Well, I think they are all asleep now and we can go on up and begin."

Upon hearing those words, I am sorry to say I sat bolt upright in bed. Auntie was already asleep across the room. Her form had become a dark mountain of blanket folds and peaceful breathing. I blinked my eyes. The door to our room was open and the light from the hall fell across our rug in a comforting, homey way, but I was not to be comforted. Not tonight. I intended to listen to all that was said, every word.

In a while I heard them climb the stairs without speaking. I saw them walk silently past my room, Mr. Donovan carrying his projector and briefcase. Mr. Stephenson was carrying a box and some papers. I waited. The Gram led them into the gymnasium. And then she closed the door. Then I heard only Auntie's breathing and the silent shifting of Captain Bathburn's old house.

Soon, I climbed from my bed and tiptoed out of the room. In the hall I stood in my nightdress, looking at the crack of light under the door. The Gram always complained that this house didn't have enough closets. There wasn't any place to put our clothes. Uncle Gideon then would say, "Well, back in 1854, they didn't have very many clothes, Mother. You had a good suit or a good dress and an everyday outfit and that was all."

"Well, Miami would have surely perished back then without her enormous wardrobe," The Gram would answer. "That daughter of mine has more fancy dresses than the Queen of the May!" I was thinking about closets just then because there was a closet in Derek's room. It was long and narrow and covered in pine paneling and led to a second door, which opened onto the gymnasium. It was a shared closet but we called it a secret passageway. I needed to be in that passageway right now with the door slightly ajar. I needed to walk right into Derek's room while he slept and wake him up.

Anyone who has ever been in love before with someone as dashing and moody and charming and changeable as Derek Blakely would know that it would be very hard indeed to enter his room while he slept. Wasn't it improper? Winnie would surely scold me when she came back. Would Derek growl at me for waking him? Would he think me dreadful? I felt shy and awkward and nervous and yet at the same time I felt itchy and jumpy and jittery and absolutely certain I needed to go in that passageway. Now.

And so I did what all British children do when they are in a pinch. I closed my eyes and I plunged ahead. I turned Derek's doorknob and I stepped quietly into his moonlit room. I shut the door behind me.

I stood in the center of the room. In the moonlight, Derek's face on the pillow looked to be made of porcelain or marble, polished and fine like a statue of a beautiful sleeping boy. I wished then that all his troubles would be gone, that the father he loved would truly be his real father, forever and ever, so that Derek no longer would feel an emptiness, a loss, and a longing. "Derek," I whispered. "Derek, wake up."

I cannot imagine what Derek thought when he opened his eyes, with the moon's light falling across the room in a long, dreamlike shaft and me standing in the midst of it in my white nightdress. Derek looked at me and I looked back at him in a very shy way. "I'm dreadfully sorry to disturb you, but we absolutely must go in your closet immediately," I said. Then I threw my hand over my mouth and said, "Oops, I mean, what I mean is, um, I have to hear what is going on in the gymnasium just now. They're all in there, Derek. They've got the movie projector with them. Get up, would you? I mean, I do hope you'll excuse me but I need to look from your closet door into their room."

Wrapped all in silence, Derek slipped out of bed, in an almost magic way, as if the statue of the sleeping boy had suddenly come to life. He was wearing the cowboy pajamas that The Gram had made for him for Christmas. It had been my idea. The Gram and I had found the flannel fabric at the dime store in Bottlebay. I had picked the tan fabric with red-and-white horses and cowboys wearing ten-gallon hats. The Gram could sew anything. I had helped her stitch the buttonholes. I had learned to do that in school in England.

Derek moved without a sound across the room. He

went right for his closet door, opened it gently, and we both crawled down the long space to the other door, which was already open a crack.

My heart sank as we sat there together on the floor, looking into the dark gymnasium and listening to the rattle and click of the film as it ran through the projector. On the screen in the long room, the film brightened, halted, and became shadowy and dark and then brightened again. There was a German soldier, an officer walking towards the camera. His face flickered by. He was getting in a car. A Nazi flag fluttered behind him.

Mr. Stephenson said, "Okay, now, this is Colonel Helmut Ludswig, a Gestapo officer, who will be taking over as head of the prison on February second. And as you can see, it's rather remarkable. We were quite excited when we realized how much he resembles you, Gideon, with the exception of the mustache, of course. You'll start growing your mustache soon, I hope?"

"Yes," said Gideon.

"So you will be posing as this man. You will arrive on February first, a day early, unexpectedly, at his prison post in Limoges. The man in charge, who will be leaving, is the only man who has met Colonel Ludswig face-to-face and knows what he actually looks like. Therefore we must make sure this man is off duty the night that Gideon arrives. Perhaps a woman agent of ours could invite him out to dinner."

"We already have someone in place for that job," said The Gram.

"Excellent," said Big Bill. Now there were photos of the large, dark-looking prison. Nazi soldiers stood at attention outside the gate. "We'll work it all out in advance. The whole procedure down to the smallest detail. We are building a simulation of the prison now. The movie-set designer from California is working on it. When you come up to the facility outside of Toronto, it should be all finished."

I sat back against the wall. I held my hand over my mouth because I was afraid I might shout out. A terrible tornado was ripping through my heart. Then Derek pulled gently on my arm. "Hush," he whispered. "Shhh."

I was on my knees but I fell to my face. I put my hands over my ears. I didn't want to hear any more. Then Derek tugged on my sleeve, pulling me back through the passageway. As soon as I was in his room, I dropped forward, facedown on the floor again. My tears fell on the wooden surface, my mouth pressed against the polished pine. "Why is Uncle Gideon going to a prison?" I whispered. Derek closed the closet door. I could feel more tears and sobs threatening to come up out of me in a howling sort of way.

Derek put his hand on the back of my head as I lay there. "Oh, Fliss, don't think about it," he said. "Don't worry, Gideon will get them out."

"Get who out?" I said, sitting up and shaking my head back and forth. "Who do you mean? Who?" I put my hands over my ears again.

"Flissy," said Derek, "listen to me."

"No, no. Leave me alone. You don't mean Winnie and Danny. You don't mean that Winnie and Danny have been caught? Are they in prison, Derek? Don't say that. Don't say one more word!"

★ Twenty-Eight ★

The next morning, Big and Little Bill and Uncle Gideon were full of jokes. They were calling my father Colonel and asking him where his mustache went. "Lost it on the way to the races, did you, Colonel?" Big Bill said, slapping him on the back. We all went out on to the front porch before breakfast to see the sun rise. I hadn't wanted to. Everyone kept making jokes but nothing seemed funny to me at all.

Even when Sir William Percy came flying in for some food, I wasn't cheered. "You see, Gideon," said The Gram, "I told you that seagull would become a nuisance." When Sir William Percy took a liking to Little Bill and put his head in Little Bill's jacket pocket and pecked at the top of his fountain pen, I still didn't laugh. My beautiful Winnie and Danny were in prison in France. After all this waiting and hoping and wondering, now I knew. I knew and it hurt. It hurt more than any of the other hurts I had been feeling. It had come like a bomb and blown Brie and the dance away. It had swept away all the other worries that had seemed to be tumbling down on me in a constant stream. But at least they were not dead. No, not yet anyway.

During breakfast, I couldn't eat a bite. Derek got all my toast and blueberry jam. I think he had been waiting for just such an opportunity. He gobbled up my scrambled eggs as well. Uncle Gideon was looking at me with soft brown eyes that for some reason reminded me of Wink again. Then he glanced up at The Gram quickly and shook his head. I did not know if I could bear the thought that he too would soon be in danger.

Little Bill was talking about when he was a fighter pilot during World War I. "Did you attack any enemy planes?" said Derek.

"Well, actually, I shot down the Red Baron's brother. Didn't kill him but he didn't fly again for the rest of the war."

"Hey, that's pretty hotsy totsy," said Derek, finishing off my portion of blueberry jam. It was very impressive the way he said that, but I didn't feel like smiling.

I went to school then, but I couldn't listen to anything anyone said to me. Winnie and Danny, my beautiful Winnie and Danny, were in prison. At the end of the day I couldn't remember anything that had happened in class.

Stu Barker walked home from school with Derek and me in the afternoon. Stu was a devoted Boy Scout. He could start a fire by rubbing two sticks together. He could pitch a tent anywhere, even in the middle of a storm. He could make a water purifier out of an old coffee tin. Stu

Barker was quite a small fellow, the size of a fifth grader. Derek towered over him. But Stu was very bossy.

"You got to listen to me, kiddo," he said as we walked along the road out of town. "I'm an Eagle Scout now. I've got everything figured out." He looked way up at Derek and nodded his head at him. "I'm going to be a page next year and work at the state house part-time. You go to government studies program in the spring and when you're done with it, you are an official page. Then you're on your way to being a senator or even the president of the United States." Then he nudged me with his little elbow. "Isn't it the truth, Flissy? Come on, say it's so."

"I daresay I know nothing at all about government studies," I said. They went rattling along, talking away, as if everything were hunky-dory (another Derek word). But everything wasn't hunky-dory at all. Not at all. My beloved Winnie and Danny had been caught. They had been put in prison. Were they hungry or cold? Were they together? Were they in danger of being shot?

On top of my worries for Winnie and Danny, I had become more suspicious of Derek's father, which caused a bit of a rift between Derek and me. He refused to hear my worries about this. When I had mentioned the Gray Moth, he had exploded and stormed out of the room. Whenever I brought it up, he would simply walk away.

"Derek," I had cried when we were alone for a moment after school. "Why wouldn't he take off his hat?"

"What!" he had almost yelled back at me. "He told us why. He likes his hat to keep its shape. You are meddling, Flissy."

Derek had invited his father to the house again this week and I had begged him not to. And I felt we needed to tell someone about the invisible-ink letter. And the eyeglasses and everything else. No, nothing was hunky-dory. Not at all.

"And by the way, who are you going to the dance with, kiddo?" said Stu, putting his hands in his pockets and looking up at Derek.

"I'm going with Brie. You knew that, Stu," Derek said.

"Oh, Brie," said Stu, punching Derek's good arm. "Brie's the bee's knees. Come on, put 'em up, buddy. Winner takes all. How'd you get so lucky?"

"Dunno," said Derek, kicking a rock up into the brush ahead of us.

Nothing was worse than having two show-off American boys fighting over a snooty, pretty American girl, even if she did wear braces. I was standing there, feeling like a foreign pip-squeak. A twerp. A twerp who knew too much. And my parents were in prison.

When we got home, Derek and Stu went into the kitchen for a cup of Ovaltine, and I went up to the room I shared with Auntie. I sat on Auntie's canopy bed. And then I flopped against her pillow. As I dropped back into the softness of it, I felt a crinkly paper at the back of my head. I turned round and picked up an envelope. It was a letter addressed to Miami Bathburn from a USO Camp Show office in New York City. My heart dropped then, like a terrible submarine going down even farther to the very bottom of the ocean. *Oh, Auntie, don't leave. Stay here forever. I couldn't bear to wander about this house without your voice calling out, "Sweetest! Oh, sweetest, where are you?"*

I held the letter up to the light, hoping to see through it. I did have a little bit of luck. I could almost read the typed words *Dear Miss Bathburn.* Then I thought I could read, *We are sneezed to inform you.* No, the words were too jumbled. I couldn't make them out and so I just sat there holding the envelope. I knew quite well in all my dreadful American snooping how to steam open a letter and then reseal it. Derek had taught me how. But for once the better part of me got hold and I resisted, though I knew already it was an acceptance. My aunt was going to be an actress traveling round to entertain the soldiers in America. It rather killed me and thrilled me at the same time.

★ Twenty-Nine ★

I felt so sad and worried for my Winnie and Danny that it almost didn't matter that the dreadful rose corsage was finally taken out of the icebox. It now sat on the table in the hallway, its petals glowing, waiting to be pinned on Cousin Brie's shoulder. How could Derek do this? Did he not hug me in the darkness on the road last week? Did he not hold my hand in Portland? Had he not spent weeks practicing dancing with me? How could he now be going to the dance with Brie?

It was evening and The Gram was in the garden taking the dry sheets off the clothesline. I could see her through the open window. There was the smell of burning autumn leaves in the air and the sun was going down, making The Gram and her sheets into dark shadows turning in the wind. How mysterious she seemed now to me after hearing her speak in the gymnasium with the two Bills. Somehow I was in the middle of something, as if in a dark funnel, everything circling round the Bathburn house.

Derek came down the stairs and stopped in the parlor. He was dressed in a dark blue suit with a bow tie at his throat. He kept his one paralyzed hand in his jacket pocket. When Uncle Gideon saw him, he said,

"Well, if it isn't Humphrey Bogart from *The Maltese Falcon*!" Derek smiled. He had the corsage in his right hand.

Auntie was lying on the sofa, reading a script for *Romeo and Juliet.* Yes, she had been accepted into the theater troop and there would be tryouts for Juliet later. She had her hair in bobby pins for curlers. She sat up and loosely tied a silk scarf round her head and said, "Oh, Derek, you are simply handsome tonight. Oh, you must always wear a bow tie!"

I sat in the corner. I had a book propped up in front of my face and I am quite sorry to report that I was rather hiding behind that book and not reading one word of it. If anyone had looked closely, they would have known that I would never be reading a book called *The History of Linguistic Development in Northern European Civilizations.*

The Gram came back in the front screen door with the laundry basket full of folded sheets. Just then a car pulled into the driveway. Its lights rode up and down the walls, momentarily flashing across the portrait of the middle daughter, Ella Bathburn, painted when she was just my age — twelve and a half years old. Oh, if only Ella Bathburn could have helped me. If only she could have flown forward through the one hundred years between us. If only she could have told me what to do about Derek and Brie and how to stop this terrible night from happening. But Ella Bathburn was caught in her painted portrait. She could not break free. She could only look at me with her serious face of warning.

"Well then, it's time to close the blackout curtains," I announced quite loudly over the top of my book. "And Brie's mother should put red cellophane over her headlights. That's what the air-raid warden told me." Then I popped back down behind the heavy history of linguistics.

Suddenly, Brie and her mother were standing in the parlor. It was startling to see them all dressed up and sparkling as I nosed round my book. Brie was fresh, lovely, sure, hopeful, nervous, and snippy all at the same time. Brie waved to me. "Hi, L.C.," she said. It sounded nice enough but I knew it stood for *Little Creep*.

Then Derek came forward with the glowing purple corsage and he pinned it to Brie's dress. But perhaps he was a bit shy because he pinned the corsage in a crooked way by mistake and it then looked as if it were trying to leap off Brie's shoulder and run away. And besides, the purple color didn't quite match her dress, but Brie flashed her silver smile above the crooked, jarring corsage. Derek put his arm round her. He too gave me a great smile. He even blew me a kiss but I let it bounce against the spine of the book I was holding. I turned my cheek and let Derek's kiss dissolve into nothing, because that was what it was. Nothing. Nothing. Nothing.

★ Thirty ★

They left the house in a flurry of kisses and good cheer. After all, Brie was Uncle Gideon's niece. Aunt Miami loved her as well. And she was The Gram's most beloved first granddaughter. So Brie moved about the Bathburn house as if it belonged to her. Perhaps it did, though I had grown to love the house and I felt it was partly mine. I had felt myself to be truly a Bathburn. Brie was wearing one of The Gram's beautiful homemade dresses to the dance. The Gram of course had wanted to see it from all angles, and Brie's mother and The Gram discussed the hem as if it were the solution to world peace. When I had done anything at all in the house, it always turned out that Brie had done it also, long before me. I loved sliding down the banister on the back stairs. "Oh, I started doing that when I was four years old," Brie said once, "and there are tons of photographs of me sliding on it. It's really mine but you can borrow it, if you don't break it."

It seemed as if Derek had always loved her. She marched in with her long blond braids and set the Bathburn house on end. If only she had liked me. But she didn't. And so I sat there alone in my sadness, alone because I couldn't really even mention it to Auntie.

Auntie's very voice was comforting and kind and I needed to tell her about this, but she had a big framed photograph of Brie on her dressing table and underneath it on the margin she had written, *darling Brie*.

I watched the grandfather clock in the parlor tick. The great hand slowly clicked by, minute by minute. The air still smelled of Brie's Blue Waltz perfume. I knew that perfume. You could buy it at the dime store. It came in a little blue bottle. It was very posh and made you feel sweetly sick if you opened the bottle and smelled it too closely. I had a bottle as well, though I had only doused my old bear Wink with it. I hadn't used it on myself. But you could smell Wink a mile away for a long time after that.

I went round and shut all the curtains in the house. It seemed a very dark night. Someone downstairs put a record on the Victrola. It was that song "I Think of You" again.

When the clouds roll by
and the moon drifts through
When the haze is high
I think of you.

Suddenly, something in me just snapped and I kind of broke into millions of pieces, like a biscuit when it's dropped on the floor. I was pieces and crumbs and particles and shards and nothing at all. I wanted my mum.

I needed her right now. Don't say she was locked up in some horrible, dark hole. Don't say she was hungry or cold or lost and lonely. Don't say my mum wasn't coming home to me. Don't say it. She was my mum. She belonged to me. She didn't even know Brie. She was mine. All mine. I was her Felicity and I wanted her back. Now.

I ran down the front stairs. I opened the door and it slammed behind me. I went out on the porch. I breathed in the dark, broken sky. I breathed in terrible, gray-black clouds that sailed over my head, the searchlights streaking the sky from a faraway harbor, searching for enemy planes. I ran down the many steps to the sea. The tide was out and the water rolled back, leaving the shore exposed and raw. I ran first along the great slabs of jutting rocks and then down into the sand and seaweed and mud and pebbles along the shore. The wind blew me to pieces too. My skirt battered and ripped against me. My hair blew back and then forward, flying into my eyes and mouth. The sea and sky raged round me. I had lost everything now. I had lost Derek to Brie. I had lost my mother to the wind. And Danny too. I had lost my beautiful England and soon I would lose America too. Everything would be washed away, battered and beaten and broken by the war that would soon come here to these shores. Derek's father was the Gray Moth. We would all soon be dead.

I ran towards the ocean. The mud and sand squishy and wet, my skirt wet, my hair wet, the tide coming in.

I would meet it. I would be there so it could take me away. Suddenly, all the tears I hadn't cried came up out of me in a terrible scream. I shouted and screamed at the wind. "I want my mother. I want my Winnie. Now." I cried and cried and cried and I ran faster and faster. Soon the cold, cold water was splashing over my legs. I turned back to look behind me. I could not see the Bathburn house in the darkness. All its light was hidden. All the houses along the ridge were black shadows now and I was alone, the sea crashing up round my legs higher and higher.

And then I heard someone calling me. "Flissy? Flissy Bathburn, where are you? Flissy dear, Fliss, tell me where you are! Please, Fliss. Come back to me. Don't leave me in this world without you. I love you and need you, Fliss. Please, please tell me where you are." It was the voice of my father, Gideon. He was crying for me. "Fliss, don't leave me. Please, little girl, come home to your father. Your father wants you now. Fliss, come back."

I turned round again and I called out, "Daddy, I'm here." And the wind wrapped me in its horrible arms and pulled me down into the cold water.

I don't remember how long it took my father to get to me. I don't remember how long or how much water I swallowed. I don't remember or know how I ended up in his arms, with my head on his shoulder, as he carried me along the shore. I know I was shaking and coughing and crying. And he held me tightly. "Flissy, my little girl. My little girl," he said. "I've got you and I'm not going to let anything happen to you. Ever again." He was crying too and as he carried me back to the house, I told him everything. I told him about Derek's father and his visits to the house. I told him about my suspicions, the clear glasses, the hat, the song "Lily Marlene." I told him about Mr. Fitzwilliam and the invisible-ink letter. I told my father everything. I told him too that I was in love with Derek. I kept back nothing. Nothing. And then I started sobbing again. Everything poured out of me . . . tears and words and all my sorrow all at once.

And when I was done with it and I had stopped crying and was sitting in front of the fire in the fireplace with a blanket round my shoulders and a cup of hot cocoa in my hands, I had a name for Uncle Gideon. I hadn't planned on it. I hadn't chosen it. It came out on its own and it was *Daddy*.

★ Thirty-One ★

I was so exhausted that evening and the fire warmed and soothed me so much that I almost was dozing off later. I was in that strange, blurry, warm state in which voices tumble past and objects float without meaning in the dark space behind your eyelids. I was just looking through a vague cupboard door in my mind when I heard my father on the landing, almost shouting into the telephone. His voice had a dangerous, gruff edge that I'd never heard before. "Look, Fitzwilliam," he was saying, "I want to talk to you in my study this evening. No excuses."

I lay on the sofa then, with one of The Gram's knitted afghans over me. I was counting the red squares and then the white squares, watching the fire leaping. I was trying to measure how high it leapt. I was planning on pretending to sleep. If they looked in on me, I would be snoring away, faking of course, though I wasn't proud of it.

I thought of Derek, for a moment, at the dance with Brie. I wondered which song they were bebopping to. I wondered if he was holding Brie tight. Were his eyes closed? Was he feeling dazzled and warm and dreamy, like I used to feel when he and I danced? Now I had told on Derek. I had ruined his dream of his father. Although he didn't know it yet, I had taken from him the only father he ever had. Surely he would hate me forever. He would call me a tattletale. How could I love Derek so much and at the same time tell on him? Why was my father calling Fitzwilliam now?

Soon I fell into a lost sleep. Mixed-up dreams came at me in the veils of shadows, the glowing fire, the wind at the windows, the ocean crashing below, never pausing or resting or stopping. Then the old doorbell buzzed at the front door and the house shook and screeched into alert. My father came down the stairs, casting a long, dark form on the walls and floor round him. The front door was opened, letting the stirred-up sky and air and cold rain and wind rush into the hallway. With all of that came Mr. Fitzwilliam in a waterproof and scarf, shaking himself dry like a great, arching cat. The two of them climbed the stairs and went down the hall and into my father's study, which surprised me. Why would my father allow a possible criminal into his private study, where even I was not allowed?

Once again I must confess that I climbed the stairs behind them.

I stood outside my father's study door and listened. My father's voice was still on edge, jagged, rough, almost shouting. "FBI or not," he was saying. "How could you do this to me? How could you put my children at risk like this? Why?"

"Well, Mr. Bathburn, the FBI has been waiting. We became aware of a very important German agent in the area. Code name, the Gray Moth. *Die Graue Motte*. We didn't know what he looked like, so we had no way of finding him. We had no way of identifying him. We have no tools without knowing who he is. I mean, what he looks like."

"I see," said Gideon. "I see. So you used my children."

"Well, we put an ad in the classifieds in the Portland paper asking for the birth father of Derek Bathburn Blakely to write. We knew the Gray Moth would take the bait. He wanted access to the Bathburn house. Did he not?"

"Well, haven't you identified him yet?" said Gideon, his voice gaining speed and strength.

"No," said Fitzwilliam. "He has eluded us. Your boy has helped him. He hasn't told anyone. He's kept his meetings secret. We think he may have even visited the house here several times. We haven't been able to see the man. Yet."

"How could you do this to my children? How could you jeopardize their safety?" shouted Gideon. The sound of his voice roared and shook and shattered the air. "To say nothing of the fact that you have compromised my circuit."

"Yes, the Butterfly Circuit. I have been admiring all the accomplishments that circuit has under its belt. I am a fan, really, in a way. I am rather thrilled to meet you."

"Look here," shouted Gideon. "You had no business jeopardizing my work and my children. What made you think you could bring my children into all of this?"

"Mr. Bathburn, you have forgotten. Has it slipped your mind? Mr. Bathburn, this is war."

When I crept back downstairs, I put more wood on the fire. The flame snapped and flickered and seemed to consume the log instantly. That fire was always hungry, never satisfied, consuming one log after another. The room was warm but I was shivering.

Mr. Fitzwilliam had left in a dark blur, leaving my father storming about the house, making phone calls and pacing the halls upstairs. Finally, he went into his bedroom and closed the door.

I knew The Gram was still awake. I knew she would be waiting for Derek to come home and the light in her room burned from under the crack at the bottom of the door, burned in a patient, quiet, persistent way. In the dining room the paintings on the walls seemed to grow darker. When I looked at Captain Bathburn's face, he seemed to tell me with his eyes that the journey home from India that winter was bitter, that the sea was ferocious and icy, that he had felt completely alone in 1855. The closed curtains, the shadow-covered ceilings, and the glowing fire surrounded me. Closed in about me. Mr.

Fitzwilliam was an FBI agent. That had certainly surprised me.

Soon, I heard an automobile pull up at the front of the house. I went out on the wraparound porch that faced the sea and leaned off the railing towards the garden. It was dark and windy and the houses down the shore loomed black and lifeless in the night. I could see the blaring lights from Brie's mother's car. Brie's mom was my aunt Maggie. But she didn't feel much like an aunt. I barely knew her. She popped round occasionally to play whist with Gideon and Miami, all the while making jokes I didn't quite understand. She was tall like Gideon and she called Aunt Miami *Mouse*. "Oh, Mouse darling, don't be so dramatic," she would say. And then she would swoop off in her fancy car with the soft leather seats, calling out something like, "Ta-ta, I really must go. Brie will be waiting at the club. We will be lunching with the governor." I knew Brie lived in a grand, pink-stone house on Cape Elizabeth. They called the place a cottage, which quite baffled and impressed Derek.

"If that place is a cottage, I'll eat my hat," Derek would say sometimes after Brie had left.

I slipped back to the parlor and soon Aunt Maggie and Derek opened the front door and came in. Aunt Maggie never used the back door. She always made a point of walking round the long porch and ringing the bell in front. Derek now plowed off into the kitchen and

I could hear him rustling through the shelves for something to eat.

Aunt Maggie stood at the bottom of the stairs and called out, "Mother, I've brought Derek back. He was marvelous. His fox-trot just swept everybody away. Didn't it, Derek? Brie was in heaven. He was so darling with her. What a little gentleman you've raised, Mother. I have to say, I think my darling Brie is rather starry eyed over him."

"Come up here, dear, and say good night," called The Gram.

"Oh, Mother, I can't. Brie's waiting in the car. She has a million and one things to do tomorrow. Love you all. Where's Mouse? I hope she has given up that dreadful postman. Ta-ta, as they say."

Soon she left. We heard the car drive off. Then the house was still. I mean, it wasn't just quiet; it was silent all the way down to its Bathburn stone foundations. I sat in the middle of that silence, listening to it. Derek came into the parlor with a sandwich and a glass of milk. He sat down in front of the fire next to me on the sofa. But the silence continued. It seemed to go on and on.

Finally, I said in a very low, slow voice, "Did you have fun?"

"Yeah, of course. Fun. Yup," said Derek. He took a bite of his sandwich.

"And how was Brie tonight? Was it lovely, the dance?"

Derek said, "You know, Flissy, when I was a little boy, I used to hear about you all the time. I knew Gideon longed to have you here. He began talking about you from the moment I can remember. I could never escape it. My birthday was picked out because no one knew when I was born and they chose *your* birthday. That used to hurt me. Even my birthday wasn't my own. The room I slept in would have been *your* room. Fliss, you were everywhere and nowhere. Everyone talked about you all the time. I think that after a while, I began to hate you."

"Oh, Derek," I said. "Don't say that, please."

"Well, no, not to say that The Gram and Gideon and Miami didn't love me. They did and they were so good to me, but there was something temporary about it, while I sensed *you* were permanent, even though they'd never met you."

"You mustn't think that, Derek. It's not true," I said.

"And then one day last year, you arrived. And when I met you, Fliss, right away you were nice. You were fun. Right away, even though I hated you, I liked you."

"I am so glad, Derek. I would have felt —"

"I used to have a crush on Brie, but something happened to it. You did something to it."

"Me? I didn't do anything," I said.

Now we could hear The Gram at the top of the stairs. "Derek, Flissy McBee, time for bed."

"Yes, you did, Fliss. You did something to my crush on Brie," Derek whispered. He was blushing. "I don't love her anymore. Instead, um. Instead. It isn't Brie anymore. It's someone else. Do you know who it is?"

"No," I said. "I don't."

"Guess," he said. "Guess who it is."

"I can't," I said.

"Guess," he said again, his voice growing louder and gruffer.

"No," I said.

"I dare you. Guess! Now!"

"Please, no," I said.

"You. You! It's you, Fliss! *You*." He leaned round me then and kissed me in an angry, awkward, melting way. All of a sudden I was a candle burning brightly. I was the fire in the fireplace, leaping out of itself in a blue-and-orange flame.

★ Thirty-Two ★

On Sunday mornings Derek and I always made breakfast for everyone in the Bathburn house. It gave us a
chance to use the dumbwaiter. We loved hoisting the
trays up and then carrying them to each room. A pot of
coffee for my father, a pot of tea for Miami, and a pot
of hot chocolate for The Gram (very rare these days, but
we had some saved). That morning we were lucky to
have a dozen fresh eggs given to us by Miss Elkin, who
kept chickens in her garden.

Oh, why must all the best things in your life happen
at the same time all the worst things are happening?
Derek's eyes, as he looked at me this morning in the
kitchen, were as brown and warm and sweet as the hot,
dark chocolate we were stirring. I felt dreamy and delicious and sorrowful all at once. I could not tell him what
happened last night while he was at the dance, what Uncle
Gideon and the FBI agents were planning. I felt joyous
this morning because Derek loved me and I felt terrified
and terrible because I was betraying him. I hadn't wanted
to, but I had to.

"We should make some muffins for my father's visit
today, after everyone leaves. He likes muffins," Derek
whispered. As he looked at me, I remembered last night.

I closed my eyes and happiness poured through me. Then terror. Cold fear. What had I done?

I didn't say anything. Instead I just began preparing my father's breakfast tray. I set the plate of scrambled eggs on the little white damask cloth, along with the bread and jam. As I tucked the newspaper under the coffeepot, I saw photographs of an oil tanker with smoke pouring out everywhere and sailors being picked up out of the water by rescue boats.

I carried the tray up to my father's room but my hands were shaking. With every step I took, I could hear the cup and saucer rattling. *Die Graue Motte. Die Graue Motte.* When I carried the tray into the front bedroom, my father looked at me darkly and said quietly, "Fliss, you must promise me you will go to Bob Henley's this afternoon. I do not want you here when Derek's father arrives. Promise me, Fliss. Promise me that."

I nodded my head, but my heart did not answer. My head went up and down, but inside my heart I was sure that I would not ever be able to leave Derek alone to face what I felt had somehow been my fault. My hands trembled, my whole being trembled. I had not planned on betraying my Derek. I had not planned on lying now to my father. *Daddy. Oh, Daddy, forgive me. Forgive your mixed-up daughter.* I was surely being ripped into a million pieces. I was no longer Felicity Budwig Bathburn at all. No, I was just a million conflicting particles, battering and bumping and battering and bumping into nothingness.

I did go that afternoon to Bob Henley's house. Before I went I had baked muffins with Derek for his father's visit. When everyone was upstairs, Derek and I stood very close to each other. We stood there with beautiful, swimming, shimmering air between us.

Now as I sat in Bob Henley's dark cottage, I thought of that moment. I thought and thought about it and I worried. I was afraid Derek would never speak to me again after he found out it was I who had betrayed him and his father. But he wasn't Derek's father. He was a German agent, a spy. He was the Gray Moth, *die Graue Motte*. Why hadn't Derek believed me? Why had he held so tightly to a father made of nothing but lies and tricks and traps? What would happen when the FBI agents descended on the house? Would Derek be in jeopardy? Would my father be in danger? I worried and I worried.

Mr. Henley was making me tea. He was working in his small kitchen nearby and calling out to me now and then. As he talked along I realized that he seemed to know nothing of the true nature of the Bathburns. He did not know, as I did, that the favorite sixth-grade teacher, Mr. Bathtub, was a US intelligence agent. He did not know that FBI agents and a Nazi agent would soon descend on the house. He did not know that the Bathburn house seemed to be at the center of something enormous and terrible. He did not know that I was caught in the middle of it all, as if in a whirlpool circling downward into darkness.

I was not even sure Bobby Henley knew anything about my aunt's intention to go away to join the USO traveling troop. Winnie always said to me that life was like a kaleidoscope: With just the slightest movement the pattern changed. The pattern was constantly regrouping. It never stayed the same.

Mr. Henley brought out sandwiches and tea. He sat down on his sofa, which he called a couch. "No sofas in this house, Flissy miss, only couches. Well, I have some bad news and I have not been able to tell your beautiful aunt. I haven't been able to find the words. Perhaps you will help me, Flissy. You are like Miami's little sister. Perhaps you can tell her." He had an envelope in his hand. Above him on the mantel, fishing nets draped. He had starfish in the netting and two old lobster traps were settled on a wide shelf under the window. He put the envelope down on the table. "This letter is from the US government. I am in the reserves and I have been called up. I will be shipping out immediately."

"Oh, Bobby," I said, forgetting to use his proper name, forgetting everything. "I am so very sad and sorry."

"Well, I should have expected it. I want to go, of course. I couldn't sit by and not help. But there will not be time to marry Miami before I leave." He tilted his head back and looked at the old, rough, pine-paneled ceiling.

"Auntie said to me that you and she will be spending the rest of your lives together after the war," I said.

"She really said that?" said Mr. Henley.

"Yes," I said. "And perhaps Miami can find something to do while you are gone, something that will truly engage her."

"I hope so," he said softly.

Minutes later Aunt Miami came in the cottage door of Henley's haven. She was wearing a silk scarf with starfish on it. She matched the room perfectly and she pulled the scarf off her hair and it went floating down to the sofa like a small silk parachute. It made me think of a local girl we knew who was having her wedding dress made out of her fiancé's white silk parachute. He was in the air force and his parachute had been retired because it was full of bullet holes where it had been shot at as he floated out of his plane and landed safely on the ground.

Bob Henley drew my auntie towards him now and they disappeared into the kitchen together. As they closed the door, I noticed he had the envelope from the US government in one of his hands.

The very second I found myself sitting all alone on Mr. Henley's sofa, I made my plans for escape. Now was the moment to slip out the door quickly and quietly and race back to the Bathburn house. Nothing was going to keep me away. Nothing in the world would stop me from helping if I could. I had to go. I wasn't afraid. I didn't care. I had to be there.

As soon as I was outside, I ran as if I had no legs at all. I ran till my lungs squeezed and shuddered and burned. I ran as if the wind and the sea and the sky and the whole world were lifting me up and pulling me along.

★ *Thirty-Three* ★

As I drew closer, the Bathburn house loomed in its usual large, brown, imposing way over the point. Its many windows seemed empty for some reason, voiceless, as if no one at all were inside. Even Captain A. E. Bathburn and his wife and daughters seemed to have vanished, leaving only a great wooden shell holding up against the wind. Still I had passed some black cars parked in a neighbor's driveway several houses down from ours and I knew who those cars probably belonged to. Isn't it odd how a gray day can make colors brighter? A red dress, for instance, on a gray day can glow like a burning flame. Those dark cars glowed with rich, fearful blackness.

It was just November and a hazy, lonely, mild afternoon and the Bathburn house was utterly silent before me. Nothing moved. Not a twig, nor a stick, nor a fallen leaf.

Then I suddenly saw a man in a dark suit at the back door. He had a gun in his hand. He was not going to let me in; I was sure of that. I stopped on the path and before he saw me, I quickly turned the corner and went for the kitchen window at the other side of the house. There was a ledge outside the window where we often set our laundry baskets, full of wet clothes, before hanging them on the clothesline. We had done some laundry earlier. I knew the window would still be ajar. I got up on that ledge and slowly lifted it open and slipped in.

Now I was in the kitchen. How silent everything was. Mr. Fitzwilliam's men were in the hallway. I could see their shadows. I could feel their heavy presence. They were standing stock-still, leaning back against the walls. They had holsters with guns strapped across their chests, all of them. One of them saw me and startled and then began shaking his head back and forth. Then he put up his hand, stopping me. He swung his arms about, motioning for me to stay where I was. So I froze and leaned against the doors of the dumbwaiter.

Derek and I and even Stu Barker used to play with that dumbwaiter. It was supposed to be loaded with trays of food and those trays could be pulled up to the next floor on ropes and pulleys, but we often loaded it up with trays of shells and rocks and sent them up the shaft during one of our games. Because he was small, Derek and I once hoisted Stu Barker up to the gymnasium that way. Now I slowly opened one of those little doors of the dumbwaiter. I could see then a slice of the parlor through the doors on the opposite side. I could see my father on one end of the room and Derek's father on the other. Derek was standing in the center of the room between them. It looked to me as if the Gray Moth had just dropped his gun, because Derek was holding it in his palm. He wasn't aiming the gun at anyone but it was lying in his good hand. He was looking down at it as if his hand were on fire.

"Derek," my father called out, "give me the gun so we can arrest this man. He is not your father. He is a Nazi spy. Please. Stand back and give me the weapon."

"No," shouted Derek, holding the gun now with his finger on the trigger and pointing it up to the ceiling. "He is not a spy. He is my father and my friend. I have been waiting all these years for him. We have been taking photographs together. He likes my portraits. You don't understand. You're wrong."

"Derek," said Gideon, "I do understand. I know you need a father. But this man is a Nazi and a spy. Hand me the gun!"

"Derek, you must give the gun back to me," said the Gray Moth. "A son should stand by his father. We have so much to learn about each other, so much to know. Time has separated us. A father and son should stand together."

"Derek, a gun is a dangerous thing," Gideon called out. "You could get hurt!"

"No!" shouted Derek.

"Please, please, Derek!" said Gideon. "Hand me the gun now so we can arrest this man."

"Don't listen," said the Gray Moth. "They will take away our time together. It will be vanished!"

I did not know why Mr. Fitzwilliam's men, hidden out in the hall, were not moving. What were they waiting for?

Why were they standing like dark marble statues? Was it because Derek had the gun? Were they afraid he would be harmed or shoot someone if they charged in now?

"Derek," I called through the doors of the dumb-waiter. "Derek, Derek. I found out Mr. Fitzwilliam put the ad in the paper on purpose, to catch this man. They didn't know what he looked like. You were set up. We were part of this without knowing it. He's not your father. He's a fake."

"Leave us alone," Derek shouted. "We were going to work on a scrapbook today. You've ruined everything, Felicity."

"Derek," said Gideon again, "if I have been amiss, tell me. I can change. Let me be the father I would like to be for you, forever. I love you so much, Derek. Please give me the gun."

"No. No. No!" cried Derek. "No. No. No. No!"

The next things happened so fast, I could not say in what order they fell. I could not say how or why I did what I did. Sometimes some other part of me acts and it feels like it has nothing to do with me. Somehow, suddenly, some other part of me was up inside the dumbwaiter and then in a blurry instant I hurled myself out the doors on the other side and I fell and rolled into the parlor and knocked against Derek with quite a force, though I claimed later that it did not hurt at all. I felt nothing, only the whole room seemed to spin and faces and voices churned and shattered about me. When I knocked against

Derek, the gun he had in his good hand went flying across the room and landed in front of my father.

Gideon reached for it quickly. "Okay, Derek," he said, "back away carefully now. Move way over now. Slowly. Fliss, back away! Stand back!"

He roared like a great grizzly bear and rushed forward towards Derek's father. At that same moment the house snapped, exploded with the sound of Mr. Fitzwilliam's men moving in quickly. I heard the rumble of their shuffling feet. It sounded like a whole flock of birds coming to rest in a tree. I saw some of the dark jackets plunging into the room. They circled and enclosed *die Graue Motte*. He pressed himself against the wall, his arms out, as if struggling to fly. They surrounded him and cornered him. Fitzwilliam put handcuffs on the man who had claimed to be Derek's father.

Now Derek began crying. He cried and he sobbed and he called out, "No."

"Derek, listen to me, if this man truly is the German agent we think he is, then he will have a birthmark on his forehead," said Gideon.

"No, he won't!" Derek said.

"Yes, he will," Gideon said, his voice thundering like the wind when it rushes through the tower room at night, like the ocean when the waves pound the shore in winter.

"Well then, we'll have a look won't we?" said Mr. Fitzwilliam. He pulled off Derek's father's hat and pushed his hair away from his forehead and there, at the very top of it, near the hairline, was a gray-and-black birthmark. It was distinct and clearly had two triangle shapes to the mark. It reminded me of the wings of a moth.

"Get away. Go away," shouted Derek, pushing past Mr. Fitzwilliam. "No. No. No!" He ran out of the room, knocking over the tea tray and the muffins we had made earlier that day. He pelted down into the hall. Then he barreled through the kitchen and I heard the back door slam. I rushed out into the hall, and through the window in the dining room, I saw him run along the ledge above the sea.

★ Thirty-Four ★

Later when I looked out the window to the north of the house, I could see a line of black cars leaving the point, headed back towards Portland.

But what happens after an arrest? What happens to those who are left behind to clean up the muffins that were ground into the carpet, to sweep away the broken crystal and the shattered teacups? What do you do about the terrible emptiness that sits amongst the disarray?

"Derek!" my father called as soon as the cars had pulled away. "Derek." He plunged through the house and he found me crouching in a corner in the kitchen. I was crying and he was crying. "My God," he said, "what were you doing here? You could have been killed. I thought you were with Miami. And where is Derek? Where has he gone? Oh my God, Derek."

We both stood at the back door for a moment, looking off towards the top of the hill where we could see Derek sitting alone up high on a rock ledge above the sea. My father and I stood there, unable to move or to decide what to do for him. How helpless I felt. My father put his head against the wall and he put his fists up and he pounded on the wall over and over again.

Then he went outside and stood in the garden in a

helpless kind of way. He stood there and he called out to Derek. I watched him climb the hill towards Derek. I heard him calling and calling out his name. But Derek did not turn round. I wanted to rush out and comfort Derek but I knew he needed time to be alone. He had been cruelly hurt and there was nothing to be said or done.

I waited until dusk when a swath of early stars appeared in the fading sky. Then I climbed the hill towards Derek. He was now a silhouette in a fiery sunset. I sat beside him and for the longest time we didn't speak. We let the ocean say it all. We were children in the midst of a war. We had no choice but to accept the waves as they rolled in and out. We were caught in the sea of it. But those new stars, like fireflies, beamed and blinked and lit their tiny lights all round us. I waited and waited and hoped as I sat there that he might say something but he did not. Finally, in the darkening air, Derek got up and walked away from me.

★ Thirty-Five ★

Derek's anger at me now was slow burning and constant. He was extremely quiet that next week. If I walked into a room, Derek would leave or else he'd stick his head out the window or under a table or turn towards any corner where I wasn't.

That week in Bottlebay, about fifty boys were drafted and when The Gram and I went to town, there was a bit of a gloom in the air, especially in Mr. King's hardware shop because Mr. King's son was one of them. He was shipping out to a training camp somewhere faraway. Mr. King hung an American flag outside the shop and there were little flags sticking out of watering cans and waving from flowerpots in the window.

Perhaps I could find a gift for Derek, something to cheer him up, something to make him forgive me. So when The Gram and I stopped at the five-and-dime, I had a look round in the bins. I knew that I had betrayed Derek and the memory of it went through me like knives. It felt a bit like Derek was a knife thrower in a circus these days and I was the girl holding balloons in her mouth while he threw knives and popped the balloons with great precision, just barely missing me at each turn.

I hadn't wanted to betray him, really. I had saved him, hadn't I?

I looked at the selection of trinkets in rows at the five-and-dime store. The wooden floor sagged and creaked under my feet. There was a bin full of little birds made of china or porcelain. They were ten cents each and I fancied a small white dove. The Gram was just picking out rolls of fly tape and a new flyswatter, so I handed my ten cents to the woman behind the counter and she wrapped the dove in brown paper. Her daughter was a WAAC, that is, a woman in the auxiliary army corps. There was a framed photograph of her behind the cash register. She was wearing a lovely, smart uniform.

As we left the five-and-dime the wind picked up and the sky was a promising blue. When I was younger I might have skipped away my worries, but I had grown too old for skipping. What if someone from school were to see me? I thought of the little dove I had bought. It had the dearest little bird face. Surely Derek would smile when he saw it? Out of habit, I finally gave way to the skipping urge and I started in, passing a poster that said, WAR SHIPMENTS MEAN LESS FUEL FOR ALL. DRESS WARMLY INDOORS. And another one farther down the street that said, OUR GOVERNMENT SAYS, "DON'T WASTE FOOD. SAVE DRIED BREAD. MAKE BREAD CRUMBS!"

I skipped and skipped until I had left The Gram

way back behind me, walking under the awnings of the shops. But skipping didn't change my mood anymore. My worry seemed to catch up with me and take hold easily. I didn't know when I would give Derek the little dove or when his dreadful anger would subside.

★ Thirty-Six ★

Of all the people I desperately loved in Bottlebay, Mr. Henley was the first to leave. It was early November now and Mr. Henley appeared in the hall one afternoon, shadowy looking because the sun behind him was so bright, the way it can be just before it begins to set. He was a silhouette, a kind of vision in the dark hall, a mirage. "Hey, gang," he called out, "where is everyone?"

Miami rushed down the steps and fell on the last one and collapsed in a silken heap at Mr. Henley's feet. He picked her up and she was crying. And then he kissed her. I had never seen Bobby Henley do anything like that before.

I pretended to be searching for something inside one of the overcoats hanging in the hallway. I looked in the empty pockets while he took her in his arms. Miami tilted back and then it was as if they were floating together in our hallway, gently swirling in circles in their kiss.

"My bags are packed. I'm off later tonight by train and then by plane. I'll keep you posted," Mr. Henley said, giving us an army salute. Then he clicked his heels together.

"But do you know where you will be stationed?" I asked, buttoning and unbuttoning the overcoat. And then for some unknown reason, I got behind the coat and stood there in the darkness and called out, "I shall miss you awfully, Mr. Henley."

"Oh, Flissy McBee," he said. "I hear we're being sent immediately over to the other side of the pond. That's all I can say. But because I don't have any family, I put you Bathburns as my next of kin. Your auntie won't be here most of the time so I've included you in something very important to me."

"You have?" I said, peeking out from behind the coat.

"Oh gosh, yes. I am planning to have all my mail sent here. I may send off some poetry from the front with a return address in care of you, Flissy. For safekeeping. You'll take care of stuff for me, won't you, kiddo?"

"Yes," I said. "I shall be honored."

Then Bobby Henley kissed Auntie again. And I soon expected to find them both on the ceiling. If ever there were a true Romeo, it was Bobby Henley just then.

Mr. Henley's train was leaving at midnight. It was a starry, crisp evening and after dinner he and I were out on the porch, waiting for Miami. They planned to take a walk together. Even though it was chilly I sat on the porch swing, gliding back and forth, looking at the Big Dipper in the sky above us.

Then Mr. Henley handed me something small and square. It was dark and I couldn't see exactly, but I was pretty sure it was the little box that held the beautiful ring. "Hang on to this for me, will you, Flissy McBee?

Miami and I, we don't have time for it now, but we will when I come back on leave! It will be a surprise. Keep it safe for me, will you?"

Soon Miami came swimming out on the porch, a slice of light splashing across the floor as she slipped through the door. Then she and Bobby set off together for one last walk.

★ Thirty-Seven ★

Derek continued to be angry and silent. And later that week I wanted to talk to Auntie about him. She was always so full of pleasant advice for me. Once I had shrunk up one of my knitted sweaters by washing it in hot water and Auntie showed me how to wash a wool sweater in cold water and then how to block it and reshape it on a towel in the sunlight while it was drying. Perhaps she would have some advice for me now. So I went upstairs to her room one evening.

Aunt Miami was packing. Since Bobby left, there was a somber, quiet air in our room. She had a photo of him in a shell-covered frame hanging near her bed. She wouldn't be leaving for a while but she needed to be busy. She couldn't quite decide which outfits to bring with her to the USO traveling theater. She trailed silky dresses across the room from her cupboard to her bed, where a suitcase was propped open, and silk scarves and kid gloves and little straw hats were laid in tidy piles.

"Oh, Auntie," I said. "Will you be Juliet over and over again for the army and the navy and the air force?"

"The theater troop will be performing *Romeo and Juliet* at all the army bases in the good old US of A. We will be doing camp shows, especially for Christmas.

That's when we're needed most. I hope I get the part of Juliet."

"You won't be here for the holidays and Bobby Henley won't be here either," I said.

"No," Miami said, looking up and out across the room. A lamp with a blue lampshade cast a blue light across her face, Juliet tinted blue for just a brief moment.

Then suddenly she clapped her hands. "What do you say to taking these little white gloves?" she said, turning her head back towards me. "They are too small for me, you know. Perfect for twelve-year-old hands. And what do you say to this clutch bag? Are you growing old enough for a little purse? Tell me, yes or no?"

"Yes!" I said. "Oh, Auntie, I shall treasure them. Auntie, may I ask you a tiny, little question?"

"Oh, Flissy Miss," said Miami. "The smaller your questions, the harder they are to answer."

"How did Derek come to live here?" I asked.

Miami closed her suitcase with a tight snap. She looked at me with her head tilted.

"The longer I stay in the Bathburn house, the more questions pop up. It's not my fault, honestly. Do you find me meddlesome? Derek said so. I was only trying to help," I said.

"Oh, Flissy," said Auntie. "Sweetest. I am going to miss you when I'm away. Derek knows this stuff but he's funny about it. He won't talk about it. He was brought here by the children's services in town. It had been The

Gram's summer project. It was only meant to be a temporary stay until his father reappeared."

She handed me another pair of gloves. I tried them on but all I could think of was Derek disappearing down the hall or walking out of a room or closing a door behind him, turning his back on me.

"I can still remember the first night the baby was here," said Miami. "I'd say he was about one and a half. Perhaps he was more of a toddler. We had a storm, a hurricane, actually. It was big enough for people to give it a name. Everyone on the coast was told to go into the school for shelter, but we Bathburns never do that sort of thing. We chose to weather it."

"And what about Gideon?" I said. "Was he here then as well?"

"Oh yes, Gideon had come home from England a few months earlier and he practically lived in his room, the way the Bathburns tend to do when they are hurt. You know his heart had been broken. His brother had taken his wife and baby away. The Gram was frantic. She tried to interest him in anything and everything. But nothing really was working. He sat in his room and all he did was stare out the window. He's really quite a mush, that brother of mine."

"Yes," I said. And I felt sad and torn again, loving Danny as I did and now loving Gideon as my father as well. And not knowing anymore whose side I should be on, if there was a side at all. I could not imagine any twelve-year-old having been more mixed up than me. I wanted so much to make all the wrongs right. I wanted an answer to everything. Now.

Miami went on with the story and I leaned back against her pink-flowered cushions and simply listened.

"The wind was extremely strong that night," she said. "It howled and battered at the house. And of course the waves roared over the steps and almost up to the porch. When a couple of shutters were torn off in the back, Gideon was called down to help. He went ripping off into the wind after the old shutters and when he'd captured them, he returned. He was standing in the hall. I can remember that clearly. He was about to climb the stairs to his room when he saw The Gram with the toddler in her arms. It was just for a split second but I remember clearly a kind of light passing across Gideon's eyes. We all saw it.

"The next few days it was Gideon who called children's services in town to discuss everything. It was Gideon who spent hours on the telephone talking about every possibility. The baby's date of birth was unknown. They said we could give him a first name. He came to us as Baby Blakely, but they were quite clear that in this case, he was not up for legal adoption. His mother had died but the father could come back at any time. We had to live with that.

"So you see," said Miami. "As we grew to love Derek, we grew to fear the return of his father. It felt as if

Derek came to us in the middle of a storm. How long would he be ours? When would he be taken away? And can you guess what they were calling the storm in Bottlebay?"

"No," I said.

"Well, they usually give people's names to the hurricanes around here, don't they? That storm was named Hurricane Derek."

★ Thirty-Eight ★

I kept the little wrapped dove in my skirt pocket. I kept it with me even at school, for there was always the possibility that I might see Derek in the halls and find a moment to give it to him and to explain how sorry I was about everything I had done. I often looked for him in the lunchroom and in the auditorium when we had an assembly about how to save and repair and reuse things for the war effort. How to patch clothes. How to use both sides of all paper at school. How to save old cardboard. But I never saw Derek anywhere. Now that I knew most of his story, I rather loved him even more.

This morning I sat at breakfast in the kitchen with Auntie and Gideon, who was behind his newspaper as usual. I tipped my head like a teapot when it's being poured so that I could see the headline. It read, GREAT WAVES OF AMERICAN TROOPS HAVE LANDED IN NORTH AFRICA IN FRENCH MOROCCO AND IN ALGERIA. NEWS COMING IN SLOWLY AS BATTLES RAGE.

Most of the war news had not been so good recently. But this North African landing seemed to be a grand thing. I could tell by the way my daddy stretched and leaned back in his chair. "Hot diggity. This is a good move. We need control of the Mediterranean!" He put his arm over me and drew me towards him. "Come on, look at this. Are you happy about it, Fliss, or are you still my melancholy baby?" And then he started to hum that song "My Melancholy Baby." He smiled at me but I wouldn't smile back.

He was right. I was not at all happy. What did Morocco or Algeria mean to my Winnie and Danny? What did it mean to me and to Derek? Would Derek let go of his anger soon? Would he let go of it just like that kite we let loose into the wind when we used to be friends? We let that kite go and it sailed so high, so very high and it headed out over the ocean. We watched it with the binoculars for almost an hour as it got smaller and smaller and fainter and fainter until we could no longer see it. We thought maybe it would go all the way to France, to fly above the Limoges prison where Winnie and Danny were held. Perhaps they would look up from their cell windows and see a blue kite bobbing away in the sky above and perhaps they would know deep in their hearts that the kite was mine, a message from me, their daughter, waiting, forever waiting, across the ocean.

I went into the hallway and stood at the library door, catching a glimpse of handsome Derek sealed away behind a book, refusing to even look my way. And I thought about my friend Dimples, in Selsey, West Sussex, in England. One morning she said to me, when the sun was unbearably bright, "My mum has a friend who has found the answer to everything. All her problems went away after she grew up and found this answer."

"What is the answer?" I asked Dimples.

"Oh, I shall never tell. I was promised to secrecy," said Dimples and she skipped away, her curly hair making wild shadows on the pavement.

I should have liked to talk to Dimples today. Back in England I should have offered to loan Wink to her for a fortnight in exchange for that answer to everything. I should have been much more clever about getting the answer out of her, as I think it could have been rather useful to me just now.

★ Thirty-Nine ★

In the late afternoon we had more good news about the landings in North Africa and my father was even happier. He was galloping through the house like a great big horse, neighing and pawing at the floor and trying to get me to act like a child as well. He snorted at The Gram and galloped by her. I *was* tempted to become a lovely purebred racehorse but I resisted because I was too old for that sort of thing.

And later, as darkness fell, the mood in the house shifted. I could feel it change. Derek and Miami were listening to *The Shadow* on the wireless. I loved *The Shadow*. It was deliciously scary. The Shadow had the power to cloud people's minds so they couldn't see him. The show always started with the line, "Who knows what evil lurks in the minds of men? The Shadow knows." Then there was the terrible laughter and scary music. I was not going to go into the parlor and have Derek march out.

I sat on the stairs outside the parlor instead, listening to some of the story. But then I got it into my mind to climb the stairs. Sometimes things just came to me for no reason and I usually followed those things. It was as if the wind had decided to pull me along and I decided to go, because who could say no to the wind?

I suddenly found myself outside The Gram's room, leaning my head against the closed door. I could hear Gideon saying, "Mother, you must try not to worry, that's all."

"Well," said The Gram, "you are risking your life and I am very nervous. What mother wouldn't be?"

"I am doing it for Winnie, for all that she has done."

"Oh, I see. You still love her," said The Gram. "She still has you in her grip. Even though she's hurt you so much. And she could still take Felicity away from us. Have you thought about that?"

"Mother, I am doing it for both Winnie and Danny and for the circuit," he said.

"You still love her. You would risk everything for her."

"Do you realize how much good they have done? Yes, I would risk everything."

"This is all Winifred's fault," said The Gram. "I will never forgive her."

"Don't speak of Winnie that way!" Gideon said, his voice growing louder and suddenly rumbling like thunder in the distance.

"I do not like Winifred," said The Gram. "And that will never change. And I do not want you to go. If anything happened to you, I could not endure it."

"Hush, Mother. Hush," said Gideon. "Even though

the Gray Moth was here in the house, we will proceed as planned. But I shall worry about you and Flissy and Derek all the more."

I sank to the floor for a moment. In my ears, an ocean, in my heart, the pounding surf. Soon I rolled away from the door and lay on my back, staring at the hall ceiling. I could hear the show on the radio downstairs: "The Shadow can cloud the minds of men. With mist and fog they see him not and yet the Shadow knows." And then the terrible laughter ringing through the hall.

★ *Forty* ★

Perhaps it was the wind that pulled me along that next day. It pulled me down Main Street in Bottlebay. Yes, it was the sky that called me and who can say no to the sky?

So many things were going round and round in the Bathburn house. Strange and scary things. And because I had lost Derek's friendship, I felt terribly alone. More so than ever. I put my hand in my pocket and I touched the little white dove. I had to think of a way to help Derek feel better. I needed to win him back. It was all too much without him.

As I headed towards the shops in Bottlebay, I stopped at the newsstand, hoping to buy a package of Fleer Dubble Bubble Gum. The store smelled of newspapers and cigar smoke. For some reason a newspaper from this summer lay on a chair near the counter. Someone had circled the headline. I looked down and read: SUNDAY JUNE 28, 1942. FBI SEIZES 8 NAZI SABOTEURS LANDED BY U-BOATS IN NEW YORK AND IN FLORIDA.

Is that how *die Graue Motte*, the Gray Moth, had come to America? Did he endure a long journey on a German U-boat, living in airless, cramped quarters with darkness and fear? Did he finally arrive at night, leaving the submarine and paddling quietly to shore in a rubber raft? Were there others with him or was he alone? Or had he already been living here in some plain, little house by the sea, like that woman who hung her laundry in certain patterns on her clothesline? Red. Yellow. Green. Upside down, inside out. Orange.

I bought the Dubble Bubble Gum and I walked back outside, studying the offices above the shops, looking for a certain sign. There it was, above the greengrocer's. The sign read, BUTTONS, BUTTONS AND BABBIT, ATTORNEYS AT LAW.

I opened the door and climbed the stairs and all of a sudden I got the urge to leap two steps at a time. Then I tried three. I always did that when I got on a staircase. I blamed it on my feet. Twelve years old or not, my feet didn't care. If they thought I wasn't noticing, they took over. I had tried to be quite corrective towards them, but they jumped when they wanted to. I was going for a four-stair leap when a gentleman coming down from above nearly knocked me over. I didn't know if it was Mr. Babbit or Mr. Buttons. Either way he was quite tall and had a satchel and he was leaving.

I sagged to the top step and sat down. I was too late. He was going out. The man, Babbit or Buttons, stopped on the bottom step and looked round and up at me. "Can I help you?" he said.

"Are you an attorney at law?" I asked.

"Yes, Mr. Buttons here. I'm just stopping by the office

to pick up some folders. It's Sunday, you know. We're closed."

"Oh. Very nice to meet you, I'm sure. May I ask you a question, Mr. Buttons, even though you are not really at work today?"

"Yes, you may, but briefly. I do try to relax now and again," he said.

"If there was a someone who was sort of adopted but not exactly . . ."

"Yes," said Mr. Buttons.

"And that someone wanted to find his birth parents, say, perhaps a father. Would you be able to help that someone?"

"Possibly," said Mr. Buttons. "Mr. Babbit would have to see this person in person, if you know what I mean. What I mean is, it would be a private matter discussed only after . . . discussed only with . . . You see what I mean."

"Yes," I said. "Thank you ever so much."

"And take my card. Whoever, whatever, they can contact me. On a regular work day, of course." Mr. Buttons then disappeared out the front door. Soon he came back in the building and looked up at me sitting as I was on the top step, all scrunched up and thinking. "Come along, then," he said. "We're closed up. You mustn't sit up there all day."

Then I was back out in the Sunday morning air. I had Buttons, Buttons and Babbit's card in my pocket. I could feel it next to the white dove. Now I certainly had things to give Derek.

Oh, if I'd only known that what I had just done might come back to haunt me. But I didn't know. As I walked along, I jumped over every single crack on the American sidewalk because of that horrid jump-rope song Dimples used to sing. "Step on a crack, break your mother's back." I never, ever stepped on one crack, hoping to protect my mum from everything. Hoping to right all the wrongs, looking for the one answer.

Forty-One

All that autumn there were losses and gains in the war and the Bathburn house would rise with the wins and fall with the losses, like the tide in the ocean rising and falling. Battles that we lost always caused Gideon to go upstairs into his bedroom and slam his door. Sometimes he would miss dinner altogether. But battles like the one in Midway Island last summer or battles in French Morocco, which the Allies won, made my father all happy and bubbly and fizzy like Coca-Cola when you stir it up with your straw till it steams and snorts and pops. Still, Coca-Cola was rather rare these days. There was something called a black market where you could buy anything in the world, even rationed and rare things. Derek talked about it with Stu Barker. It sounded mysterious and dark and dangerous — just those words *the black market*.

There were fewer and fewer older brothers and fathers seen about town because many of them had enlisted or had been drafted. Though I still saw the ragpicker in the park, swinging his long stick with a sharp metal point on the end, looking to stab old papers and rags and poke them into his cloth bag on his back. I did not think he was anybody's father. He had a skinny, red, old face and a dreadfully scrawny body, all bent over and sorrowful and dusty. I did not think he would ever be drafted.

It was November 20 and we teetered on the edge of winter. Flurries of snowflakes fluttered here and there and because it was earlier in the morning than we usually got up, the sky was full of raw, painful light. It was Auntie's turn to leave. I was not sure I could bear another farewell. Everyone was clustered near her on the porch. I stayed in the house, just at the doorway. I did not want to go out and say good-bye.

Gideon stood there, holding one of Miami's suitcases. "I see you've got enough of a wardrobe here to outfit the entire USO theater troop!" he said. "Maybe even the whole US Army for that matter, though all that chiffon could prove a problem on the battlefield."

"Very funny, Gideon," she said, leaning her head on his shoulder.

Our pet seagull, Sir William Percy, had even flapped over and settled down on one of the hatboxes from Porteous department store. Derek was there too, slouched against the porch railing, fiddling with a yo-yo.

Then Aunt Miami's carpool to the train station arrived. Someone was beeping a loud horn. It jolted me and I tore out on the porch. I tripped over a chair, landed on my face, and almost started to cry. I suddenly remembered Auntie falling into Bobby Henley's arms the night he left.

I looked at Derek. He had a growling, early-morning smile on his face. He was watching me as I limped over to hug Auntie. I saw his eyes follow me and stay fixed on me as his yo-yo droned up and down and then "slept" at the end of the string. Soon he tossed it forward and it went "around the world" and came back "to walk the dog," all the while he seemed to watch me as I struggled not to cry. Oh, he was a dreadful beast and I think I hated him just then. His anger had smoldered and kept on spinning like a sleeping yo-yo for a long time, it seemed. I had grown almost impatient with it. Almost.

We followed Auntie out to the car. We were a raggedy, tearful, shivering group as she climbed into the backseat. Auntie was all settled in amongst her boxes and suitcases when suddenly she scrambled out of the car. She rushed towards Gideon and hugged him again for a long moment, making my heart drop like piano notes falling down the scale. Then she climbed back in and the car pulled away in a flood of exhaust from a dragging tailpipe. We stood there in a line, not making a sound. Finally, I shouted out, "Write to me, Auntie!" But the car was near the crest of the little hill by then and I did not think she heard me.

Soon The Gram and Gideon wandered back into the house. But Derek was still outside, working his yo-yo in circles. Suddenly, he caught it up in the palm of his hand and tucked it away in his jacket.

"Derek," I said, "I have something for you. I've had it a while now." And I reached in my pocket and held out the little white china dove. "It's for your windowsill. Won't it be ever so lovely in the sunlight in the morning when you first wake up?"

Derek reached for the dove. He closed his eyes and took a deep breath.

"I am awfully sorry I hurt you," I said. "I mean, terribly, truly, really."

Derek shook his head up and down and then sideways, all the while his eyes closed.

"And I've done something else," I said. "And I do hope it will please you."

"Oh no, Fliss," said Derek, opening one eye and taking a good peek at me. "What have you done now?"

"I've been to see Buttons, Buttons and Babbit for you. They're solicitors. I mean lawyers. Perhaps they can help you find your true parents," I said.

Derek frowned and squeezed his eyes even more tightly shut, as if he were avoiding a wild fly ball heading his way on the baseball field. Actually, because of his paralyzed arm, Derek couldn't play baseball anymore and so he played soccer and his feet were as fast as the wind.

"I mean of course it has to be *you* who goes to them and you who makes the request. But I might add that Mr. Buttons wanted you to have his card. He asked me to give it to you." I did hope it wasn't dreadfully meddlesome of me to say he wanted Derek to have his card, which wasn't exactly what he had said. It was the truth, but I had stretched it and pulled it a little bit, just as if it were long, stretchy, sweet molasses taffy.

Derek was quiet for a minute. An airplane was roaring and thundering overhead. Suddenly, he took the card and put it in his shirt pocket. When the plane had passed, he looked at me with his swimming-pool eyes, deep brown and changing, like water. His eyes rippled into my eyes for a moment. And then in a very mumbling way, Derek looked down at his black high-top tennis shoes and said, "Thank you, Fliss."

★ *Forty-Two* ★

That next week we had a small Thanksgiving. They had announced on the radio that cooking a turkey would help the war effort, if everyone saved the turkey fat in tins and handed it in. The glycerin in the fat, they said, was greatly needed to make explosives.

I was often busy with The Gram during that time doing things about the house. I was making Christmas decorations out of odd, forgotten things like old silk ribbons found at the bottom of a drawer. We made sweet-smelling clove balls by sticking cloves into unpeeled oranges and tying ribbons round them. Then we hung them over doorways, filling the rooms with the scent of cinnamon and cloves. (Mr. Donovan sent us a box of oranges from Florida for Thanksgiving. It was a great moment when they arrived! Perhaps he got them on the black market.)

I was very busy and so there were times in the day when I had no idea where Derek was at all. Had he gone into Bottlebay to see Mr. Buttons? It was hard for me to know.

When I was helping The Gram clean rooms upstairs one Saturday in December, I saw the gold-printed card of Buttons, Buttons and Babbit lying out on Derek's desk but that didn't tell me much. I remembered that night by the fire when he had come back from the dance with Brie. I remembered what he had said to me. "Guess who it is. Guess!" It seemed now that any love he had for me had vanished in a terrible blast.

In the middle of December, winter came at us with full force, bringing sleet and ice and snow, which whirled and whined and wrapped itself all round our house. Sometimes the snow sifted in at the old windowsills and thin ice formed on the glass most exposed to the wind. Then, looking out the windows, we had to peer through white castles and caves and stars of ice patterns.

One blustery day my father said, "Fliss, shall we take a walk?" He meant to put his arm around me, but he reached too far and he knocked the wall behind me and bumped the painting of Ella Bathburn by mistake. Suddenly, she looked all tilted and confused, staring at the floor. Then we had to stop and try to straighten her out and that became difficult because the Bathburn house itself wasn't terribly level.

After we'd decided on the perfect angle for Ella, my father looked at me shyly. "Sorry, Fliss," he said. "Shall we carry on? We haven't had a walk together in ages, have we?"

"Very well, then," I said. But I held my breath for a moment because a walk seemed to mean that my father might be leaving soon. And it was almost Christmas. Oh, I didn't want him to go and, oh, I *did* want him to go.

Then I felt all pulled and stretched and twisted because I knew he was going to help Winnie and Danny. I wondered if Winnie and Danny would be allowed to have Christmas in prison. And then, of course, I knew they wouldn't. I couldn't bear to think of Christmas morning and bells ringing and Winnie being hungry and cold and alone. I couldn't bear to think of Danny sitting on the floor in a dirty cell on Christmas morning.

"Oh, Fliss, if only these times we live in were normal, regular times," my father said. We were walking down to the water's edge and heading north. It started to snow and at first the snowflakes seemed to dance about in a playful way and then they fell faster and thicker and harder. Even though the wind was quiet and we were not far from the house, suddenly it felt as if we were lost in a white storm.

"Do you realize it was a miracle for me when you came to live here?" my father said.

"A miracle?" I said.

"Yes," he said. "I had waited so long to know you." We stopped and he wrapped his scarf about his neck and looked at the sea, which was quite rough in this area. "Oh, but these are not normal and regular times. Not at all," he said and he turned his face away. When he brought it round again, I looked up at him. His eyes were watery and there were sad snowflakes all over his cheeks. "Fliss, I need you to be especially careful now that we've had the Gray Moth here."

"Yes, but he's been captured," I said.

"I know," said Gideon, "but there could be others. You see, these people are looking for things, information. While I am gone, take good care of yourself. And don't allow anyone other than family into the house." He clapped his gloved hands together. "I wish you didn't have to think about all this. It is not right. Still, we cannot hide our work from you, though we tried." Gideon ruffled the top of my head, knocking snow from my hat. Then he smiled at me. "I guess you are one of us now."

"Will you really have to leave before Christmas?" I said.

"Fliss, there are terrible, unthinkable tragedies going on in Europe. We must do all we can. It's more important than anything in the world right now."

"Yes, I know," I said.

"And you are my lovely, almost partway grown-up daughter and I think you know why I am going to France."

"Yes," I said.

"Good. I want you to know what I am doing and why I am doing it. I do not want to abandon you. I know you felt abandoned by your mother and by Danny."

"No, I did not!" I shouted out, suddenly feeling all wound up, like a skein of wool wrapped too tightly. "No, I did not feel abandoned." But I started to cry because I *had* felt abandoned and I still felt abandoned. "If only Winnie and Danny had told me everything first. And now you are going away as well."

"What I am scheduled to do *must* be done. Oh, Fliss, I will try so hard to ease your worry while I am gone," he said. "And I shall not forget you, Fliss, not for one moment in my long voyage. And don't forget me. Not ever. No matter what." Then he buttoned the top button of his overcoat, turned up his collar, and looked at the dizzying, snow-filled sky. He finally closed his eyes. Snowflakes collected along his eyelashes and eyebrows and covered his new mustache until it too was lost in whiteness. "You'll see. Keep a lookout for cards from me, then. I'll send them to you and Derek," he said. "And our Christmas will just have to wait until a brighter, better year."

Forty-Three

Soon enough, snapping suitcase sounds, unmistakable getting-ready-to-leave noises were coming from my father's room. It was soon to be Christmas vacation at school, but my father did not go in wearing his Mr. Bathtub, Christmas-red velvet bathrobe over his regular clothes or hand out favors from its large pockets to the youngest kids as he used to do.

There was a substitute teacher at his desk now when I passed his room at school, and the whole of Babbington El seemed already to miss Mr. Bathtub. A few months before, people at school had started calling the point where we lived Bathtub Point. Now when I walked down the hall at school, someone would usually call out something like, "How is Mr. Bathtub? Did it snow last night on Bathtub Point?"

At the house a man from the FBI came to search and check all the rooms one more time for listening devices. My father was uneasy, worrying that the Gray Moth might have tucked a device somewhere in the house.

And then one evening my father was saying his good-byes. He pulled me into his huge arms and I felt his rough, prickly cheeks and chin and I smelled the warm, tweedy, pipe-smoking, book-reading air that was all round him. I had known the time was upon us when he had grown his mustache as planned. He looked quite handsome really, a little like Auntie's favorite actor, Clark Gable, in *Gone with the Wind*.

"Mother, take care of my little daughter," said Gideon. And he squeezed me tightly. When my father released me, I saw Derek standing nearby, dark and like a fire burning all alone in a stove, unattended.

"Oh, Derek," said Gideon, "come here. I shall miss you with all my heart. Perhaps it is not on paper but you are surely a son to me." He threw his great, long arms round Derek, who suddenly looked skinny and all swallowed up. "I know you will hold down the fort. I shall be very proud of you."

Derek began to cry. It was a small sound muffled against Gideon's shoulder, but the sound ripped and stomped on my heart. Whenever a boy cried, it was so much more wrenching than a girl crying because it didn't happen very often.

"Daddy," I called down the stairs after dinner, when our blackout curtains were closed and the house had that lonely, dark, shut-away feeling. From where I stood I could see a few empty branches of the tall Christmas tree in the parlor. "Daddy," I called before I went to bed, knowing he would be gone in the morning when I awoke. "Bring Winnie and Danny home safely. Make them be safe," I said. "And promise me you will come home to us."

He put his fingers over his lips to hush me. And then he blew me a kiss.

The next day my father was gone and his room at the front of the house was no longer full of coffee cups and newspapers. It was oddly clean and organized. When I went in there, it was chilly and empty and full of light. I kept thinking that my father hadn't promised me that he would come home. He hadn't *promised*.

Derek and The Gram and I managed alone through Christmas. We sang carols at the Last Point Church on Christmas Eve. The Gram held Derek's hand on one side and my hand on the other. Her grasp was so tight and so strong, my fingers felt numb.

We planned very few presents for Christmas Day but that morning I couldn't find my slippers and so I went down on my knees and looked under the bed. There I saw a tiny gold ring in a crack in the floor. It was shining in the darkness under there, next to my slippers. I could just barely reach it. It proved to be quite sweet, stamped inside with the initials E.B. In swirling old writing, there was a date, 1864. It had been Ella Bathburn's little gold ring. I wondered when she lost it or why. It had been found nearly one hundred years too late, but because it was Christmas morning, it almost felt as if Ella Bathburn had given me a gift.

We made it through New Year's Eve and New Year's Day and the long white stretch of sledding days before school resumed. Derek was friendly now, but he didn't love me anymore the way he once had. It was over and gone. And that ragged and nagged and pulled on me. It just wouldn't quit, for I still loved Derek.

But we did everything together because there was no one else about, I suppose. We stacked wood together for the woodstoves. We did the washing up after tea. We rushed home to read *Life* magazine together every week. There we saw photographs of battles, of fighter planes and parachutes dropping and we read stories of USO canteen belles like Auntie. I liked the advertisement for the lipstick called Patriot Red by Louis Philippe. I wanted to wear Patriot Red lipstick and I wanted Derek to notice it and stare at me, thinking me very patriotic indeed.

Derek and I had the same birthday on January 29 and that wasn't very far off. I would soon be thirteen. But it wasn't really Derek's true birthday. It had been chosen for him because it was the day I was born. It had been done to make up for Gideon's loss. Derek boiled and simmered about his birthday through all of early January.

Where did love go when it went away? It was as if Derek had opened a door and had thrown his feelings for me out into the wind. I wondered if perhaps his love would be restored if he would just let Buttons, Buttons and Babbit find his true parents.

One day I came in from a walk along the water, watching frozen convoys move across the icy horizon. The Gram was in the dining room, leaning over Derek. They were whispering. She had her arm across Derek's back. And then she had her cheek resting on the top of his head.

"What is it?" I said when I came brushing into the dining room, where the morning mail was scattered across the table.

"Oh, nothing," said The Gram. But she had the card with the gold writing on it in her hand. I could see part of it, half a word here and there. I could read *uttons* on one end and *Bab* on the other.

The Gram then quickly slipped the card in her apron pocket and said, "Well, Flissy, we've a job to do now. We have been asked to knit socks for soldiers overseas and that will include our Mr. Henley."

"Good," I said, "because he never seemed to have matching socks, did he? But that's because he's a poet. Poets are like that."

"I know you are a crack knitter, Flissy McBee. We'll get the wool from Miss Elkin because she keeps sheep now along with her chickens. She spins it herself, the way we have been churning our own butter here. It's the best way to get butter these days." As she was talking, she was putting stamps on a pile of letters. The Gram had elegant handwriting. I always liked to see the curls and the extra circles she added at the ends of words. I looked down as she went through the pile. Most of the letters seemed to be going to Washington, DC. I looked away.

Yes, my father and The Gram had asked me to stop noticing things and I was going to try. But things still went on in the house. Things I did not completely understand. In the middle of the next night I awoke in Aunt Miami's huge canopy bed. I heard someone in the hallway slowly passing my room. I heard each measured step so clearly as that person moved along the hall. Then I heard keys rattling on a large, circular key holder. I heard a key being inserted into the lock. And then someone stepped into my father's study and clicked the door shut behind them. I knew it was The Gram and I lay in my bed, chilled in spite of the piles of quilts and the soft pillow under my head.

★ *Forty-Four* ★

We began our great sock-knitting project that next week. Well, I should say I began knitting. Derek made up a chart showing how many socks should be knitted each day and how long each sock should take and which sizes would be most useful. By evening Derek had a lovely graph showing all sorts of complicated information that I couldn't follow and I had in my lap a pink-and-purple-striped wool sock on the large side. I was already knitting and purling the second sock, wondering all along if the soldier who would be wearing these socks would fancy the lovely, bright colors I had chosen.

The Gram wasn't getting very far with her sock because she was on edge and flying up to the landing and lifting the receiver off the telephone and then dropping it back down. She changed her apron three times and paced through the house, like a small fox in a cage.

She checked the mailbox constantly and came back inside now, looking windblown and anxious. "You've gotten a letter, Flissy McBee," she said and handed me an envelope. My heart started drumming inside me, as usual. Letters always made me leap and lunge, hoping still to hear from Winnie and Danny. If they wrote to me, I would have their address and then I could send them both a pair of warm socks. Did they let people write from prisons in France? By now my parents had grown thin as mist, vague as clouds, distant as faraway smoke. But I had the habit of loving them and waiting for them and once you acquire a habit, it stays with you. It stands by you. It won't leave you, just like hope.

I rather ripped open the letter.

Dear Felicity Bathburn Budwig,

I have been in Canada, as my mum sent me on a boat with the others. I am staying in Montreal with Monsieur Laport and his sister-in-law. She only speaks French. Montreal is close to Maine, said my mum in a letter. She thought I should come for a visit by train. May I? I saw a ghost last night and Madame Laport chased it out of the larder with a ghost detector. It is my greatest wish to own one of those myself. Do write back soon.

Sincerely yours,
Dimples McFarland

When The Gram read the letter, her eyes became two blue stars spinning and twinkling at me. It was the first time I had seen her eyes lighten since Gideon left. "Well, if she is your little friend, of course Dimples can come to visit," she said. "Perhaps it will take my mind off things."

"Um, Dimples is five years younger than me and she does much more gallivanting and hopping about than I ever did, if you know what I mean. But she doesn't break things, actually," I said.

"That's good. And can she knit?" said The Gram.

"She learned at three," I said. "She makes odd things, like capes for invisible tiny people. But she's quite good at it when she settles down."

"Well, that's it, then. Knitters are more than welcome. We'll have all the soldiers in Europe wearing a nice pair of wool socks before the year is out," said The Gram, sitting down to work on her first sock. Her needles began clicking and flashing and a brown-and-gray argyle sock slowly began appearing right before my eyes. "But I should ask the office about the correct colors to use before we really get started," said The Gram. "Pink-and-purple stripes for the army might not be the best choice, Flissy B. Bathburn."

★ Forty-Five ★

Soon The Gram and Dimples's mum were exchanging telegrams. The first one from England read:

*Dimples needs happy place to stay STOP Can
she visit you STOP I shall be grateful STOP*

After all that *stopping* in the telegrams, I was quite happy to be *going* one morning to pick up Dimples at the Grand Trunk Railway station, the one that serviced the north, including Montreal. In the Packard, The Gram and I dropped Derek off in Bottlebay. He planned to walk home, he said. He had something important to do, but of course he wouldn't say what it was. When I asked about it, The Gram said, "Oh, tra la la, Flissy B. Bathburn. Must you stick your little nose in everything?"

Train stations always made me breathless, the ceilings stretching off into almost forever. The Grand Trunk Railway station was on India Street and today it was full of soldiers in khaki uniforms. And there were sailors milling about with long duffle bags slung over their shoulders. Everything echoed and murmured in that huge, vaulted area, as if it were a kind of cathedral.

Dimples, as she rushed towards me, looked tiny and jumpy and rosy. She was bobbing about like a fish on a line. "Felicity!" she called out, running into me. "I've got a suitcase that used to be Monsieur Laport's typewriter case. Look," she said, opening it. "It's got clamps in here where the typewriter was attached. See that, do you?"

"Come along, you little nipper, close all that up now," said The Gram.

But Dimples pulled out a nightdress and held it up. "This is brand-new. I didn't pinch it. Madame Laport bought it off a lady in a frock shop only yesterday."

"Come along now, close all that up," said The Gram, pulling on Dimples's little sleeve.

Then Dimples threw herself down on the station floor and looked up at the ceiling. "Oh, but I did want Madame to buy me a new pair of galoshes because mine are full of holes, but she said no."

"Little nipper, up on your feet," said The Gram. "And pack away your things now."

In the car riding home, Dimples suddenly grew quiet and wouldn't answer anyone. She kept kicking her foot on the back of the seat and her curly hair was quite messy looking.

"She's an odd little thing," whispered The Gram to

me when we got out of the car. "She can stay here but, please, not a word about certain matters. You know what I mean, dear. Good girl."

Dimples was very subdued when we walked in the house. She mostly seemed to look down at her shoes, which were a scruffy brown and worn-out. She had all sorts of cuts and bruises on her knees and her socks quite sagged about her ankles.

Finally, she said, "I should like to have a look at your Wink again. Do you still love him?"

I wasn't sure at all how to answer a question like that. Of course I still loved my old brown bear. But it was different now that I was soon to be thirteen. I was above all that. The thought of his fuzzy ears and cheerful smile did not make my heart soar the way it used to. In fact, when the war was over, I was planning to mail him off to a friend in England. But it's very hard for an almost thirteen-year-old to explain that to an eight-year-old. And so I said, "The problem with Wink is that he is up in my tower room in a box under the bed and that room is locked up for winter. There used to be a key to the room hanging in the library but it is gone now."

Just as those words left my mouth, I suddenly felt a rush of sorrowful air blowing through me. I remembered Gideon, when he was still my uncle, cutting out and sawing the headboard for Wink's bed, measuring Wink, making sure he had plenty of foot room. How I missed my father. Where was he now? When would he come home to us? Would he be able to rescue Winnie and Danny? He didn't promise. He forgot to *promise* to me he would come home. His German uniform floated before me, the bright red armband and the swastika spinning and turning in the air.

★ Forty-Six ★

Derek had come back on his own from Bottlebay before us. He was awfully secretive these days and I was dreadfully curious about his trip.

Dimples was now sitting on the bottom step in the hall. "Come along, then," I said to her. She picked up her typewriter suitcase and we walked into the parlor. Derek was stretched out on the sofa, sipping something through a paper straw. He sat up and looked at Dimples. He seemed a bit perplexed, like a dog with his ears perked up, looking down at a very feisty new puppy.

"Hmm," he said. "Figures, Fliss. Your friend *would* be another Brit. Isn't she kind of small, though?"

"Size really has nothing to do with friendship," I said.

"I'm quite good at figures anyway," Dimples said. "It doesn't matter about my being small. Ask me anything with figures and I'll have an answer."

"What is the largest number in the world?" said Derek, eyeing Dimples with his dark Derek frown.

"Infinity," said Dimples with her hands on her hips. "So where are my sleeping quarters, Felicity?"

I took Dimples upstairs and offered her my little cot in Auntie's room and she sat on it, testing the softness, looking quite messy and pleased the way you do when you've just been on a long journey and haven't had a chance to peek in a mirror to see that your hair has all gone wild and that there are crumbs on your coat.

"Felicity, shall I read your palm?" Dimples said. "I know it will say that you love that boy downstairs."

"Oh, hush, Dimples! You mustn't say that. You see he doesn't love me back anymore."

"Very well, then, I shan't sing the little song I had planned. Perhaps later," she said. "And can we trade beds, possibly? I can offer you two boiled sweets and a special rock brought all the way from England. I think we can make a nice little trade."

"I'd rather not. It's my Auntie's bed, really. She promised it to me for the duration," I said. "The canopy with birds flying all round on it makes me hopeful about my mum and my dad and Daddy. I'm always waiting for them, you know." And then I had to explain everything.

"You have two papas, then, haven't you?" said Dimples after we'd unscrambled the whole story.

"Yes," I said, "I do, actually."

"And I don't even have a one," said Dimples. "Mine packed off and hasn't come back since I was a baby. And here you have two. Aren't you the lucky one?"

"Well, not really, actually," I said. "Oh, all right, then, Dimples, you can have the canopy bed. I'm used to my little cot. Go on, then, take it."

In return, I got two boiled sweets and a small rock,

which I set on a shelf next to my old cot. The rock was quite plain looking really.

Then Derek appeared at the door, leaning on the jamb, with his jacket back on and his paralyzed hand tucked in one of the pockets. "Grab your coats. As a treat, The Gram is taking us all out for supper," he said.

"*Supper* is our *tea*, Dimples," I said.

"I'll be back in a tick, then," said Dimples. And she ran off and we couldn't find her for the longest time. When we did find her, she was in the linen closet, writing a letter to her mum.

The Gram had won a prize for one of her quilts at the winter church bazaar, when we were helping with Bundles for Britain last week. The prize was a free meal at Hank's Hamburger House. And so that evening we drove the Packard into town just before dark, with wind and a light snow blowing all round our car.

Hank's hamburgers were smashingly delicious. Dimples called them hangabers. When Hank came out to congratulate The Gram on her winning quilt, Dimples looked up at him and said, "You don't have a seawall in Bottlebay. We had one in Selsey, but the sea knocked it down and flooded the town. They found fourteen sofas floating in the water the next day."

"Hush now, little nipper," said The Gram.

It was a jolly nice evening with Dimples singing. She had a "hungry song" that she made up and then she sang a "full song" and finally she sang a "tired song" for Derek. He was quite pleased, I thought.

But later when we pulled up to the house, everything changed again. It was a pitch-black night since the moon had gone away to shine somewhere else. And we quickly saw that the wind had taken out our electricity because the house was terribly dark and the tiny red lightbulb The Gram left on for us in the kitchen was off. We got out of the car and we didn't have a match or a candle or flashlight. That's when the sea seemed almost spooky. Because you couldn't see it, you could only hear it and it seemed to be calling for you in a strange, lonely way.

We were just at the gate when we saw someone or a shadow of someone rush from the back door to the front of the house. We heard footsteps on the wraparound porch and then more footsteps on the stairs down to the sea. The snow blew across the garden in gales, making drifts and tunnels, yet leaving some patches of ground barren and exposed. The Gram reached out towards us, her arms waving about. She grabbed me in a fearsome clutch. And Dimples let out an odd little screech.

When we got into the house, we had to stomp the snow off our frozen shoes. Then we had to light candles and close the blackout curtains. Dimples offered to do the job. She said she loved the dark and she rushed through the house, saying there were ghosts in the hall and ghosts in the kitchen.

When the candles were lit, The Gram went to the window in the dining room and parted the curtains and looked out into the night.

"Perhaps we should call the police," I said.

"Oh no," said The Gram, "that wouldn't do at all, Flissy. Too much attention. No. No. We must handle this ourselves."

We both stood there in the dining room, listening to the moan of the wind and the snow. The ocean too was singing and calling in its lonely voice, whispering words that seemed to slip away before we could truly hear them.

The next night, The Gram rang up Mr. Stephenson in New York. I could only hear The Gram's part of the conversation and her voice echoed from the landing. "Bill," she said, "I must know how Gideon is. Did he arrive safely? I can wait no longer. You must inquire. You must tell us. And we must have some kind of protection. I worry for the children. Someone was here last night. But I don't think they got in the house."

The sleet hammered against the windows and Dimples jumped rope and sang in the next room.

> "The old moon came down for a cup of milk
> But he got tangled up in a pile of silk.
> The sun couldn't set and the night couldn't fall
> And the moon rolled away like a big silk ball."

★ Forty-Seven ★

The Bathburns always kept their Christmas trees up until February 2, Groundhog Day. And so today Derek and I and Dimples took down all the old decorations and dragged the long, dry tree out into the garden and started to chop it up into little pieces so we could chuck them into the stove when the temperature dropped at night.

Dimples was jumping on one of the branches. "Oh, I wish I had been here on Christmas Day. Did you have Christmas pudding? Was it lovely and yummy?" she said. Then suddenly she rolled on the ground in the snow and shot at Derek with an invisible gun and he pretended to shoot back at her. I daresay Dimples was a very war-like little girl. She threw a fake hand grenade at Derek and he rolled to the ground and pretended to be dead. I was left to chop at the poor Christmas tree.

Soon Derek shot at me and I fell to the ground, rolling under the tree and dying as well. I stared up through the brittle branches at the sky. I lay there for a long time. It started snowing harder and millions of snowflakes came falling at me. "Come on, Fliss, we should get back to hacking up this tree," said Derek, poking at me with his foot, but I just stayed there, staring at the sky, thinking about everything.

"Perhaps she really is dead," said Dimples, peering down at me sadly. I didn't move one bone or one eyelash. I was quite still, like an ice statue. I hated chopping up our lovely Christmas tree and I hated the loneliness and worry about Winnie and Danny and Gideon. And I was lying there thinking about Derek too. Where had his love for me gone? I decided perhaps it all had disappeared, as if it had been chopped to pieces, like an old Christmas tree when you are done and finished with it.

Then The Gram came out into the snow and stood near us. She kept staring at us, as if she were a boat and we were the faraway shore. And I remembered yesterday was February 1 and that was the day Gideon was to arrive at the prison in Limoges. The Gram just stood there as the snow fell all round her.

Derek got up quickly and brushed himself off. He had been covered in snow and wood chips. He straightened his shoulders, cleared his throat, and stood back away from Dimples, as if to say he hadn't just been playing war with an eight-year-old child. Not at all. Not at all. I too came back to life quickly and stood up.

Dimples looked joyful to see me again. She rushed towards me, throwing her arms round me. "Oh, Felicity, I was worried and sad. You looked like that poor lass who washed up on the broken seawall in Selsey. She was dead, she was. She wasn't faking. But you were faking, weren't you?"

Now The Gram pulled a letter from her pocket and handed it to me. The stamps had rows of palm trees on them and looked a bit like North Africa. The wet snow blurred the ink on the envelope but I could see it was from Mr. Henley. I nearly jumped into the sky. I raced to the house and threw myself down on the sofa in the parlor. The letter said:

> Dear gang,
>
> Thanks a ton for your letters. They cheer a soldier up. I sure do miss Miami. Well, let me know if Doubleday ever answers my letter about my submission. I sent them one hundred poems, return address in care of you, Flissy B. You'll have to be my secretary. I wrote the poems at night. They are my best to date. Love to all, you busy Bathburns.
>
> Bobby Henley
>
> P.S. Has Gideon been drafted? Do you know how he's doing?

Well, we could not answer that last question. We did not know what had happened on February 1 in France. And yet everything in the world seemed to hang on that day. Winnie and Danny and Gideon were perched on the edge of the unknown. As if on the rim of a dark hole, as big as the universe in my mind. And all we could do was wait.

Later in the evening, Dimples came into the parlor and lay on the rug in front of the radio. She had her knitting with her. The socks she knitted had a strange look about them, but she was fast, faster than The Gram or me. "Felicity," she said, lying on her stomach with her face and cheek resting on the floor, "I should really like to see Wink again. I've always had a fondness for that bear. Where is the key to that room anyway? I must have a look at Wink."

But I didn't answer her. I was worrying and wondering about my father wearing that Nazi officer uniform. What if he made a mistake in his German accent? What if Winnie and Danny weren't in the prison after all?

Forty-Eight

Dear Bobby Henley,

 Here is some news from Bottlebay. America no longer has hot dogs. We have victory sausages. It was announced on the radio recently. And January 17, 1943, was declared official Tin Can Drive Day. All day people collected as many tin cans as they could for the war effort. Derek found eight tins and I helped him but we had to rummage about in an old dump not far from the house. You'd better hotfoot it home; they say shoe rationing could start. You'd better not loaf about! So, Bobby Henley, be good and don't forget Miami is yours 4 ever!

 Love,

 Flissy B. Bathburn

We had a little government brochure that told how to write to our GIs overseas. You were expected to be cheerful and jovial and not to mention anything gloomy. Don't talk about sacrifices and shortages, the brochure said. Make jokes.

Dimples had written a letter too, even though she didn't know Bobby Henley. But hers was very hard to read because her handwriting was messy and she only talked about ghosts. I told her that it didn't fit with the government brochure and she became grumpy with me and tore it up.

The Gram told me that Dimples had settled into the third grade at school quite well. The Gram had sent off a telegram to her mum all about it. And Miss Elkin adored Dimples. I could always see Dimples nipping along after Miss Elkin in the halls or sitting with her at lunch. And right off I knew Dimples went mad keen on a little boy named Stucky in her class. She found a small piece of driftwood that was shaped like an elephant and she painted it with gray poster paint. Then she wrapped it up and gave it to Stucky at school. The next day the elephant was sitting on her desk with a note under it that said, *No thanks.*

So Dimples was a bit cross that afternoon and wouldn't go to school the following morning and The Gram had to climb a ladder and pull her out of a cupboard in the gymnasium. But she wasn't the type to mope about for too long and before you knew it, she was racing round the house again.

But she kept after me about Wink. She really wanted to see him again. On Saturday morning Derek and I were gathering up laundry. We were dragging baskets of sheets into the laundry room. Most of the time we couldn't get Dimples to help.

When we were piling cotton pillowcases on the ironing board, I remembered the invisible-ink letter that

Derek and I had ironed in here. I wondered if the person we saw on the porch in the darkness recently was another agent. Derek was standing so close to me, I could hear him breathing. I loved the sound of it. Perhaps it was dreadfully strange but I loved even the gruffness about him. I wanted to tell him that I still cared for him. I wanted to say so many things. "Derek," I began, "I . . ."

Just then Dimples pushed into the laundry room. She was dancing and laughing and singing her "Wink song," which I'd heard before in Selsey. But she hadn't sung that song at all since she had been in Bottlebay.

> *"Wink is woolly brown with spice.*
> *His bearlike heart is awfully nice.*
> *Wink loves winter sun and snow.*
> *He has a happy, fuzzy glow."*

I looked up, rather startled. "Dimples," I said. "Is that Wink you are holding in your arms? It is, isn't it? You've got Wink! Now, how did you get him out of the tower room?"

Dimples looked quite cheerful and she gave Wink a great kiss on his smashed-up nose. He was wearing his old overcoat and his wool sweater. "Oh, he's lovely, Felicity. He's every bit as friendly as I remembered him," she said.

"Dimples, how did you get him?" I said. "The tower door was locked."

"I know," she said. "Well, I just had to get the key and I did and I opened the door and got Wink out. He smells lovely, doesn't he?"

"Where did you get that key, Dimples? It wasn't on the hook in the library anymore."

"Oh, well, I found it quite easily, didn't I?" she said, pushing up the sleeves of her raggedy dress. "The key was taped into the back of a book, *The Secret Garden*, by Frances Hodgson Burnett. It's a jolly good book and I know you've read it eight times, Flissy Bee Bee, but *I'm* reading it for the first time."

"Well, *I* won't be reading it again," I said but in my heart I felt a little tug, because I rather missed reading that book.

Later I became a bit blue as I watched Derek, tall and gruff, bringing in a load of wood for the stove. I wished I'd had a chance to talk to him alone. And seeing Dimples with *The Secret Garden* made me remember all the times my daddy-uncle read aloud to me from that book, before I got too old for all that sort of thing. I so hoped he was safe, wherever he was.

★ *Forty-Nine* ★

But as the weeks stretched on and on and we had not heard from my father at all, I worried more and more about everyone. And The Gram was stewing too. I could tell by the way she did things, even little things, like knitting. One moment her needles would be clicking along like lightning and then those needles would freeze, stop cold for no reason and The Gram would stare at the empty air, looking still and distant, like a stark tree in winter.

Today as we were knitting away on our wool socks for the soldiers, Dimples said, "My mum's working now. You want to know what she does?"

"Oh," I said, "Dimples, are you supposed to say what she does?"

"I don't give a toss. She's working at a factory, making parts for bombers. Halifax bombers!"

"You're not to say that, Dimples," I said.

"She sent me off with the others 'cause she had to work at night and because they bombed Coventry in West Midlands, the Jerries did. It was all rubbish afterwards and heaps of brick from the cottages," said Dimples.

"You shouldn't say *Jerries*," I said. "It isn't polite."

"Well, Dimples, I've gotten to know your mother through all this and I think she is very caring and loyal and responsible. A wonderful mother!" said The Gram. She then smoothed my hair and leaned her head against mine and looked out towards the ocean.

I suddenly wanted to shout out, "Is my mum caring and loyal and responsible? Do I have a wonderful mum too?" Why had she left me for so long? Why hadn't she explained things to me? What would happen when Gideon came to rescue her? And then I closed my eyes and everything nagged at me, like a dark bird caught in a room, trying to get out by flying at the walls, bumping at them over and over again.

Later that afternoon I was having a little tea party for Dimples in the dining room to cheer her up because she had a nightmare last night. She woke up screaming and was all red and sweaty. The Gram had come in to comfort her. In the morning Dimples said, "I didn't have a bad dream, Felicity. I was faking." Well, she got herself a tea party out of the deal anyway.

Just as I was pouring out tea from a little child's teapot that we found in a glass cupboard, The Gram walked into the room. She handed me another letter. Dimples was a bit of a crosspatch then because I was getting all the mail these days.

The envelope said the letter came from New York City. I opened it quickly. Was it from my father? The inside said:

Derek and Fliss,

I think Captain Bathburn has something to say to you! Have a look, won't you?

I studied the card carefully. Yes, it was Gideon's handwriting.

The way The Gram watched me reading it, I could tell she knew my father had written the card before he left and that a secretary at Mr. Stephenson's office in New York had mailed it. The card was dated properly, as if planned ahead. On the front was a picture of Porky Pig and Bugs Bunny on a sailing ship.

Even though I knew my father had written it before he left and I didn't understand what he meant by the words he wrote, I still felt joyous to have the note from him in my hands and to remember when he had taken me and Derek to see *Bambi* at the movie theater last year. Bugs Bunny cartoons were played at the intermission. But at the same time I was suddenly filled with anxiousness, as if the gates had been opened up farther and all the worry in the world had flooded in like rushing water.

When Derek saw the card, he said, "That's Gideon for you. Perhaps we should have a peek at the painting of Captain Bathburn."

So we went into the dining room and looked up close at the captain staring out at us with his green, finely painted eyes. Derek checked behind the painting and there was a little tag hanging from the wire. It said:

Derek and Fliss,
I shall miss you both terribly. But please know you can depend on me. No matter where I am, I will always love you.

★ Fifty ★

All of January and February the snow whirled and whined and washed and whittled at our windows. We huddled near the fireplace in the parlor or by the stove in the dining room because coal was hard to get for the old furnace and we ran the furnace only on the worst days to keep our pipes from freezing.

Derek and I tried all winter to keep track of the war. After *The Shadow* was on the wireless, there was usually a news broadcast. There had been victories in North Africa before Christmas and then some setbacks after that. Mr. Henley had been stationed, we thought, in Morocco. In his last letter he had included a photograph of himself wearing a kind of turban and a long, flowing cloak on his day off. But now we decided he had been transferred somewhere else because we had not heard from him in a while.

On Valentine's Day I got fourteen crumpled valentines from Dimples. She'd made them all herself. They were mostly all of ghosts walking among heart-shaped flowers.

I had hoped and hoped and waited, but I did not receive a valentine from Derek. I had made one for *him* that said, *Derek, I still love you. Do you still love me?* But of course, I had torn it up at the last minute and I had thrown the scraps in the cold woodstove.

Though later when I opened the stove to light it, Dimples said, "Is that a sad, torn-up valentine in there? Oh, it looks so lonely. I should like to paste it back together." Well, I threw a match quickly into the stove and that was the end of it.

Just before supper on Valentine's Day, the phone rang. I made a great dash and beat Dimples to it by a long margin.

"Hello," I said. "This is the Bathburn residence. To whom am I speaking?"

"Sweetest!" Aunt Miami said over the telephone. "Happy Valentine's Day. How are things going at the old homestead? Oh, I do miss it so, in a way."

"Will you be coming home soon?" I said.

"Well, they say things are turning around for the war. Perhaps if we win and the war ends. In North Africa, where Bobby is, they are winning some of the time against the Germans. There was a big battle that Bobby was a part of. He sent me a terrific poem. Have you heard from him? I haven't had a letter in weeks and he usually sends me one a day. And there was no valentine."

"No," I said, "we haven't had a letter in a fortnight."

"I am worried about that. Are you worried, Flissy McBee?" said Auntie.

"Oh, not at all. But guess what? Derek gets to order a pair of Sky Rider shoes. They give you a free model airplane with them," I said. And then later, after we hung up, I felt a bit dreadful because I had stretched the truth about not being worried.

Russia was the front Derek was most interested in. There was a miserable fight that lasted months over the great Russian city Stalingrad and the surrounding area, and finally on February 2, the German general Paulus and his troops were cut off, cornered, and had to surrender. Over ninety thousand German troops were taken prisoner. It was a great victory for the Allies and in the next few weeks the newspapers were full of stories about it.

The Gram and I stood out on the porch for a moment on a cold windy day at the end of February. A Coast Guard boat was cruising the shoreline, always keeping watch. A coastie even waved at us and called out, "Helen, did you hear about that German general who surrendered in Russia?"

I think The Gram smiled for a moment before she wrapped her coat closely round her. Then she tilted her head against her woolen scarf, as if looking for comfort in the soft weave.

★ Fifty-One ★

The next day the sky was dark with more falling snow. But it was snow that wasn't sticking. It just blew about in wisps and worries. I was out for a walk when I saw Dimples running along the shore towards me. Her hair was all wild and windy and she almost looked like she was flying through the cold air. "Felicity," she shouted, "someone has written Mr. Henley a letter and they've put your name on the envelope as well."

I ran towards her as she zigzagged and skipped over the ground, reminding me of a little top spinning along. When I got to her, I saw she had a long white envelope from Doubleday, Doran Publishers in New York City. It was addressed to Mr. Henley and was in care of me! Felicity Budwig Bathburn. Perhaps the reason we hadn't heard from Mr. Henley was because his squadron had been moved somewhere and he couldn't say where. Censors read all the soldiers' letters before they were mailed and if they found something that a soldier shouldn't be saying, the letter was not sent.

When we got back to the house, I left the envelope on the dining room table as we usually did. Was I to open it? Or should we wait for the return of Mr. Henley? He hadn't given me any true instructions. I must say, I felt a bit stuck about it. In fact I felt dreadfully stuck all afternoon.

"Open it now!" Dimples shouted later as she marched round the dining room table, wearing a paper sailor hat that Derek had folded for her out of the *New York Times* front page. She was carrying a stick and she played the part of a soldier with great tragedy.

"Halt," called Derek. "About face!" Dimples froze and turned like a perfect soldier.

"Open it," said Derek. "I command you. Now! Dimples, march! Hup, two, three, four. Halt."

Derek looked back at me, with all kinds of new freckles scattered over his nose. Extra freckles were always popping up on his face, even on dark winter days! Soon he gave me a coaxing Derek smile and I felt like I had just taken a sip of Hershey's Syrup, straight from the tin with no milk added.

I looked at Mr. Henley's letter. I wanted to ask Aunt Miami if it was proper for me to open Mr. Henley's mail. But she had been gone already three months. All we had was a photograph of her wearing a very smart USO uniform with a pin on her lapel with a tiny metal bell hanging from it. She had won the part and by now had been Juliet almost twenty times across the country.

Along the way she had learned all sorts of things that soldiers at boot camp do, like how to make a bed so the sheets were so tight, you could drop a penny on them and the penny would bounce. If Auntie had been here, she would have known whether I should open the letter or not.

Dimples kept marching and Derek played along with her for the lark of it, even though he was fourteen now. "Open it!" they both kept chanting. "Open it!"

And finally in a great moment, like a rush of wind, I dove for the letter. I tore it open and I read it out loud.

"Dear Private Robert Henley,

We received your package of poetry sent to us from the northern African front. These poems are full of the flavor of Morocco and Tunisia and the desert. Each one seems to capture the feeling of longing and of the wish to go home and the sorrow and pity of battle. They remind us of the poems of Rupert Brooke, who wrote during World War I (though not at all in style). We would like very much to publish this collection of poetry you have titled Oh Morocco! *Thank you for giving us this opportunity. We look forward to hearing from you. As soon as we do, we will begin the process of publishing this special book.*

Sincerely yours,
Pike Jemson
Doubleday, Doran Publishing"

"Oh, Derek," I called out. "Mr. Henley will be so very pleased. He has tried for so many years to get published." I threw my arms round Dimples. She wrapped one of her little arms round Derek and pulled him towards us. And her *New York Times* sailor hat fell off and got smashed by mistake by our joyous, jumping feet.

★ *Fifty-Two* ★

It was the very first of March now. They say, "March comes in like a lion and goes out like a lamb." Well then, this March was a wet, soupy lion with ice in his whiskers and sleet in his mane. Still, walking home from school, I could feel a bit of melt in the air. Dimples was wearing her old galoshes that were full of holes. She didn't care at all that her feet were soaking wet. She was jumping in every icy puddle we passed. Perhaps last year I would have done the same but I was taller now and puddles no longer interested me, except to look at the clouds and sky in them. Sometimes it seemed as if the whole world was displayed upside down in a puddle. Perhaps there were answers there in the deep reflection of the sky. I wanted those answers. And yet every time I looked down into a puddle, Dimples splashed the whole thing with her galoshes and the reflection scattered. "Derek's gone off today, hasn't he?" said Dimples.

"Yes, I looked for him after school, but I didn't see him," I said.

"That's because he's gone off with Mr. Babbit to find his mum and his dad."

"How do you know that, Dimples?" I said.

"I don't say," said Dimples, "I just don't say." She was about to call it out one more time but instead she looked straight ahead and fell silent.

A black car had pulled into the driveway in front of our house. A soldier got out and waved slowly to us. He was all dressed up in his somber, freshly ironed uniform.

I suddenly hated him. My stomach turned over. The ground underneath my feet seemed to fall away. I wanted to shout out, "No. Don't come here. Don't come to our house."

Dimples called out, "What does it mean when a soldier comes to your door, Felicity? Does it mean something bad?"

I ran inside and went upstairs. I wanted to go to bed. I wanted to be far away under my covers.

Dimples came pounding into the room after me. "Felicity, his number plates are from New York State. He has driven a long way. I invited him in. He's in the parlor. Shouldn't we get him a cup of tea?"

The Gram was in the upstairs hall when I looked out my door. She was walking very slowly and with great care, as if she were balancing a large book on her head, as if she were carrying a basket of glass eggs, as if she were walking on a narrow white line above a drop-off. "Flissy, get my glasses for me, dear. They are on my dresser," she said.

We followed her downstairs. "Dimples, stand up straight and offer the young man a chair. Girls, go in the library, then, and do some knitting. Dimples, work on your sums. Flissy, don't jump about. Be still. Be quiet. Don't make a sound. Excuse me, have you a letter? For me? Can this wait? Is it urgent? I . . ." She put her face in the crook of her arm. She started to cry. She stopped. She wiped her hands on her skirt. "Is this from Little Bill? He sent you all the way up here? For this? Did you drive all the way today? I'm so sorry. Do I need to read this now? Could we do this later? Flissy, come here. Flissy." She reached out to me and pulled me against her. "Flissy, don't go, dear. This nice man has something for me to read and I don't want to read it. Could you please . . ." She sat down in a chair and she started to cry again. "Could you please hand it to me, young man? Could you please do me the kindness of handing me the letter? I'm really too tired to do anything at all."

He held out the envelope and The Gram took it. Then she squeezed me even more tightly against her. She looked down and read the letter and I read it too. Her hand was shaking. The paper was shaking but I read the words.

Dear Helen,
I was sorry I could not be more forthcoming on the telephone when you called. For security reasons, of course, and I'm sure you understand. Anyway,

*Helen, you have my greatest respect and admira-
tion for your own work and for the work of your
sons. Both of them. They are by far and away our
best in the field and it's due to your superb training and support, so you must feel great pride, dear
friend.*

*Meanwhile, I do have some news to report. It's
not conclusive so you mustn't fret.*

*I delayed in sending this until a certain
amount of time had passed, again for the sake of
security. I am pleased to tell you that the escape
and rescue maneuver by the Blue Piano to free
the Butterfly and the Bear was successful. It went
off flawlessly. However, we understand that some
miles from Limoges, the Blue Piano was driving
the car and we believe he was shot at a checkpoint
or by the local police. We don't know the extent
of his injuries. It's unclear. We do know, however,
that the Butterfly did reach the convent near the
Spanish border. Helen, dear, this is the best and the
worst possible news. Please take care and do not
fret. I shall keep you posted further as information
comes in.*

I remain your friend and admirer,
William Stephenson

The Gram then put the letter on the table. She walked
out into the hall and pulled herself up the stairs, holding

on to the railing. She went into her room and she closed the door. All that evening we could hear her crying. It got into the wind and it got into the walls. You could hear it all through the house. No one fetched wood for the fire. No one made any dinner. The house was cold and empty.

The soldier had stood in the driveway earlier, fussing with his briefcase. He kept shuffling his feet, not knowing what to do and then he got in his car and drove off, waving to Dimples. Derek came home at six from where, I did not know, and he didn't ever take off his jacket. All three of us wore our coats and our wool hats. One light alone burned in the parlor. The rest of the house was dark. Dimples sat on the floor in the parlor and played chutes and ladders with Wink. Derek curled up in a chair and didn't speak. I lay on the sofa under a quilt and stared up at the ceiling while Dimples talked to Wink about good children getting to climb a ladder and have lovely sweets and bad children having to go down a dark chute all by themselves.

We ended up staying the night in the parlor, Derek on the floor, rolled up in a blanket, me on the sofa, and Dimples sleeping on two stuffed chairs pushed together. In the morning she said Wink hogged the bed and that she had fallen through the crack two times in the night.

The Gram was up already and was making scrambled eggs and toast for us in the kitchen. There wasn't a trace of a tear in her eyes. And I rarely saw her cry again.

The fires were going but when we went in the kitchen to eat, we were still wearing our coats and hats. Dimples stood quite soberly by the door, her hair in a bit of a tangle and some peanut butter and jelly from yesterday still on her cheeks. When I looked at her, I realized she was alone outside the circle of tears, while The Gram and Derek and I were standing in the middle of it. Dimples had not met my father. She had never talked to him. She could not understand how it felt to know he had been shot. He was the Blue Piano and he had rescued the Butterfly and the Bear. The Blue Piano had been brave and daring and courageous and he had saved Winnie and Danny. I burst into tears over and over again. I felt so different now from Dimples. As if there were a very long expanse, an endless, lonely field of winter grass between us. And yet my mum had been freed. She was no longer in a horrid prison. She was safe in a kindly convent. The nuns would feed her. They would let her rest there. I still had a mother. And I still longed for her. And my Danny too was still alive. And yet the Blue Piano had been shot.

We didn't go to school that day and I spent most of the afternoon in the library because that was truly my daddy's room. I took my hand and ran it across the backs of all his books on the shelves. I picked up the sharpened pencils standing in their jar on his desk. I went to the piano and let my hands rest on the keys. Then I opened his writing box. I pulled out a little flat drawer at the bottom. Some old, half-finished letters lay in there, covered with my father's big, easy, open handwriting.

Darling Winnie,

If you only knew how I feel tonight. If I could be sitting in the same room with you now, that alone would ease my longing. Even if you were in my brother's arms, I would still choose to be near you. We love so few people in our lives. Love does not come easily or often. It is rare and stubborn and unyielding. And my love for you, Winnie, in spite of what has happened, is unstoppable. I cannot control or steer its course.

The letter was never finished and never sent. There appeared to be others and all of them were never mailed. In one he spoke of me and his great longing and sadness over not seeing me or knowing me. I closed up the writing box and went over to the Victrola and put on a record. I chose "I Think of You." Not because I wanted to wallow or drown in tears but because it had been Gideon's favorite song and I wanted Dimples to know my father. "Dimples, do come in here and listen to this song," I said.

She wove her way into the library a bit cautiously. She was dragging Wink by his ear.

"You're hurting Wink. He always had very sensitive ears, actually. I never carried him that way," I said.

"He likes it," shouted Dimples. "He likes being dragged about by his ears. He told me. He told me." She kept shouting and shouting and finally she started to cry.

I went over to her and I put my arm round her. I suddenly realized how confused and alone she felt. After all, she was far away from her home and from her own mum. "We shall be all right, Dimples," I said. "We shall go on waiting and waiting and hoping. And I think we should ask The Gram if she could make Wink some new clothes. I bet she can make him the best pajamas any bear ever had."

★ Fifty-Three ★

Derek was shattered by all this. He had a look about him, like a sturdy plate that had been dropped too many times. Every morning before school, he walked off way down the shore and I could see him tossing small rocks into the water over and over again. Now we were like other families in Bottlebay, not knowing anything about their brothers or fathers or uncles or cousins. We did not know where Danny was. We did not know if my father was alive or dead. Not knowing left you feeling heavy and confused, with your feelings all in a bottle inside you.

Last week our seagull, Sir William, had shown up on our porch with three fat gray children, all of them waiting to be fed. Miss Elkin was visiting and confirmed Sir William was a girl seagull and not a boy as we had previously thought. We now needed to change her name. I did not think a girl should go flying about with a name like *Sir William*. I would have loved so to tell my father about his pet. But I could not. Perhaps he would never know now.

We sent packages of biscuits and our homemade jam and sweaters and socks to the last address we had for Mr. Henley but we got no reply. And it was Dimples who asked after we'd mailed off the package if a soldier would need a wool sweater in North Africa. And The Gram rolled her eyes and said, "Oh, how could I be so foolish? You're right, Dimples, of course. No one wears wool in that climate in the spring, which is, God willing, just around the corner."

In the middle of March, Dimples found a whole collection of ladybugs that had wintered over in the house, upstairs. She captured about five of them and had them in a jar in our room. She put a tiny thimble of water in for them and sometimes she let them out to wander about on her arms. One day one of them got lost under the dresser and Dimples had a terrible fit until Derek helped her find it.

We read in the *New York Times* that month that the Allies were planning to send planes to bomb Germany "around the clock." And I did hope that didn't make the Nazis bomb London all the more. We had real baths, instead of sponge baths, that month too, when it began to warm up enough in the bathroom to be able to stand it. Dimples told us that when she took a bath in England, the government said you could only have five inches of water in the bathtub. Did they measure the water with a ruler? I wondered. And I hated war and I said so every night before I went to sleep.

And then on a warm evening in late March, the sort of evening at the end of winter that appears out of nowhere, when the air is strangely thick and balmy and new, we decided to pull out the wicker porch chairs and sit outside. The four of us, on the darkened porch, were rocking away all bundled up in our coats. We were rocking in rhythm with the surf and watching the searchlights across the water, when the telephone rang.

The Gram began to shake and she wouldn't get up even when I tugged and pulled at her. But she wouldn't budge. She just kept calling out, "No. No. I can't do it. I won't do it." And finally I ran to the phone and grabbed the receiver. I too did not think I could bear any more bad news.

"Hello," I called into the phone.

"Hello," a voice called back. "Is it Felicity?"

"Yes," I called, "who is this?"

"It's your mum, Winnie, darling. Can you hear me? Are you there? You sound so grown up. I'm just arrived back in the States. Are you there? Hello, darling? Say something. Have we been cut off? Hello?"

"Winnie! Winnie!" I said. "Is it really you?"

The phone started buzzing and sputtering. "Hello? It's your mum, darling. I have so wanted to hear your voice, my baby. I am going to be trying to come there tomorrow, although Bill thinks I'm too weak." She started to cry. "But I shall be fine. Can you make up a bed for me? I'm awfully tired, darling. Can you hear me?"

"Oh, Winnie, yes, we can make you a lovely bed. Oh, Winnie, I've missed you so. I nearly died waiting for you," I said.

"I shall see you tomorrow. I have a ride, says Bill. It's all arranged." Her words trailed off and grew faint. "He's been so very nice. I'm awfully tired, darling. I shall see you tomorrow, perhaps. Is that just lovely, then? Okay, my darling. Good night, then."

"Winnie! Winnie!" I called out again. "Winnie. Oh, Winnie. Don't hang up. I have waited so long. Good night. Will I really see you tomorrow? How will you get here?"

"Yes, darling. It's all been arranged." The phone began buzzing and sputtering again. "I've lost a bit of weight, you know. Don't be shocked, will you? And I imagine you are a big girl now."

"Oh, Winnie, shall I tell The Gram? What shall I say?" But I don't think she heard me because, soon enough, the line was empty and an operator broke in. And then I held the receiver in my arms and I shrieked and cried at the very top of my lungs. I screamed at the very tippy top of my whole being. "Winnie! Winnie! Winnie! My mum, Winnie, is coming home. She is back. Winnie is coming home!"

★ Fifty-Four ★

The next day the sky was as gray and blue as the pearly inside of a mussel shell. The wind was coming in from the south, the clouds high and tumbling. I don't know how Winnie ended up approaching the house from way down the shore. Perhaps her ride had left her off at the wrong spot along the water or she had taken a wrong turn herself or maybe she just wanted to look at the ocean first before knocking on our door, but there she was, walking up the shore just as I always knew she would, just the way I had seen my mother coming towards me so many times in my mind. The water pearly blue, her dress the same color, the sky too chiming in, matching that soft blue note. All of it melting into wind and wholeness, her hair loosened and blowing. She was limping. *God, Winnie, don't limp. Don't look so thin and so tired. The wind could carry you away. Don't let it. Don't move. Be there really. Really.* I ran towards my mother. She seemed farther and farther away, the faster I ran. And she seemed hardly aware of the wind that battered and ruffled her.

"Winnie," I called out, rushing along the shingles and sand and mud. I raced and ran and for a moment it felt like I would never reach her, that I would run and run and I would never get to her. She suddenly seemed so far away, so far away. Then in a cloud of wind and salt spray I rushed upon her. "Winnie!" I shouted again. I threw myself into her arms and she fell into mine and as soon as I had my head on her shoulder, I realized I was bigger and taller and older now, that I wasn't the same little girl anymore. Winnie felt small to me and her eyes were huge and full of something new, something I did not recognize.

It was all a jumble of sky and sea and tears. Winnie's voice sounded lost and wavering and her arms were thin. When she and I stumbled up to the porch, The Gram stood at the screen door. Her face was frozen and still. Winnie leaned against my shoulder and looked at The Gram. "Helen," she said through the mesh of the screen, "Helen, may I come in? I've been on a long, long journey and I am very tired and I have lost so much."

The Gram didn't answer.

"May I ask you for a place to rest, just for the time being?" said Winnie. She laughed in a weakened, soft way. "I shan't take up much room and I promise to be quiet."

The Gram stood there saying nothing for the longest time and then she backed away from the door and I led my mother into the parlor. In the moments that followed, The Gram began to step back a little more and a little more until finally she turned and went upstairs into her room and shut her bedroom door.

Winnie sat down on the sofa and took off her shoes. Her feet and legs were dotted with faded bruises and old scratches and for some reason she began to shiver. She pulled a crocheted blanket across her lap so that I wouldn't see the marks on her legs. She was shy about that and about her wrists as well. "It's been almost two months and they are practically all gone now," she said and she took my hand and I sat down beside her. And for a moment I too felt shy, as if a stranger had come for a visit.

"Would you care for some tea?" I said finally. I spotted Dimples then, peeking round the corner and I shook my head and waved her away.

"Yes, thank you, darling," said Winnie, closing her eyes and squeezing my hand. "Yes, oh yes, tea would be lovely."

"The Gram must be tired today, if she forgot to say hello. Sometimes she can be forgetful, especially because of Gideon. We've been so very worried about him."

Winnie rested her head on the back of the sofa and closed her eyes. "Hush, darling. Yes. We'll talk about all that when I've rested. Now I need to sleep. Did I tell you how lovely you are, do you know? And you are so much taller! But you are still my pretty little child. Oh, I have missed you."

She spoke with her eyes still closed and she squeezed my hand again and I suddenly wanted to shout at The Gram, "Come downstairs and greet my Winnie. She did not mean to hurt anyone. She's been gone so long and she's tired!"

But The Gram did not come out of her room. I thought for a moment I heard her on the stairs but it was only the sound of the sea that always seemed to transform itself and rise up and become yet again a kind of unexpected visitor in the Bathburn house. I made a pot of tea but Winnie fell asleep on the sofa and never drank any of it.

And then I went upstairs into the spare bedroom at the back of the house. Dimples followed me without saying one word. I opened the curtains and put fresh sheets on the bed. The sheets were cold and smelled of sweet cedar when I took them from the wooden chest. This room had hand-stenciled birds as wallpaper. Cardinals and orchard orioles flew all over the walls and above the doors. In the cupboard was an old doll with a wax head and a calico dress. Dimples watched me as I put the doll on the pillow next to where my mum would lie. Winnie had a small shopping bag of clothes with her. They were new, with tags hanging from them and they did not look like clothes she would pick out for herself.

Derek finally helped me lead Winnie to her room. He called her Aunt Winifred. When she sat at the edge of her bed, she looked at Derek and said, "I don't believe we've met and I'm so sorry about that. I suppose you're my nephew, but are you Miami's son?"

"No," said Derek, looking down.

"Am I unaware of Gideon's marriage? Are you Gideon's son?"

"No," said Derek, turning to the window.

"Well then, dear heart, we will talk about it. I'm a good listener. You will tell me all about it when I wake up later."

Derek turned round quickly and his face lit up. Every freckle seemed suddenly a tiny point of light. Later that afternoon as Winnie slept, Derek disappeared and I stood at the back window in Winnie's room and watched him bicycling along the road to town.

Fifty-Five

The white snowdrops bloomed along the south side of the house in the morning sun the next day and Derek picked a bouquet for my mother. And Dimples said, "Did you want a bouquet too, Flissy Bee Bee Bee?" Then she started singing:

> "*Derek, Derek, won't you marry Miss Fliss?*
> *And if you won't marry, won't you give her a kiss?*"

"Oh, Dimples, hush," I said. "I shall be quite embarrassed if Derek hears you. He doesn't love me anymore so please don't sing that song."

"Very well, then, can we make a trade?" she said to me. "I shall stop singing the song and in exchange I shall have your mum for mine and you can have the canopy bed back." And then Dimples got all pouty and wouldn't say anything else and finally she started to cry.

I poked about the room and fetched Wink for her. He was at his most huggable in the mornings. He was all fuzzy and ready to be supportive. I straightened his red bow at his neck and I handed him to Dimples. I told her we could share my mum but I couldn't give her over completely the way I could with Wink.

"Wink is not just a toy bear. He's real, Felicity! Oh and I don't like sharing. I just need a mum to hug me, that's all," said Dimples, kicking at the tassels along the bottom of the pink stuffed chair in the bedroom.

"When she wakes up, I am sure my mum will hug you," I said and I looked out Miami's tall windows. From this angle the sea seemed quite elegant and reserved, like a grown-up sea that never slipped over the proper borders or did anything wild. I was used to sharing my mum with others, with everyone in the world, in fact. But I did hope she would have a moment for me. I did hope too that The Gram would let her stay. I knew it was up to me to unravel all that wrong between them and fix the break in the knitted pattern.

★ *Fifty-Six* ★

My mum slept and slept and slept. And I waited and waited' and waited. And I worried about the bruises and scars on her legs and wrists and I hated to think what they meant. Still, it was to me a great relief to have her back here safely in the house. For once my heart was light and soaring like the bluebirds that appeared in our garden that late March when the last patches of snow were melting. How those bluebirds dipped and trailed, as if they were strewing ribbons in the air. At last that gnawing pain, that longing for my mother was gone. The pain was quieted. She was here!

In that next week when she was still mostly sleeping, waking up only for very small sips of tea and toast, she had called me her pretty little child again. Somehow that made me feel a bit uncomfortable. I wasn't sure why. And then she said, "I noticed some long, old-fashioned skirts and old hats in the cupboard. When I'm rested, I will play dress-up with you, darling, the way we used to. I am sure we can find you a fairy gown. You used to ask me all the time to bring you a fairy gown. Remember, darling?"

"I don't really play dress-up anymore, Winnie," I said.

"But I can't believe it! It's your favorite! What have they done to you here? I can still see your little face and that starry little crown you made. Remember? And who is Flissy Bee Bee Bee?" she said in an awkward, tired, and pitiful way, her face lying deep against the starched cotton pillowcase and feather pillow.

"That's me," I said, standing up tall and smiling.

"Oh, I prefer your name the way it was given to you, Felicity Budwig," she said. "That's you. That's my little girl."

But I was Flissy all the way down to the tips of my Pink Passion toenails. (Auntie had given me the bottle of nail varnish before she left.) Couldn't Winnie see that?

And then I had whispered quietly as I set a tea tray down on the table next to her bed, "Do you think we can have hope for Gideon? And what about Danny? I mean, you know more than we do and . . ."

"Hush now. I cannot answer your questions just yet. I don't have any answers, darling. It's still so soon and hurts so much. Perhaps later, my little baby. Later."

I didn't know if I wanted to be called a "little baby" and I had hoped Winnie would talk to me about my father. But she didn't seem to want to.

Oh, but those bluebirds fluttered and soared and dove about in the garden. My mother was here. She was here. I couldn't believe it. I felt relief and joy and something else. Something else.

In the next few days I was able to leave the windows open in Winnie's room. It was soothing and peaceful to see the curtains breathing in and out in the first spring air. She arrived at the end of March and it was the very beginning of April now. I think she had only been freed from prison a short time, but I didn't know for sure. I would ask her everything when she was rested.

I was in the parlor knitting socks alone, waiting for Winnie to wake up from her endless sleep when the telephone rang again. We had one of the few telephones along the coast in this area and recently a neighbor who lived behind the Last Point Church had come in to use the telephone. He wanted to call Washington to ask the whereabouts of his two sons, who were in the same squadron in the Pacific. He did not receive an answer that day.

And so it was with our Mr. Henley too. We thought he had been moved somewhere and hadn't been able to tell us. Whenever Miami called, I reminded her of that. "But it has been months now," Miami had said, crying at the end of the line from so many miles away. She cried from Portland, Oregon. She cried from Santa Fe, New Mexico. And she even cried from Sacramento, California.

The telephone rang and rang now but The Gram did not come out of her room except once every evening to make dinner for us. And so I was left to answer it, as

Dimples and Derek were playing horseshoes in the garden. I could hear the *clang clang* every time a horseshoe hit the iron pole to score.

"With whom do I have the pleasure of speaking?" I said.

"Hello, there. This is Pike Jemson from Doubleday Publishing. We hadn't heard anything from you or from Private Henley with regard to this marvelous and extraordinary poetry manuscript. Is there any way we could go forward with this project through you, madam?" he said.

"Um," I said. "Um."

"Am I speaking with Mrs. Felicity Budwig Bathburn?" said the voice.

"Um, well, um, yes, sort of," I said.

"Well, Mrs. Bathburn, Private Henley indicated in his letter to us that the matter would be in your hands while he is away."

"I see," I said. "Um, well, you see, Private Henley is in a special squadron, I believe, and we can't contact him. But I know he will be ever so happy, Mr. Pike."

"Mr. Jemson, if you will," he said.

"Mr. Jemson. I am sorry," I said. "Mr. Henley will be, in fact, pleased as Punch, as they say. He loves to write poetry. It's what he lives for. He thought no one would want his poems. He got rejected about a hundred times, I think. Perhaps you should speak with his fiancée. Her name is Miami." Then I felt dreadfully bold, as Mr.

Henley had not yet asked my aunt to marry him. It was I who still had the engagement ring stored secretly in my room.

"Where can we contact her?" said Mr. Jemson.

"Well, she moves about, you see. She's always moving with the USO. I don't know where you might find her just now. She was in Wyoming last we spoke but she was leaving that night."

"I see. Can we send *you* a contract, Mrs. Bathburn, for your signature and approval, with a check for one thousand dollars payable to Private Henley upon his return? He indicated that you were his contact."

I paused. I took a deep breath. I did not think Mr. Pike Jemson knew he was speaking with a thirteen-year-old child. Well, perhaps I wasn't a child. No, of course I wasn't. It was clear when I stood next to Dimples and when she jumped from her bed to mine, pretending the beds were battleships; it was clear then that I was no longer a child. I hadn't wanted to jump. I had been too busy to jump. And I didn't believe my bed was a battle-ship. "Um," I said, "um."

"Well," said Mr. Jemson, "the reason we are acting so quickly is because this book must come out while the war is on. It will be so meaningful to so many people. It will *help* so many people and it really can't wait, Mrs. Bathburn."

"Oh, I see," I said again and that word *help* sort of floated round in my head, like a bumblebee moving amongst the lilac buds outside. "Yes," I called out. "Yes, go ahead and send the papers. Mr. Henley will be over the moon because of this."

And then I hung up the phone and I started crying. I cried for my daddy-uncle, who had been shot while saving my mum and Danny and I cried for my sweet Danny because I didn't know where he was. I cried for my mum, asleep and silent, recovering in her bed upstairs. I cried for Derek because he was unfinished and waiting and wanting. I cried for The Gram, locked away in her room in her anger and for the neighbor who did not yet have an answer about his sons. And I cried for myself because I had made a decision without asking anyone and I could see clearly that I was no longer a child.

Fifty-Seven

I sat in my auntie's room, looking at all the photographs of movie stars she had sent away for. All of them were signed *to Miami Bathburn*, some with *love* and some with *best wishes*. There was a photograph of the dashing Clark Gable. He had been in the movie *Gone with the Wind*, which The Gram had finally taken us to see last spring. Miami had sent off for his autograph long ago and she adored Clark Gable. Now he had joined the air force and was seen in the news in uniform. His wife, who was also an actress, had gone down in a plane while on a tour promoting the sale of war bonds to Americans to help raise money for the war. Even movie stars had mixed-up and broken lives because of the war.

Oh, what could I do to make The Gram forgive my Winnie? I decided to write The Gram a letter.

> *For The Gram,*
> *I love being here at the Bathburn house. I love the bedrooms upstairs, the way they smell of lilacs even when the lilacs haven't yet bloomed for the season. I love the Lifebuoy soap in the long porce-lain bathtub upstairs. I love bathing in it. I have never floated in such a long bathtub. Do you think*

the captain was an extremely tall man? I love
seeing Ella Bathburn's doll and her whalebone
knitting and embroidery needles tucked in baskets
about the house. I love seeing her embroidered bed
curtains on Miami's canopy bed. I love the soft,
murmuring sound of you being in the kitchen
when I wake up in the morning. I love your muf-
fins even without sugar, as they have been recently.
I love the sky above the Bathburn house, even full
of fighter planes and Coast Guard planes. I love
your son Gideon, my daddy-uncle, and I love your
handsome son, Danny, my uncle-daddy. But best of
all I love you so very much. You are my favorite
grandmother. Won't you come out and greet my
Winnie? You cannot blame her anymore. She is
part of the family. Come out and hug my Winnie.
Do it for me because I love you so.

Love,
Your granddaughter, Flissy B. Bathburn

I stuffed the letter under her bedroom door and
waited. For a half hour I sat there in the window seat in
the hallway, watching the door and the sun slide slowly
across it. Finally, I heard my grandmother stirring.
She came out into the hall and she threw her arms
all round me. She rocked me tightly, just the way she
rocked her bread dough, rolling and coaxing it with care.
And then we went downstairs together, grandmother and

granddaughter, and put on the kettle for tea. There was something about the sound of the water heating in a kettle on the cooker that seemed always to offer such promise, as if that sound would cure or heal any wound.

It was I who took the tray up to Winnie later. The Gram still refused. But she stayed downstairs all day. She did the washing up and the cooking and some laundry. She did not speak of Winnie but she no longer stayed behind closed doors in her bedroom.

During that first week of April, The Gram made a tart using the last of our homemade wild strawberry jam. "The wild strawberries will be out in June and I wanted to use up last year's supply of jam," The Gram said and she pulled from the oven a blistering, bubbling, cooing, wild strawberry tart.

"A piece of this will be wonderful for my Winnie," I said. "She isn't eating much. She must be losing more weight. I'm dreadfully worried."

The Gram drew a long breath and went to the kitchen window with her back to me and said, "I did not make this tart for *her*."

It was then that an idea came to me. You never know when an idea may decide to choose you. It's a bit like a dragonfly coming to rest on the tip of your nose. You either acknowledge it or shoo it away. But I would never advise shooing away a great idea.

I tucked my idea away for now and let it ripen, like a green tomato put in a bag to turn red in the darkness.

When I nosed open Winnie's door quietly with a tray of tea and a slice of strawberry tart that The Gram had finally given up, Winnie was brushing her lovely hair and sitting up in bed. "Darling, how sweet of you. I was just thinking about how we used to play that board game Uncle Wiggily together. Shall we again? Oh, poppet, we will leave here soon. When I am feeling stronger, we'll rent a sports car and go off on holiday, you and I. Perhaps we won't come back to this old, gloomy place."

"But I love this house with all my heart," I said. "Winnie, I don't play Uncle Wiggily anymore. I am thirteen years old."

"Oh, tomorrow I shall get up and be a normal mum for you. I promise. I do promise, poppet." She closed her eyes again and held my hand. "I am so sorry I left you so long in this dreadful, awful house. You seem to care terribly for The Gram. Have you forgotten me, darling?"

"Oh no, Winnie, it's just that I would like to know what happened with Gideon and you, I mean, before . . . I mean . . ."

"You are only a child. You are far too young for me to talk about this with you," said Winnie quite firmly and then she covered her eyes with her delicate hand.

"No, Winnie, you don't understand. I want to know," I said.

Right then Dimples plowed into the room with a jar of jam from the cellar in her hands. She put it on the small table next to the bed and she stood there, staring at Winnie and not saying a word. Winnie reached out and put her arm round Dimples and pulled her up onto the bed next to her. "There you go, you little dumpling," she said.

★ Fifty-Eight ★

I was so glad and relieved to have my mother back! And yet there were clouds forming between Winnie and me. This morning The Gram and Derek and I were in the kitchen unwrapping and setting up our brand-new clock-size Taylor Stormoguide that had just arrived in the mail. It would help predict storms for us since there were no more weather reports on the radio or in the newspapers. The government thought a weather report might help the enemy, so weather was never mentioned on the air.

"It is very attractive, isn't it? I'm glad we chose the ivory color instead of the walnut," I said, admiring the chrome along the bottom of the Stormoguide. Then Winnie appeared in the doorway, like a beautiful ghost in a new starched housedress that was too big for her.

I startled. Derek got up and offered her his chair and as she was sitting down, she looked towards The Gram and said, "My sister calls her mother-in-law Mother. May I call you that? After all you are Danny's mother. You are Gideon's mother."

"Don't mention his name," The Gram said and then she turned and left the room.

"She wants to call you Mother," shouted Derek. "Let her. Let her call you what she wants."

I felt shadows and dismay pour through me. I wasn't upset with Winnie but I wished she would call The Gram something else.

Dimples had just woken up and come downstairs. She was a very late sleeper and still wearing her pink, wrinkled nightdress. She sort of wandered into the room with Wink. Dimples could be grumpy and cross in the morning and I feared she might be dreadful but she walked over to Winnie and climbed up in her lap with Wink.

Suddenly, I wanted to cry. *Why didn't you tell me where you were and what you were doing, Winnie? Why did you leave me here and not explain about my real father? Why didn't Danny write to me and tell me he loved me? And why do you think I am too young to know the truth?* I bit my lower lip and was about to burst into tears when under the table, I felt a gentle nudge of someone's foot against my foot. It turned out to be Derek's. He was looking at me, steadying me, as if I were a sailboat that had gone off course in the wind.

Perhaps the Stormoguide could have helped us with the hurricanes or thunderclouds that threatened in the sky above, but that barometer could not have helped with the storm brewing inside the Bathburn house.

When the mail came later that morning, I received another card from my father. As the postman handed it to me, I felt a wave of fear. Would this be the letter that would say for sure where he and Danny were? Or would we never know? Would we go on wondering all the rest of our lives, the way it was with some families?

Dimples was down on the rocks below singing and her small flutelike voice wafted through the air. I opened the letter, my hands trembling, hoping it might be a real letter. But it proved to be another prewritten card. On the front of the card was another picture of Bugs Bunny. This time that bucktoothed rabbit was playing the piano. My father had added an arrow pointing to the piano keys.

Derek took one look at the card and drew me towards the piano in the library and opened the top. There we saw all the metal strings lined up and all the little padded hammers ready to tap each string loudly or softly to make the music. On the last, heaviest string that would sound the deepest note was a little piece of paper. It read:

Fliss and Derek,
I do hope one of you plays this old contraption.
I always loved it. It would mean a lot to me, and if
you learn to play it, I will surely hear each note

and chord in my mind and think of you. Don't
forget I love you both.

It is the very saddest thing in the whole world to receive a message from someone who might now be dead. It was perhaps like looking at a star that was so far away that it took millions of years for its light to arrive. By the time you saw that shining light, the faraway star was long dead and gone. I put the card against my heart as if to somehow soak it in or absorb it or at least hold it close.

What would my father say of the small, lovely tornado in the house that was my Winnie? Did he know she would come to stay here and every moment would be a windstorm because The Gram hated her? I was quite sure that The Gram and Winnie needed to talk. I knew that my father would want them to talk. He would not like to see The Gram leaving every room that my Winnie entered.

Derek went into the parlor now and turned on the radio and the song "Stormy Weather," sung by Ethel Waters, played into the room. That song was always being aired.

Don't know why, there's no sun up in the sky,
Stormy weather.

For me it was the perfect coincidence. As I watched Winnie take a walk down the beach all by herself, I rocked in the porch swing, listening to the song. I did not follow Winnie. I did not know whose child I was anymore.

Derek cheered me up by stuffing a clipping from a magazine under my door the next morning. The article and photograph showed a cute black dog wearing a sailor's uniform. The caption read, "This dog is named Blackout. He is a mascot of a Coast Guard cutter. There are many dogs and cats serving in the US Navy and Coast Guard and they are treated as servicemen. They all have uniforms. They all have military ID cards and they all get shore leave." I pinned the photograph up on my wall and it made me laugh. Derek made me laugh. I liked feeling his foot knock against mine under the table.

I looked at my father's last card, Bugs Bunny playing the piano. I decided then to ask Miss Elkin if I could take piano lessons from her. I would help her with spinning wool later in exchange. I would begin practicing the piano right away. I could hear the Bathburn house stirring now and I thought again of how much it would mean to my father if The Gram could somehow find a way to accept Winnie. I had that plan in mind and I decided this morning to put it into action. Winnie had been here for well over a week and it seemed like a perfect day for my idea, since The Gram was planning to go into town for groceries.

I tucked my father's card into my pocket and when Dimples came running down the hall at top speed, I whispered my plan in her ear. Her eyes became very large indeed and she looked very solemn and serious. She walked down the hall with her arms flat against her body, not saying a word. She took forever going down the stairs. But finally I led her out into the garden at the front of the house and we stood by the Packard, which was parked by the wild rosebushes.

Then I am rather sorry to report that we went to work. Derek helped. He came darting out the back door with a tool kit in hand and we chose a tire at the back of the car and we went about releasing the valve that held the air in the tire, but of course we didn't twist it all the way open, so the air would escape slowly.

Later Winnie came downstairs in another awkward, brand-new, a little on the too-big side housedress. "Stephenson's office purchased these dresses for me, poppet," she said. "Very sweet of them but they are too big and must look ridiculous."

I said, "Winnie, we will have breakfast on the porch but would you care for some steamed dandelion greens this morning? There's a wonderful early patch of them up the road near an old cellar where a house once was."

"Oh, darling, how lovely," she said, stepping out into the sunlight. I handed her a colander.

"Shall we ride up on bikes to pick some?" I said.

"What a grand idea!" said Winnie, smiling, but I could see her eyes were filled with shadows. Since she had arrived, they were always filled with shadows.

We set off in the early morning down the road, headed a mile away for the best dandelions growing near an old lilac bush in an overgrown garden long ago abandoned. As we biked along, Winnie called out, "Pretty as this area is, I can't wait to get you out of here. The Gram is so cross. It must have been just dreadful being here. I wouldn't have left you if I had any other choice."

"She's not really cross," I said. "She can be quite sweet in her own kind of way. And I do love it here."

"Oh, I see," said Winnie. "Well, they let you run wild. You sound American. You don't even use British words anymore. We'll have to have a lesson. Get you back on track."

"I am half American," I said.

"I see, you'd rather stay here, then. You'd turn down a chance to go off somewhere amusing. You'd rather stay here with that cross woman."

Soon enough we were picking dandelion greens silently, with more and more clouds piling up between us, just as the greens were piling up in our colander. Hearing the distant sound of the Packard coming along the road, I said to Winnie, "I shall be back in a moment. I need to go get another container. Will you wait here?"

"Yes, poppet," said Winnie, her housedress full of warm spring wind and sky. I biked off, passing The Gram in the Packard, tootling along. I waved and kept going. I biked a little farther and turned to see The Gram's car coming to a halt. The tire must finally have gone flat. It was rather perfect timing because it seemed to happen right in front of the old cellar where, soon, returning daffodils would skirt the tumble of rocks and brambles. I could see, in the distance, Winnie running over towards the stopped car. I knew she could fix anything with wheels.

I wasn't there and I did not know exactly what happened then. I could see Winnie looking at the tire. After that I turned and biked back towards the house. From there on I could only guess. Perhaps Winnie fixed the tire for The Gram, which would have impressed my grandmother beyond measure. She could do nothing with that old car. The Gram couldn't even back it up. Perhaps then they rode into town together, maybe even yelling and screaming all the way. I do not know exactly what they said but I do know they were gone all morning. They had clearly driven away into town. It seemed to me that the front seat of an automobile was always a good place for a nice chat.

★ Fifty-Nine ★

Derek and Dimples and Winnie played crazy eights in the back bedroom the next week and I could often hear them shrieking and stamping their feet as one of them won. Winnie had charmed both Derek and Dimples entirely, as if she were a butterfly flitting over the tops of flowers in the garden. Sometimes I would go in and Winnie would say, "Oh, won't you join us, poppet, my sweet little baby?"

Then I would stand in the doorway. I did not feel at all like a sweet little baby and I didn't want to go in and play crazy eights. I began to feel Winnie was avoiding talking to me. She never seemed to be alone. She slipped out of it every time I asked her the things I needed to and I felt awkward bringing up her life with Gideon. I seemed every moment to grow more out of step with myself as well, as if being thirteen meant that your old self was constantly bumping into your new self and that neither one of your selves felt entirely at home.

But the storm between The Gram and Winnie had dispersed a little after the dandelion day. The Gram had eased up a tiny bit. At least they were civil now. But I hoped that soon The Gram would soften like butter, like the butter we churned in the old wooden butter churn. Then we wrapped the new butter in white paper and stored it in our icebox, right on top of the ice. I knew how soft and kind The Gram could be.

The next morning I was waiting for the mail as usual when it began to rain and I thought I would close the windows in the parlor. But when I reached the parlor doors they were shut tight. But old houses are known to leak secrets. Doors never close tightly. Rusty latches do not hold, and voices travel easily through open seams, cracks, and crevices.

I could hear The Gram saying, "Mr. Fitzwilliam has sent you another invitation to tea, Winifred. You have a kind of myth around you. But I am asking you not to cause any more trouble. Both my sons love you. Isn't that enough?"

"I am not proud of what happened in the past," said Winnie. "Surely you must know that. But I have neither of your sons now. This is not the way it should have gone. I do not think I can live with the way things have gone. Oh, I wish we'd hear from someone. Where could Danny be? How could this be happening?"

"Well, I think what you did to Gideon was despicable. I don't mind saying it outright. How could you love a man enough to marry him and then when you're carrying his unborn child, leave him for his brother! I find it outrageous. And then to stay in England out of guilt and fear and not bravely come forward and let Gideon at least meet his daughter."

"That's *not* what happened. I didn't want to lose Felicity. I wanted to do so much. Too much, perhaps. And I didn't plan on falling in love with Danny. You must be pleased to see I have now lost everything." Winnie began to cry.

"Are you planning to take Flissy away again? It will break my heart. Gideon would not want that. You should leave her with us. After all, you practically abandoned her for two years."

"I did not abandon her! I love my daughter dearly. But I've already lost her. You've made sure of that."

I stood there feeling shattered and pulled and stretched and twisted between my grandmother and my mother. If only Derek had been here. He was spending the week with Stu Barker because the Barkers were moving soon. But I needed to talk to him. How could I ever hope to find an answer to anything? Everything seemed broken and missing and lost.

"Dimples," I asked that night, knowing it was a useless question, "remember when you said your mum's friend had found the answer to everything?"

"Yes," said Dimples.

"Well," I said, "what would it take in trade to get that answer?"

"What is your offer?" asked Dimples.

"I'm not sure yet," I said.

"But I was promised to silence," said Dimples and then she fell asleep. I knew she was asleep because she started snoring and that snore was so loud, it could have woken up every ghost in the house, if we had any.

★ *Sixty* ★

The longer Winnie seemed to avoid speaking about things, the more upset I grew. I was not angry. Not at all. I could never be angry at my Winnie. I had waited so long for her return. But I did *feel* angry. I knew it was painful for her, but how could she not explain what happened recently with Gideon and Danny? She must know exactly. After all, she was there.

I walked down the hall to Winnie's room. I paused at the door and then I knocked lightly. In London I never would have knocked on my mum's door. I would have pushed right in, feeling her room belonged to me. But oddly now all that had shifted and changed. I didn't know what I felt or thought about my mother.

When I walked in slowly, Winnie looked up at me. She was embroidering a group of butterflies on a white linen cloth. Finally, I said, "Lovely job you are doing, I mean, with the butterflies."

"Oh, Felicity," said Winnie. "Won't you sit down?"

"I am called Flissy mostly now," I said.

"I see. I hadn't meant for things to get out of hand the way they have. It's just been one thing after another. Such a world it is, darling. I am so sorry. Can you forgive me? Remember when we used to laugh together in London?"

"Winnie, I want to know what happened to my father and to Danny. I want to know now."

"All you talk about is your father. What about your mother? Me? What about me?"

"I want to know what happened to my father."

"Oh, poppet, I shall be a perfect mum when all this is over. I fear you will hate me for everything that happened. Danny and I should have managed on our own. Perhaps you won't forgive me, like The Gram, when you hear it all."

"I want to know, Winnie. I want to know what happened to Gideon."

"Yes, I know. Danny loves you too, darling. Danny and I raised you. You haven't forgotten?"

"What happened?" I said, looking again directly into Winnie's face.

She sighed. "Well, my baby, if you promise not to blame me," said Winnie, staring down at her hands. "Perhaps you already do. Yes, you do blame me."

Finally, she opened the drawer of the desk and got out a journal. "I've been keeping this since I arrived here. I suppose Bill's people wouldn't approve of my putting anything in writing but I did it anyway. You may read the pages about Gideon in France if you like," she said. And then she turned away and gazed out the window.

I took the journal into my room and sat on the canopy bed and began reading.

Danny's brother, Gideon, looked remarkably like Colonel Helmut Ludswig, the new, soon-to-be-head of the prison in Limoges where Danny and I were held. Gideon arrived from the United States by way of Spain. Finally, in late January, he was escorted over the Pyrenees Mountains into France. He arrived at the Limoges prison dressed as Colonel Ludswig, including a freshly grown mustache. Gideon's German was absolutely perfect, like Danny's and his mother's. They have an uncanny ear for language and mimicry.

When he arrived earlier than was expected, an underling was in charge. The head officer whom Gideon was replacing was having dinner with one of our agents. So when Gideon appeared, this young assistant was flustered by the colonel and completely caught off guard. The colonel was considered eccentric and demanding and he always traveled with a priest and a nun. So accompanying Gideon that night were two men, one dressed as a nun and the other as a priest.

When they first arrived, Gideon acted dismayed that the men had not expected him that night. He feigned anger. He went through the papers on his new desk in a fake rage. He had been instructed in training to scold the underling for an untidy facility. Gideon sent officers to the top floor to straighten up the area for inspection tomorrow. "And I will not be lenient with any messy desks!" he called out. "Presently I shall have a look around and I want you all working. May I have the keys now?" The young assistant, fumbling and nervous, handed him the ring of keys. Gideon then proceeded to the basement with his priest and his nun.

Thanks to our secret sources, Gideon had trained with maps of the prison and he knew everything, even the names of the guards on duty that night. The nun quickly approached one of the two guards outside the cells downstairs. The priest at the same moment did the same with the second guard. With syringes from their satchels, they sedated each of them until they were both in a deep sleep. Then they removed the guard uniforms and took off their priest and nun clothing and put on the guards' official clothing.

When Gideon unlocked my cell and walked in, I was sleeping. When he called softly, "Winnie, get up quickly," I thought I was dreaming. There standing before me was Gideon Bathburn, my ex-husband, the father of my little, beloved daughter, Felicity. I could not believe . . . No, I could not conceive. I could not understand. I began to cry, thinking it was a strange dream.

But then Gideon touched my shoulder. "Hurry," he said. "Put this on." He handed me the nun's habit that one of his men had worn into the building. The habit reminded me of the convent in Aubeterre. Oh, I knew that convent. I had taken many children there myself for protection on their way to escape out of the country. I rapidly put the black habit over my torn prison clothes. Then I set the white, starched headdress over my head.

Gideon took my hand. The two men now dressed as guards lugged one of the sleeping men into my bed and covered him up with the blanket. Then we quickly headed for Danny's cell. As we walked down the passageway, prisoners were calling out, "Sister, sister, listen to me, help me."

"Hush," we called. "Quiet."

"Please take this letter out with you and mail it when you can," one prisoner called. And I did. I reached for it and took it.

We found Danny's cell and he stood up from the floor where he lay, a terrible, thin scarecrow, a battered, wounded, bedraggled scarecrow. Danny was given the priest's black jacket, tunic, trousers, a black felt hat, and white priest's collar. The second sleeping man was dragged into the cell and covered under the blanket.

Then we headed for the stairs. Soon a young guard came towards us and Gideon ordered him aside. "We will be inspecting the prison tomorrow. Oh yes, young man, things will be changing around here. I suggest you go up and discuss this matter of rearranging things this evening with your higher-ups. I am under orders from the top."

Soon we walked by the front door. "I shall be back in the morning," said the colonel to the next guard. "I should warn you all that cleanliness and order will be a high priority in the inspection tomorrow. Good night for now. I will be staying at the Hôtel de France until my rooms are ready. I can be reached there if any problems arise. These guards here will help me out." He handed the assistant the keys. "You'll need these, I would imagine. Keep on your toes and I shall see you in the morning," said the colonel, smiling. "Early!"

We walked out into the courtyard where the car Gideon had driven in was waiting for us. We immediately climbed in. Gideon drove up to the gate and the guard saluted to him and let us pass. We drove off, following the prescribed route. And I must commend the planners who worked under Bill Stephenson. They thought of almost every-thing. We drove fast as we guessed within moments the whole area would be on our tail. But oddly it was quiet. The guards we tranquilized probably were sleeping peacefully, snoring away while the various lesser officers hustled about cleaning up the offices on the top floors.

On a back street in the next town, we let the two men out who were dressed as guards. They disappeared, headed for a safe house not far away. And then we drove on into the night. All was well until we came to a small town some thirty-five miles from Limoges. A sleepy, dark town, all the shutters closed up and the streets narrow and empty as we drove through. Still, on the street in front of us, two Gestapo officers were walking along, having just emerged from a bistro. They were drunk and singing, blocking the road and waving their arms at us to stop. "We're having a dance at the officers' club up the street. Why don't you join us?"

"Oh no, I must continue. I am Colonel Ludswig. I am doing inspections in the town ahead early tomorrow. I must get to my hotel before it closes."

"Colonel Helmut Ludswig? But I just talked to you by telephone an hour ago. You were in Berlin." He squinted in at us. "You don't really look quite right. I mean for one thing, Ludswig has shaved off his mustache. He did it on a bet. I only saw him a day ago."

"As a matter of fact, I am his brother. Uh, I shall telephone him tonight when I get to the hotel," said Gideon.

"He doesn't have a brother," said the man. "Perhaps you had better get out of the vehicle."

Gideon then gunned his motor and took off. But one of the men shot at us, hit the side window with the first shot and the second shot hit Gideon's back on his left side. His jacket was soon covered with blood. Danny shot at them. We do not know if he hit one officer or both of them. Perhaps he hit no one at all. We could only keep driving.

Even though he'd been shot, Gideon stayed at the wheel, keeping his foot on the gas pedal. There wasn't time to stop. At the edge of town we took a turn off the main road and careened along the river. The moon was out and the car rushed through the speckled larch trees and the wind shuddered and brushed through the empty branches around us and we listened for cars or sirens but we heard none. Finally, Gideon stopped the car and slumped at the steering wheel.

Now Danny and I carried Gideon to the backseat. He lay beside me and we pressed on, Danny driving, using only back roads and moon-light. We turned off our headlights. In the darkness a mother deer and her winter fawn

hurried across the road in front of our car and for
some reason that made me cry.

Gideon was bleeding profusely. I held his head
in my arms. I tore some fabric from my habit and
tried to make a bandage for him. He was losing so
much blood. He looked up at me as we drove and
he said, "Oh my God, Winnie, if I had known that
I would be lying here in your arms."

We drove all night along the back roads,
unpaved, some of them clotted with snow.
Sometimes cows or long-horned sheep loomed up
in the darkness.

We approached Aubeterre-sur-Dronne. It
seemed to be part of the sky, perched high on the
side of the hill above a river. As we drew up the
climbing streets, I put a blanket over Gideon in the
backseat and got in the front seat. Then we were
simply a priest and a nun headed for the convent.
We passed through the elevated town square,
where a narrow park waited among beech and oak
trees in the darkness. Farther up the hill, Danny
stopped the car in front of the large stone convent
with its heavy, arched, wooden doors.

"There you go, Winnie," Gideon whispered,
leaning forward and trying to sit up but not open-
ing his eyes. "Off you go now. A guide will take
you over the mountains when you are ready. Your
papers are all in order. Everything is in order."

"Yes, but you are not in order, Gideon," I said. "What about you? Danny, he's so badly wounded. I can't leave you. Where will you go?"

"Dr. Sachet in Chalais. He will help us. I will take my brother there," Danny said.

"I want to go with you," I said. "Please let me go with you."

"All this has been arranged. Winnie, think of what's at stake. We haven't any more time," said Gideon in his faint, breathy voice.

I leaned over and kissed him on the cheek and then I leaned forward and kissed Danny. Danny smiled at me and said, "Give my love to Felicity. Tell her I miss her." I looked back at Gideon and his face was full of pain at the mention of Felicity's name.

I forced myself to get out of the car. I struggled with reluctance up the convent steps and I knocked on the door.

The sisters surrounded me like a flock of dark swans and they pulled me in. They said when they saw me that I made a perfect nun. They fed me some thin soup. I remember the warm bowl in my hands. I was led to a plain room with a small, cold bed and I lay there awake for the rest of the night. We had not prepared for this. Danny had not told me much about Dr. Sachet. I did not know where Danny and Gideon were going. It was the last

*time I saw the Bathburn brothers and I had loved
them both so dearly.*

"Flissy McBee," The Gram called from downstairs,
"will you come here, please? Dimples has locked herself
in the pantry and she's in there eating all the cookies we
made last night. Will you talk to her, please?"

I closed the journal and I sat there for a moment. I
could not close away the image of my father lying in the
backseat as my Danny drove over bumpy roads towards
some doctor that might not even be there when they
arrived. Try as I would, I could not shut out what I had
just read and the pages of Winnie's journal seemed to
flutter and fold open even when I closed my eyes.

I went downstairs. Night was falling. Passing the
front door I saw Winnie was out on the porch, all alone
in the darkness.

Sixty-One

Winnie's journal threw me into a bit of a panic. It seemed as though everything in my life was funneling and spinning in a great vortex and I was lost in the middle. I had tried to ring up Stu Barker because I wanted and needed to talk with Derek, but their telephone had been disconnected. Well, they had a ten-party line anyway and you never could get through.

The next day I sat with The Gram in the hallway upstairs. She was unpacking a chest and stacking all the bedspreads and old linen sheets on the hall rug. Then the chest was empty except for a tortoiseshell hair comb and long, ornate hairpins lying on the bottom. One of the long pins had a silver filigree butterfly perched on a tiny spring at the end of the hairpin so whenever someone wore it in their hair, the butterfly would bob at the top of their French twist or braided bun. I picked it up. "Have you rung up Derek since he left?" I said. And then I added, "Winnie would probably like this hairpin because of the butterfly."

"It's a treasure and it's part of this house and I wouldn't give it to *her*," said The Gram. "She's caused enough trouble, hasn't she? Why should she have something that belonged to Ada Bathburn?"

"But you are talking with her now," I said.

"Well, Winifred and I do share certain interests, you being one of them. Take the hairpin for yourself, dear. It's yours. When you are a little older, you can pull back your hair with it and show off your lovely Bathburn forehead."

Perhaps The Gram was right about Winnie. I wasn't sure anymore. I had wanted to smooth out the wrinkles and rumples between the Bathburns and the Budwigs and now I too was all mixed up and muddled. I could hear Dimples shouting from the parlor, "Felicity, you've got another letter. You get all the letters here and my mum never writes to me."

"She has to send a telegram and they are expensive, Dimples," I called as I clumped downstairs to see what she had for me.

Dimples saw me and started piloting through the house in her invisible airplane, rising up in her Halifax bomber, with an envelope in her hands. She soared by me, waving it at me. I grabbed it.

I saw immediately it was another prewritten card from my father. I could tell by the stamps. The Gram swooped down from upstairs and watched me from across the room with a look of great sorrow looming over her, like a dark mountain full of rainfall. I took the card out to the porch. I tore open the envelope. On the front was a sketch of Bugs Bunny sitting in a bathtub eating a carrot. Inside it said, *Mr. Bathtub says READ!* And then in small letters it said, *But what's he reading?*

I sat on the top step of the stairs to the sea. There it felt like the whole world was falling away below me. I stared out across the ocean. From here I could not see the bombs falling or the sky burning red in Europe but I could feel it. *Mr. Bathtub says READ!* What had my father meant when he had written that card to me, so many months ago? Whose child was I? I knew *where* I belonged, but *whom* did I belong to?

★ Sixty-Two ★

It had been almost a week that Derek had been visiting the Barkers. I quite missed him and I would be glad when the Barkers left and Derek came home. If only he loved me as he had before. Of course I was beginning to understand that you could not control love. It went where it wished and it did as it pleased, just like the hiccups. Still, if he loved me, I felt I could endure the low pressure and the dense air that seemed to be hovering in the Bathburn house. The needle on the Stormoguide in the dining room almost seemed to register all that was inside my heart.

As school was soon starting again after spring break, The Gram and Dimples and I were going into town. Dimples would be allowed to buy a set of paper dolls because she had knitted so many pairs of socks. I had grown taller and hoped the five-and-dime would have a light skirt for a thirteen-year-old, size 12 girl, which I now was.

"Oh, you're going shopping for clothes. Oh, poppet, I wish I could go," Winnie said, looking sadly at me.

"No," said The Gram. "You need rest. And we're used to shopping together, aren't we, Flissy McBee?" The Gram drew me towards her.

As we got in the Packard, I waved to Winnie and I hoped while we were gone, she would manage being alone. She was working on some project in a scrapbook she wouldn't let me see. Perhaps that would occupy her. I didn't think I was still mad at Winnie for leaving me for so long or for not telling me things she should have. But now I wasn't sure. I did not think I was mad at her really for what happened in France with my father and yet when she looked at me in that sad way, I felt awkward and looked away. I knew it was hard for her to be here. She was jumpy and nervous and she didn't eat much. As we drove off she stood there in the garden, waving in a wistful way. I was torn between anger and pity. Yes, it hurt me when The Gram barked at her.

On the drive into town I was thinking about that prewritten card from my father. *Mr. Bathtub says READ!* And when The Gram pulled up to park the car near Babbington Elementary School, I looked at the pinkish-brown bricks of the school through the arch of trees and I knew I had to go in there. I had to look closer at something.

I did not want to leave Dimples to pick out her own paper dolls. I hoped I could persuade her to buy the set of army nurse paper dolls. Or perhaps the WAAC paper dolls. Those were the paper dolls of women in the army and they came with all sorts of posh uniforms and ball gowns and dancing dresses to cut out. There were hats and shoes and gloves and flags and all that. Of course I would not be playing with the paper dolls with Dimples but I might help her cut out some of the outfits. I was very good at cutting out paper doll dresses, while Dimples always chopped off the tabs on the clothes by mistake.

"I shall meet you at the dime store," I said to Dimples and The Gram.

Dimples scrunched up her nose and looked up at me. "Where are you off to, then?" she said.

"Miss Elkin asked me to pick up a music book on her desk at Babbington El," I said.

The Gram frowned at me. "Is the school open?" she said.

"I just saw a janitor go in. The door's propped open," I said and then I took off without waiting for a real answer. I ran across the shady park towards the school. I needed to look again at something. It simply couldn't wait.

The door was open but as I stepped inside, the school had a chilled emptiness about it. It was shadowy and unlit, except for the streaks of sunlight from the open front door that fell across the linoleum tiles. The halls were stark and silent. I did not even know where the janitor had gone. I hurried down the long hall towards Mr. Bathtub's old room. I hoped the janitor would not leave and lock me in by mistake.

I felt a terrible pang as I entered Mr. Bathtub's classroom, all closed up for spring break as it was, his desk empty, his bookshelves spare. The poster was still there, framed and behind glass and hanging on the wall above the shelf of collected seashells. I pulled a chair out across the room. It made a scraping noise along the quiet floor.

I stood up on the chair and stared at the picture of Mr. Bathtub in a suit and tie and bowler hat, sitting in an empty bathtub, reading a book. Underneath the photograph were the words *Mr. Bathtub says READ!* I studied it closely, my eyes rolling over every detail. I hadn't noticed before, but up close, I saw that my father was winking. It was nice to see his face from this distance. The green book he was reading was firmly in his hands and if I tilted my head, I could read the words on the spine. It was called *A Season of Butterflies.*

The whole way to the five-and-dime store I was thinking about the book. I knew that Gideon loved nature and that he was fond of bird and butterfly watching in the summer. He always let the milkweed plants grow tall in the garden at the side of the house because he said the monarchs fed on the flowers and hung their cocoons among the leaves. He always considered it a sign of luck when a monarch fluttered across his path.

In the dime store I did my best to get Dimples to buy the army nurse paper-doll book but she wouldn't listen. She bought the Shirley Temple set instead. At home later, when she cut everything out, she wasn't at all careful and Shirley Temple ended up with a missing foot.

Back at the house, when I passed Winnie in the hall that afternoon, I saw that she was wearing one of Aunt

Miami's dresses, a silk one that fit her much better than the housedresses someone had bought for her. It was a light red-and-white print and when Miami wore it, it had been one of Mr. Henley's favorites. I didn't think Winnie had asked The Gram if she could borrow a dress of Miami's. I was just going to tell her about the card and the poster, but all of a sudden I felt upset that she hadn't asked anyone if she could borrow the dress. It was odd to see Winnie wearing it and not Miami. I mean, of course, her other clothes were too big for her. Of course. I didn't think I was at all disappointed with my mum. Not at all. But I wished she'd asked about the dress first.

I thought too about Mr. Henley and I suddenly wished Miami would come home and that she would call Washington, like our neighbor had done when he wanted news of his sons. I went out on the porch and got behind a book and when Winnie stopped by out there, I pretended to be asleep and wouldn't answer her when she asked me if I had got a card from my father.

Then everyone disappeared into themselves the way they do sometimes on a long, quiet afternoon. Winnie was napping. The Gram was reading the newspaper on the porch and Dimples was having her Shirley Temple paper doll dance and sing "On the Good Ship Lollipop" (even with only one foot). It was then that I had a chance to go into the library. I began to look through the books on the shelves. Many of my father's natural history and botany books were alphabetical and there I found the book I was looking for, with its green leather cover and binding and its gold letters: *A Season of Butterflies.*

When I opened it, I found vivid colored plates of various butterflies. A purple emperor, a painted lady, a peacock butterfly, a clouded yellow, an orange mapwing. They were all beautiful. I was just about to close the book when I came across, on the last page, a lovely blue butterfly, a blue the color of heaven. The author wrote that this butterfly was called a Mazarine blue but sometimes people referred to the male as a Romeo blue. My heart shivered when I read that. It shivered and fluttered like a butterfly.

There was a folded piece of paper in between those pages. I read:

> *Dear Fliss and Derek,*
> *If all has gone well, remind everyone to listen*
> *to the radio! They will know what I mean. How*
> *proud I am of you because you found this message,*
> *as I knew you would!*

There·was a drawing of a radio and an arrow pointing to it. It looked to me like the shortwave radio set that Gideon had built himself.

But all had not gone well, so what was the use of any of it?

★ Sixty-Three ★

I jumped on my bicycle and I pedaled off down the road. I had to talk to Derek. The note from my father made me cry. All of this was too much and I needed Derek's advice and I missed him. I could hear clusters of crows cawing in the tops of the pine trees and it was such a melancholy sound, as if they were announcing my sadness to the woods and the sky. I did not think the Bathburn house would ever be the same without my father. I wondered if Danny and Gideon had been captured en route to Chalais. Perhaps the doctor turned them in upon arrival. Or perhaps they had been shot as they drove along the back roads after leaving Winnie at the convent.

Stu Barker lived down a pine-tree lane among several other houses that were not far from the tall, cement, sub-watching tower that stuck up high out of the trees. As I turned down into the woods, I passed a parked army jeep and later, a Coast Guard vehicle heading towards the tower. I pedaled on over a little bridge and found the driveway of the Barker house. I tossed my bike down in the pine needles, remembering the time Stu Barker got a terrible reaction to poison ivy in these woods.

I looked up at Stu's small house. It seemed dark and quiet and then I noticed that the windows were boarded up with shutters. People here did that when they went away for long spells to safekeep the house. "Stu!" I called out, walking over the soft floor of pine needles. "Derek! Stu!"

I went up on the little cement porch. I lifted the knocker and pounded on the door. The sound of the knocker hit with an empty thud. "Derek!" I called out again. I ran round to the back of the house only to find the windows boarded up there as well and the garage locked tight too. "Derek, you have to be here. Where are you?" I shouted, propping my hand across my forehead against a shaft of sunlight that fell through the pine trees.

I got back on my bike and pedaled up the hill. Early spring gnats buzzed round my ears. I called out again, "Derek! Where are you?" Nothing echoed in a pine-woods. Everything was softened and quiet and padded with pine needles and pine boughs and branches, matted and thick and webbed and twisted, just like a mixed-up, tangled knitting project.

I tore along the pine trail, my heart bumping and banging against my rib cage. I passed an old man hunched over as he walked. As he looked up, his splotchy, rough face reminded me of the ragpicker in the park in town. Perhaps he lived near here. "Where are the Barkers?" I called to him.

"They left a couple weeks ago," he said. "There was a moving truck blocking up the road that day."

I biked on as far as the cliffs near the Bathburn house, the rocks piled up high in a kind of lookout. I dropped my bike and climbed the rocks and sat up there, watching the ocean waves roll in and roll out. If Derek wasn't at Stu's, where was he? I imagined a Nazi submarine surfacing in the water below. There were several of those subs spotted this week, so The Gram said. She had been told by a friend who was volunteering in the sub-watching tower.

And this was the exact spot where Derek sat while the Gray Moth was back at the house being arrested. Derek sat and stared at this same sea, feeling betrayed and heartbroken, thinking he had a father when he did not. I could not imagine such disappointment. And yet I too felt a kind of disappointment about my mother. She had married one brother and then left him for the other. She hadn't told me who my father was. She had left me for almost two straight years without telling me the truth about things. She had taken Miami's clothes and was wearing them without asking.

Perhaps Derek had felt the kind of confusion that I was feeling. But where was he now? Had he run away? I tried not to cry again. Did he want me to tell everyone that he was not at Stu Barker's or would I be betraying him if I said anything? Was he off on his own or had he been taken away by someone, a Nazi agent perhaps, looking for reprisals or leverage?

I finally resolved to go back to the house to tell everyone that Derek was not at Stu Barker's, even though I was perhaps betraying him again. I threw my bike down in the garden and then I rushed in the back door, sweeping through the kitchen and down the hall, glancing in the parlor and dining room. "Winnie! Where's The Gram?" I called out. "Hurry. I need to talk to The Gram and to you. Now. It's important. It's about Derek. It's about Derek!"

Then I pushed through the screen door and rushed out on to the wraparound porch. There was someone in the porch glider, sliding back and forth slowly and reading a book and relaxing in the new spring sunlight. I took in the sight of a long pair of blue-jean legs and high-top black tennis shoes. The legs were stretched out in a casual, self-confident manner. The book propped over the face was a Hardy Boys mystery. The someone, who was wearing a brand-new shirt, peered at me in a cheerful way over the top of his book. It was Derek.

"Derek," I said, "where have you been?"

"He's back from his journey," said Dimples, who was eating an apple and reading the Bobbsey Twins. "It's lovely to see him, isn't it, Flissy Bee Bee Bee?"

I ran into the house and went upstairs and slammed my door and threw myself down on my cot. Why had Derek lied about where he had been? He had not been at Stu Barker's. The family had left two weeks ago. I did not want to say anything of course; I knew better than that, but I was angry with Derek and hurt that he hadn't told me where he had been. I lay there for a long time, until the sky darkened and Dimples went round closing all the blackout curtains.

Then there was a knock on my door. I had hoped it would be Derek with an explanation but instead it was Winnie.

"Oh, poppet," she said, "you are all upset. I am so sorry, darling. Knowing about Gideon and what happened has taken a terrible toll, hasn't it? Won't you come downstairs and make a cake with me? Remember when we used to make cakes together?"

"I'm dreadfully tired," I said.

"Too tired to decorate a cake?"

"Possibly," I said.

"Come on," said Winnie. "Just for a little while."

"I'd rather not."

Then pity came to melt me. My mother had such a hopeful and strained look on her face.

"Oh, perhaps, but I won't stay long," I said.

And so I went down to the kitchen with Winnie and we started to mix up cake batter. I didn't say much as we worked. We had only a little sugar in it. But we did have plenty of eggs since Miss Elkin's chickens produced so many. We saved the powdered sugar for the icing.

I knew the cake would be lovely. Winnie had once wanted to be a baker of cakes years ago. She had planned to have a shop full of pastel-colored biscuits and cakes with roses and ribbons of sugar. She had planned to name it Winnie's Wonders, and once, she had even picked out the perfect little shop near Kensington Gardens in London.

When we came to decorate our cake, I finally spoke. I asked for a butterfly on the top.

"What kind of butterfly?" Winnie said. "A monarch?"

"No, a Mazarine blue," I said, looking up at her.

Winnie looked startled. Then she closed her eyes.

"Mazarine blue is a pretty color, isn't it?" I said.

"Yes, it is a deep, layered sky blue, a blue with depth and variation, almost a magical blue. What made you bring up the word *Mazarine*?"

I sat down at the table where we had been creaming powdered sugar into the butter. "I saw it in a book called *A Season of Butterflies*," I said. "My father wrote me a note before he left. He told me to look in that book. And I found this between the Mazarine blue butterfly pages." I showed Winnie the paper with the drawing of a radio and the words, *If all has gone well, remind everybody to listen to the radio!*

Winnie stepped backwards. She looked down at his message and squeezed her eyes tightly closed for a moment, as if to shut out everything in the world. Then she reached for the paper and crumpled it in her sugary hands.

Sixty-Four

The contract from Doubleday, Doran for Mr. Henley arrived that next week and Derek helped me sign the papers. I wrote my name on the line at the bottom, *Ms. Felicity Bathburn Budwig* and then I crossed it out and wrote *Mrs. Felicity Budwig Bathburn*. I did not want to rock the boat. If the editors thought me a Mrs., I would be a Mrs. We put a date on the thing and folded it up and sent it back.

"Perfect. Mr. Henley will be ever so pleased," I said, smiling at Derek. And then a shadow drew across my mind, like a dark camel crossing a desert slowly. Yes, our troops were doing splendidly in North Africa. They had sent the famous German general Rommel turning on his heels. But there had been casualties. There were always losses. Still Mr. Henley did not seem like the kind of person who would die. He seemed more the type to end up in a prisoner-of-war camp, like Mrs. Boxman's brother. I imagined Mr. Henley would have all these stories to tell us about it when he came home. And yet The Gram whispered with Winnie in the parlor when Mr. Henley's name was mentioned. And Winnie took a deep breath and shook her head.

Derek and I decided to write a letter to Mr. Henley that day.

Dear Bobby,
   Please, please write to us. Miami is so worried.
She sobs and cries on the telephone. She'll be home
for a visit in a couple of weeks. And you are to have
a book of your poems published! In a few months
Oh Morocco! *will be out on bookshelves all across*
America. Let us know, if you can, how you are.
   Love,
   Flissy, Derek, and all the Bathburns

"I am not a true Bathburn," said Derek.

"Of course you are, Derek," I said.

"But it's not official," he said.

"Where did you go when you disappeared?" I said.
But Derek turned away and would not answer me.

Sixty-Five

The amazing arrival of daffodils and hyacinths and violets was not the usual happy Bathburn celebration because we had not heard from Mr. Henley or Danny and we did not know whether my daddy-uncle had died in France from his gunshot wounds. We were always afraid of a telegram or an official letter from the government. But we were not the only ones. Mr. King at King's Hardware had lost his son in the Pacific in February and in the window of his house there was a flag with a gold star. The gold star was a terrible thing to see and I always looked away.

Winnie was in her room upstairs a lot now, and at night I could hear her pacing the floor back and forth. And finally, on a warming day later in April, she set off walking along the shore past the White Whale Inn and beyond. I wondered where she was going. I had seen those letters arrive for her from Mr. Fitzwilliam. I was uneasy about her visiting him. I did not know what her intentions were. I wondered even if I could trust her at all and so I am sorry to report that I followed her.

When she climbed the rocky path towards the big, dark, granite house, I stayed back among the wild rose-bushes. Then I too climbed the path into the garden. I passed the mossy angel statue standing among drifts of purple honesty and yellow forsythia. The angel was now standing upright, her face lifted towards the sky.

I did not knock on the door but went to the windows of the drawing room and peered in. There the huge, black marble fireplace seemed to stare back at me with its vacant eye. The room was empty at first and then Winnie and Mr. Fitzwilliam walked in. Mr. Fitzwilliam swung his arms about, pointing to everything. Out here in the garden the air was full of birdsong and the sounds of spring so I could not hear their words. Mr. Fitzwilliam leaned down and looked up into the fireplace chimney. Then he pointed up into it and Winnie did the same. She got down on her knees and peered up into the chimney. When she stood up again, she had dark soot on her hands. She tried to dust the soot away, but her hands remained ashen and stained.

Then Mr. Fitzwilliam opened a closet and showed Winnie the contents. They walked round the room and he did the same on the opposite side. What were they talking about? It seemed very strange and left me a bit rattled. Finally, they went on to the atrium.

I went over to the side of the house and carefully peered in those windows too, keeping to the wooden frame and the edge of the glass. I could see clearly from there Mr. Fitzwilliam's face, which looked to me to be rather stunned and charmed at the same time. And there was Winnie, a short distance away, standing among thousands of butterflies. They fluttered all about her, the mapwings and the monarchs and the hairstreaks and the lacewings and the swallowtails. Winnie's arms were stretched out almost like butterfly wings as she turned round and round and round.

I did not discover that Winnie was listening to my father's shortwave radio upstairs by herself until one late afternoon when I was running the Hoover vacuum down the hallway upstairs. I had unplugged it and was just outside Winnie's closed door. She was always shutting her door, especially near four o'clock. Now I leaned my head against the door and I could hear a radio playing inside, music and then an announcer. I knew it was a British station because I recognized the accent, the words, the tone. It pulled on my heart in a faint old way. I remembered listening with Winnie and Danny to the wireless in London, Winnie and Danny dancing sometimes round our flat to the music. Often I would dance with them too.

Sometimes I did not think about things at all, I just rushed forwards, as if the earth and sky were pulling me. And so all of a sudden I turned the door handle and walked into Winnie's room. She was on her bed, gluing something into a book.

There on the desk was Gideon's old shortwave radio.

He had all sorts of shortwave operators' manuals in the library and build-it-yourself wireless kit manuals. I had spent so much time in my father's library that there was little I did not know of him. As I looked at Winnie, I realized she was listening to that wireless, hoping for a message from Gideon or Danny. "Winnie, why didn't you tell me you had started to listen to the shortwave radio?"

"Oh, poppet," said Winnie, "you've scared me. Sometimes you won't come in at all and other times you startle me by barging in. You are acting so strangely. I do not know you anymore."

"Why didn't you tell me? Gideon sent the note to *me*, didn't he? That meant he wanted me to listen too! Why do you keep things from me? Why did you leave me here and not explain two years ago? Why did you drop me off and not tell me even about Gideon? My father! And what were you doing at Mr. Fitzwilliam's house? What was he hiding in his chimney? Why didn't you tell me what you were doing all along in Europe? It was just as if you lied to me! I loved you, Winnie, and you lied to me," I shouted and cried and I would not stop. No, I could not stop.

Winnie sat there shaking and then she rushed towards me and tried to hug me, but I pushed her away. "Oh, poppet, you're a child. It wasn't for you to worry about the shortwave station."

"I am not exactly a child, Winnie. Can't you see that?"

She looked at me for a long time with a sad face. Then she said, "We often used that station for messages. We had friends at that station, you see, but it's too late. Things didn't go well. No not at all. You didn't need to know about that radio station because there won't be any message. You don't need to listen with me."

"Why not?" I shouted. "Why can't I listen too? It's worse not knowing and not understanding. I don't even know what you and Danny had really been doing in France before you were arrested. You've never told me."

"Oh, how could I have been so stupid? I am such a fool," said Winnie. "Of course you can listen to the short-wave with me. I didn't know how you felt. We will all listen. Even if it comes to nothing. We'll listen to nothing, then, together."

"And what about Mr. Fitzwilliam?" I shouted. Every bit of me was shaking. "What were you doing at his house? Don't you care that he hurt Derek and me? You were looking for something in the chimney. What were you doing there?"

"No, darling. Mr. Fitzwilliam is selling that house. He was showing me the chimney and the closets and all the rooms. It's for sale. That's all."

"Oh," I said, suddenly feeling dreadfully foolish. "I didn't understand that."

"And you were following me?" Winnie said, smoothing my hair.

"I didn't realize," I said.

My mum hugged me then and I let her. "Poppet," she said. "Forgive me. I've been a coward. Sometimes the bravest people can be the biggest cowards. I could not face telling you about Gideon being your father. It would have been such a shock to you and we would be leaving you right after that. It seemed better for you to grow used to the Bathburns first. And then they would tell you. It was dreadfully difficult for me to even bring you here. We wanted to keep you. But the war interfered. My work interfered. I saved so many children and all the while I was neglecting my own child." Winnie began to cry and I cried too. The old lace curtains puffed and fluttered in the open window and I cried and my mother held me.

"I will find a way to make it up to you. I promise," said Winnie. "You know that Danny and I were undercover agents working in France. We did many things. We helped downed British pilots get back to England. I worked in an airplane factory and was able to send back information here. And we did something else. I have been making you a scrapbook so you would know. Danny took photographs of every child I helped smuggle out of France. He took the passport photographs and I sewed a copy of each one inside the hem and lining of a skirt and I hid the skirt at the convent because we always started from there. When Gideon rescued us and brought me back to the convent and I left to hike over the Pyrenees to Spain, I wore the skirt. Even though it was foolish and dangerous for me. I wanted to remember the children I had saved. I wanted *you* to see what I had been doing. There are one hundred and fifty photographs, poppet. One at a time, I saved one hundred and fifty French Jewish children from dying at the hands of the Nazis. Look, you can see each child."

And she opened the scrapbook and she showed me the child on the first page. "Look, this is Sylvie. She plays the violin. And she plays beautifully. We had to leave her violin behind. And this little boy was so darling. He had a book with him. He was reading *The Secret Garden* in English on the journey. He wouldn't let go of the book. Just like you. Oh, poppet, just like you." Winnie began to cry again and I sat with her on the bed and I looked through each page of the scrapbook, at the faces of each child, sweet and smiling and hopeful, and I cried too. Winnie pointed out one and another and told me little stories about each child.

And then I hugged my mum again and said, "Oh, Winnie, forgive me. Forgive me. I am so glad, so very glad you are finally home. It's just that I wish, perhaps . . ."

"It's no use wishing and trying to change things that happened. Your father was an amazing man and you should be very proud of him," Winnie said and then she paused and looked down. "I did not choose to do the things that I did. When it comes to matters of the heart, one has no choice."

★ Sixty-Six ★

During the next week Winnie brought the shortwave radio downstairs and set it up in the dining room. Oddly it got better reception there. And at four o'clock we all would listen to the station from London. But just as we had suspected, nothing came of it. Every evening when the program was over, we would turn off the dial and feel a bit of a letdown. The good part of all that was Derek became interested in shortwave radios and he started reading my father's pamphlets on how to build a set. He still had not told me where he had gone for a week, and a couple of times recently he disappeared for long afternoons. I wondered and I guessed in a way what might be going on. I sensed The Gram knew, but I had learned to keep quiet where Derek was concerned. And how sad I was that the shortwave message didn't have an answer for us about my father.

Today Dimples came across a harbor seal pup on the shore among the rocks. "It is not with its mum," she said, frowning and stomping back and forth. "It's just lying there all alone on the shingles and sand." Derek and Dimples and I loved seals and we usually counted the ones that we saw swimming or lounging about on the rocks. So far we had already seen fifteen this spring, or sixteen if you counted the seal that was possibly a dog.

Derek was just saying to Dimples, "Was it really a baby seal? Sometimes you make things up, don't you."

Then the doorbell at the kitchen rang and Dimples and I raced to answer it. Upon opening the door, I was handed a nice fat package and it proved to be from Doubleday, Doran Publishing in New York City, addressed to me.

"Derek, Mr. Henley's book has arrived! It must be," I shouted out. Dimples started pulling at the paper and jumping up and down.

"Oh, I wish Mr. Henley were here," I said. "He will be so thrilled." We all pulled the book out of the wrapping and looked at it. It was beautiful with a simple, pale yellow dust jacket, the color of sand and the words *Oh Morocco!* written across the front in ornate script.

Inside the package there was a note from the editor. Dimples grabbed it and then Derek chased her and finally I swiped it out of Derek's hand. Then I unfolded the paper and read:

Dear Mrs. Felicity Budwig Bathburn,
    It is our great pleasure to offer to you Private Robert Henley's beautiful book, which we rushed to publication. I can assure you that because of the war, these poems will be all the more pertinent and

helpful to others. It will be a tremendous comfort
for people to be able to read this powerful testament
to faith, endurance, and longing that this soldier
has been able to convey in these poems. Thank you
again for your help in all this. Please accept our
warmest congratulations and we look forward to
hearing from Private Henley upon his return.

> *Very truly yours,*
> *Pike Jemson*
> *Doubleday, Doran Publishing*

"Oh, Derek," I cried out, "this is so wonderful!" And then my eyes fell down into the shadows that speckled the dining room floor just now.

Dimples was tugging on my sleeve. Why was she tugging on me? Her eyes looked suddenly as blue and changing as wind over water. Her face was a sad white, like unwanted, fresh spring snow. "Felicity," she said. "I must tell you about a letter that I pulled out of the letter box last week. I put it in the parlor. I set it behind the wooden ship with the tall sails on the mantel and I left it there. I didn't think you'd want it."

"What?" I said. "Why didn't you tell me?"

"It looked like a bad letter. I don't like bad letters, do you?" she said.

"Dimples, where is that letter?" I said, going into the parlor and looking behind the small model of Captain Bathburn's ship.

I pulled the envelope out and Dimples started to cry. "I hated that letter. I didn't want to see it."

I looked at the outside. It was addressed to Miss Miami Bathburn from the War Department in Washington, DC.

The War Department? Why would the War Department write to Miami? Who should open it? Who should read it? I could not.

Derek took the envelope.

Wait. Don't touch it. Stop. It's Miami's. Wait. No. Stop!

Derek did not wait. He moved very firmly and very surely. He pulled open the envelope and quickly we read:

Dear Miss Bathburn,

As you have been designated as Private Robert Henley's next of kin, it is with the utmost sympathy that I write to you now. First allow me to extend my deep condolences to you and your family. Private Robert Henley, US Army Second Corps, Tunisian Campaign, died as a result of wounds on February 14, 1943, in the Battle of Sidi Bouzid in Tunisia. I know that his fellow soldiers who lived and fought beside him will feel his loss greatly and his battalion will mourn his passing. . . .

"Winnie! Winnie! Where are you?" I screamed. "Please come here. Help me. Hurry. Winnie!"

Winnie came rushing into the room, followed by The Gram. Then everything seemed to be flying every which way, as if we were a flock of birds scared up by the wind. We flew everywhere, up and about and all round, knocking into one another. Then we rushed towards one another, Derek and Dimples and Winnie and The Gram and I. We all stood in a circle with our arms locked round one another and our heads pressing in together and we cried and screamed and shouted, "No. No. It can't be. Please don't say it is so."

And the beautiful yellow book, just published, lay on the table waiting to be opened.

Dear, dear Miami,

Please come home as soon as possible. Here is Bobby's beautiful book of poems. I know he would be so proud to see his words in print. Please telephone us as we have had some very bad news about him and I cannot bear to write it down. In the meantime, I am sending along this lovely engagement ring he had for you and asked me to keep until he came home. I send it to you now because I know you will want to have it. And as you can see, he dedicated his book of poems "To my beautiful Miami Bathburn. Here's to the future."

★ Sixty-Seven ★

Dimples drew some strange pictures of ghosts as a trib-ute to Mr. Henley and, because he was a postal worker in town, the post office hung a flag at half-mast for him. And there was a memorial service in his honor at the Last Point Church down the road from us.

Auntie came home for the service and The Gram was worried about her the whole time because she seemed almost to be wearing a mask. She didn't cry at all. At least not until she and Winnie took a long walk along the shore just before the service.

After the memorial, *Oh Morocco!* was for sale in the church entranceway. The bookstore in town had stacked all the sandy-yellow books in piles and everyone bought one. Many people wanted Auntie to sign the book because of the dedication and so she did in her very flowery handwriting, though it was then that she began to cry and had to stop signing the books altogether. Some people even asked me to sign a few but I shook my head no. Even my hands and fingers were sad and I did not think they would behave properly or be able to write in a brand-new book.

We could never go anywhere after that without someone rushing up to us to tell us how "bereaved" they were for us and how much they loved Mr. Henley's beautiful book. Oh, how that would have pleased him.

Miami and The Gram both wore black after that. It was an old-fashioned tradition that The Gram adhered to. And it seemed to soothe Miami. All her skirts were black taffeta now. All the silk flowers she tucked in her hair were black or dark and somber. And while she was at home I moved back to my tower room. But one night I heard my aunt talking with The Gram. Even with the wind outside and the ocean ever constant, their voices wavered up the stairs. "No, Mother," Miami said, "I'll go back to the traveling troop. I'll continue, though I'll never be happy again. You know, it's funny, I hardly knew Juliet before. I didn't understand her words. But now I do."

"My sweet dear, I've been through it too. I lost your father. I know how you feel," said The Gram.

"But you were older. I'm still young, Mother, and I'll never be the same," Aunt Miami cried out.

★ Sixty-Eight ★

It is so very odd when someone you love dies. The pain of it seems to come and go like waves of water rolling in and rolling out. At the school picnic that next week in the park in Bottlebay, across from Babbington Elementary, we were sitting at picnic tables, laughing and talking. Soon I spotted the ragpicker way on the other side of the park. I could see his rough cheeks and his dark, bent-over body as he poked at the earth with his sharp stick. Then the pain of losing Mr. Henley came at me in a wave or as if it had drifted in on the wind. Mr. Henley had died. He was gone. And my father had died. He was gone too. Shot. Killed. Dead.

Someone passed a bowl of potato salad and said, "Did you hear about that sixteen-year-old boy who lied about his age and enlisted right before the war? He was a gunner during the bombing at Pearl Harbor and he shot down two enemy planes."

"Really?" I said. "At sixteen?"

"Yeah and then his mother wrote a letter to his captain and told him her son's true age. They sent that kid right home with an honorable discharge after that! His name was Olen English."

We all started laughing and talking about that and I forgot Mr. Henley and my father and Danny. They disappeared as if in a draft of warm picnic air and we chattered away, eating the potato salad and macaroni salad and slabs of Spam. Everything tasted salty and sweet and I felt normal and light for a moment. And then in a wave it would all come back to me. I couldn't believe it. It couldn't be true. But it was. Mr. Henley. Postman Henley. Bobby Henley had died on Valentine's Day.

After the picnic we walked by his house. A sign that read HENLEY'S HAVEN was still in his front yard. I could not believe his house could still be here and we could still be here and yet Mr. Henley was gone. Where did he go? How could he have vanished? How was that possible? There seemed no reason for his death.

I did not want to leave his house and we sat on his steps for a long time. I wouldn't leave. I couldn't leave and finally Derek pulled at me and so did Dimples. They almost dragged me away from Mr. Henley's house.

"Mr. Henley will forever be remembered in the argyles of time," said Dimples quite loudly as all three of us walked back along the downtown street in Bottlebay.

"That doesn't sound right, Dimples. Argyles are

socks," said Derek. "Socks with a pattern, like the ones The Gram knits."

"No," said Dimples. "In Selsey, by the sea, where I live with my mum, they say 'the argyles of time.'"

"I think they say the 'annals of time,' Dimples," said Derek. "Mr. Henley will be remembered forever in the annals of time. And you're right. He will be."

Dimples got very cross then. She ran off into the five-and-dime and I rushed in after her. I couldn't find her for a while and then she turned up in the paper-doll section. When I finally got her back outside, Derek had disappeared. I looked all up and down the street and then towards the harbor where the little lobster boats knocked about on their moorings.

"He's gone back to see Buttons, Buttons and Babbit again," said Dimples. "And it's good in some ways and it's bad in others."

"How do you know all that, Dimples?" I asked, looking directly at her. She decided to turn in circles and stare up at the sky instead of answering me.

"Shall we go along there as well?" I said. "I am tired of guessing and wondering about Derek." I looked over at the green lawn in front of the courthouse. There was that ragpicker again. His wide bag on his shoulder was now full. He swung round and looked at me.

Presently, Dimples and I arrived at the street entrance of Buttons, Buttons and Babbit. Then Derek came bursting forth from the doorway as if he were just rising from the bottom of a swimming pool or the depths of the ocean, his face wet with brightness and cheer.

"It's good and it's bad," whispered Dimples. "You see, that's what it is."

★ *Sixty-Nine* ★

When Derek was ready to tell me, he would tell me. There were some things I had learned this year and that was one of them. Meanwhile, it was a lovely spring on our point in Bottlebay, Maine. The birds seemed to dive and call in the most joyous way, as if the war and the losses we had taken were nothing to them, nothing to the flowers, nothing to the bees, nothing to the Mazarine blue sky. Dimples's favorite puffins were back, floating in the water with their bright, wide, orange beaks. The lilacs were in bud again.

One morning a very nice lady in a blue uniform with a red cross on her sleeve dropped off about ten boxes of strips of cotton that we were to roll into bandages. I liked the idea of helping real soldiers with their real wounds. I wanted to do it because of Mr. Henley and I started jumping up and down in my stocking feet on one of the fat, stuffed chairs in the dining room. And then suddenly I felt foolish because I was thirteen now. Perhaps it was the last time I would do that sort of thing.

The Gram called out, "Felicity Budwig Bathburn, at your age you're just as antsy as ever! I am sorry she's so 'enthusiastic,'" she said, shaking her head sadly at the woman. "Come over here now, Flissy, and get a lesson in how to roll bandages properly."

The Red Cross woman straightened her white cap and frowned at me.

Derek and I soon were wearing clean cotton gloves. We sat at the table and we rolled and we rolled and we rolled each strip of cotton and then we would fasten it with a little clip and stack it back in the box.

Derek only had to wear one glove and he got quite good at rolling up the bandages with one hand. We sat there for the whole afternoon, the sun falling through the curtains, lacy light and shadows moving slowly across the tabletop.

Towards the end of the day Derek started tossing the rolls he had finished into the box from a distance and I did it too. We got a bit more "enthusiastic," playing a sort of ball game. "Touchdown!" Derek kept shouting. We had perfect aim and a perfect record, except that once Derek tossed a roll and it hit me on the shoulder and he started laughing. We laughed and laughed. I even got the hiccups. Suddenly, Derek and I were close to each other, almost nose to nose. He looked at me longer than usual and it made my hiccups go away. I felt myself blush.

The Gram arrived from the kitchen and I quickly dropped the roll. She swooped it up, popped it in with the others, and tied up the box with twine.

Through the lace curtains I could see Dimples out on the porch, jumping up and down. She had her arms wrapped round Mr. Henley's book. "Read one aloud, Felicity," she called and then she knocked on the window. "Read me one aloud. I want to hear the music of Mr. Henley's words."

So I went out on the porch to the glider and I began to read Dimples one of Mr. Henley's poems. Dimples was now lounging in a wicker chair with her feet up on the wicker footstool and her eyes wide open and serious, listening. She had Wink sitting next to her, wearing his checked bathrobe and plush slippers that The Gram had sewn for him.

Then Derek came busting out on the porch and flopped down next to me on the porch glider. "Dimples, can you go get me the Brer Rabbit molasses? I'm going to put some of it in my milk. Bring a spoon too," he said. He set the glass down on the wicker table in front of us. "I mean, hup, two, three, four, about face. March, Dimples!"

"Derek, I'm on shore leave. Soldiers don't march when they are on shore leave," said Dimples.

"Yes, but they always obey their captain," said Derek.

"Oh, all right, then," said Dimples, stumping off to the kitchen. We could hear cupboard doors banging about and glasses clinking.

Derek looked at me again with his velveteen eyes, his silky, brown, long lashes, his heavy, dark, handsome eyebrows. Suddenly, he moved closer to me. He put his arm round me and pulled me towards him and he kissed me. It was a fierce and gloomy kiss. It was a Hurricane

Derek kiss and I closed my eyes because my head was swimming.

Then he said in a low, whispering way, "Flissy, this is the second time I have kissed you. And it's also the last time. It's a good-bye kiss." And he looked at me as if he were trying to say more but the words were lining up and refusing to leave his mouth. "And I don't mean good-bye because I am going to Government Study Camp in a few days. No, I mean another kind of good-bye. I'm not mad at you anymore. I'm glad you did what you did. You were right. I've read about first love in a lot in books. I shall always think of you as my first love and for that reason, you will always be special to me."

"Oh, Derek," I said, "I didn't know you still . . ."

"I shall always care," he said. "But I shall never say it again or tell you again because something will be different when I get back from camp."

"How will it be different?" I said, feeling a great happiness and a great sadness all at once. "What do you mean?" But he didn't say anything else. We just held hands and glided forwards and backwards and forwards and backwards, as if moving into joy and then away from it again.

Soon Dimples plunged out onto the porch. "Don't you love this picture of Brer Rabbit? He's wearing such a grand pair of trousers. For a rabbit, I mean. When the jar is all empty, I shall soak the label off and save it forever. It's lovely, don't you think, Flissy Bee Bee Bee?" Dimples said.

I sat there with Derek, feeling as if I'd just breathed in or absorbed an entire vanilla soda or a slice of yellow cake with pink icing, the sweetest thing ever tasted. And yet everything was oddly tinged with questions. What was Derek trying to tell me? Then I thought about the bandages he and I had rolled together and I wondered what soldier would receive the bandage that Derek tossed at my shoulder by mistake. Perhaps *that* bandage would bring extra luck to the poor soldier because *that* bandage had caused Derek to finally tell me that he still loved me.

★ *Seventy* ★

Yes, I knew that Derek had applied to a camp for teens interested in government service. Many of the campers would be training to be pages next year at the Senate. Pages, Derek told me, were young messengers at the state house, who ran about with notes and messages from one senator to another and to the speakers or other politicians. The camp took place during the school year and counted for school credit. You had to have good grades and great manners to get in. Derek had been accepted recently. He would be gone almost a month and would come back ready to be a page during the summer session this year.

A month wasn't very long to be away. I was sure I could manage just fine, though as soon as Derek left, I missed him terribly. Everything would be different, he said, when he got back. I thought about it and I decided I didn't want to know what he meant. But that knowing seemed to linger anyway at the edge of my mind, like the ragpicker far off on the other side of the park.

Miami had gone back to her theater too. I had said good-bye to so many people. And we were a gold-star family now. We had lost Mr. Henley and Gideon and Danny. Nothing could mend the torn feeling inside me. I walked round the Bathburn house like one of the injured.

Walking carefully because I felt weakened by the losses. There was a quiet, unspoken wall around all the remaining Bathburns. And things seemed as if they would never be the same.

I spent every afternoon playing "I Think of You" on my father's piano. It was comforting to know that my fingers were touching the same keys that his once did. At first I was hesitant and slow and clumsy but soon my fingers knew the way and the song rolled out of me like water.

When the mist is sheer
and the shadows too
When the moon is spare
I think of you.
I think of you.

One day The Gram and Winnie went into Gideon's room and opened every drawer and laid out every piece of his clothing. I walked by and saw The Gram holding one of Gideon's shirts in her arms. She was rocking back and forth, cradling it. Winnie took the shirt and laid it down on the bed, folded it carefully, and then she hugged The Gram. "He saved his heart for you, Winnie," said The Gram sadly. It was the first time I heard The Gram call my mum Winnie and not Winifred.

I was thinking of Derek. I had certainly saved my heart for him. But I began to feel and know that things for him were changing and that something that had barely begun was coming to an end.

Dimples came round skipping and singing:

"She loves him so
but he didn't stay.
The wind can't blow
this storm away."

★ Seventy-One ★

And so the war went on and on. We could often hear the army base, not far away, testing guns over the water. There were always Coast Guard members patrolling the shores with their rifles on their shoulders.

"Do you think we will be bombed soon? Stucky thinks so. His sister is very afraid," said Dimples. We were in the gymnasium. She was riding the little unicycle round the edges of the room. The unicycle belonged to Gideon. He used to stand on his head sometimes. And then he would ride that little unicycle round and round. He used to say, "Fliss, we can always join the circus, if we ever get in a pinch. You can go as a jumping bean and I'll be a clown on this contraption. What do you say?" It seemed as if I could hear his voice almost echoing in my head now.

"Don't worry, Dimples. If any bombs fall, we can run into the cellar here," I said.

Dimples dropped the little bike and tossed herself down on the large, open floor. "I do wish I were a pilot. Don't you, Felicity? I should be pleased to fly over England and nab off with every bomb in the sky. Then I would drop each one in the ocean. I wish my old mum were here, I do. I really do."

"Go on," I said, reaching in my pocket for a Life Saver from the package I had been saving since Easter. Most candy was sent overseas to the soldiers and so it was a rare Life Saver. "The war will be over soon. Would you like a sweet?"

"Oh, not half!" said Dimples, taking it. She put it in her pocket and then she rolled across the floor like a rolling pin.

Winnie came to the door of the gymnasium and smiled at us. It was a faraway, lost sort of smile and she seemed so little in the large gymnasium doorway. I got up and ran towards her. "Oh, Winnie," I said, "are you all right?" She moved into the gymnasium, limping in her slight, graceful way. She stood in the middle of the room and looked at everything as if she were noticing Gideon for the first time, even though he was gone. She stood there and her head went up and all round the room in wonder.

The next day she wanted to go to school with me to see the *Mr. Bathtub Says READ!* poster. And when she stood in front of it, with Mr. Bathtub in his bowler hat and suit sitting in the bathtub, she shook her head back and forth and then she put her arm round me and she closed her eyes.

Then it was the first of May, May Day. I always admired an old framed photograph on the wall in the library showing Victorian children in straw bonnets and boaters carrying flowers while dancing round a maypole.

Dimples and I tried to construct a maypole in the garden but it kept falling over in the wind.

And every afternoon we continued to listen to the shortwave radio station that Winnie knew about. That wireless always whistled and screamed and roared with static as we rolled the dial until we hit the right spot. Even though we were sure it was for nothing, we kept on listening and hoping, except for Dimples. She never sat with us. She was always off trying to teach Wink to fly, making him jump off the backs of chairs. A hopeless task, I could have told her. Wink had always been a land-loving, two-feet-on-the-ground kind of bear.

The station carried all sorts of entertainment and news. The Gram and Winnie and I sat very close to the shortwave at four o'clock every evening. Sometimes a British film star would come on the air, like Laurence Olivier. The more we listened and heard nothing that meant anything to us, the quieter and more anxious Winnie became.

★ Seventy-Two ★

When it happened, it was an early May evening. I had just fed Sir William Percy and her children, who were grown now and were quite demanding about their food. Dimples had just given poor Wink a full bath upstairs in the long porcelain tub, scrubbing him with Lifebuoy soap. Now she was carrying him down the hall up there, dripping wet. The Gram was just finishing the quilt she had been working on since the beginning of the war. She was sewing in the last perfect star and square. Winnie was still working on the scrapbook of photographs of children she had helped escape to England.

It was four o'clock and the sun was beginning to lengthen its long arms of light across the water. The ocean too had a faraway-afternoon stretch about it. A group of seals was seen paddling through the waves towards some rocks. And then it happened.

The announcer on the British wireless program began to speak. Winnie and The Gram and I were all in the dining room at that moment. We all sat up and listened.

"We have a rare opportunity on this late night in London to air a tape recording sent to us earlier this month, a reel-to-reel tape sent to us from deep in occupied

France. In a hidden-away château, a group of resistance fighters and freedom fighters have joined together to send a message of hope to the free world. Tonight we are going to play this tape for our listeners to hear. Picture yourself in an old, partly bombed château. The drawing room is still intact. All round you, there are murals of angels playing violins and some gold, stuffed chairs and sofas, rough and worn and battered, but still intact, like France herself. And lo and behold! There is still a piano and it may have a few gunshot holes in it but it's mostly in tune. May I now present to you 'An Evening in Occupied France.' Yes, the tape is scratchy and missing in places, but the message rings out clearly."

The announcer then began to play on the air the reel-to-reel tape that had been recorded secretly in France and smuggled out to England to be played for the whole world.

"Good evening, ladies and gentlemen of the free world," said a man with a French accent. "We are here tonight in secret and by the time you hear this we will have all moved on. But tonight we have found some old bottles of wine in the cellar and we have found some hope in our hearts." The tape was scratchy and the short-wave wireless whistled and crackled. "First of all we would like to give a round of applause to all the American and British troops, the army and the navy and the air force and the RAF! They are doing such a fine job. We are waiting here with confidence. We have no doubts." The room then exploded with cheers and clapping and the stomping of feet.

"We have a number of musicians and poets here tonight. Each one will entertain you for a moment. Ah, is that not what we all need, a moment of entertainment? Now I should like to introduce to you our first performer, Mr. Mazarine Blue on the piano."

As soon as I heard the word *Mazarine*, I knew. As soon as Winnie heard the word, her scrapbook slipped from her lap and pages of children spiraled to the floor. The Gram too heard it and jolted forward, and spools of thread and cloth stars spilled from her sewing basket. I rushed towards the shortwave radio, as if to hug it or to jump with it or to pull it into my arms or to run with it. The Gram shrieked and threw her hands over her face and started sobbing. "Tell me. Tell me it's true. Please say it. Please," she cried.

"Wait," called Winnie. "Stop. Wait. Wait. Listen, hush. Listen!"

We held our breath while Mr. Blue sat down at the piano. Then we were sure. We could tell by the way his fingers hit the keys. We could tell by the rolls and the turns and runs we knew so well. I could play that song myself now. I knew all the chords and all the changes and all the notes. Mr. Mazarine Blue began to sing:

"When the clouds roll by
and the moon drifts through
When the haze is high
I think of you.
I wink at you.

When the mist is sheer
and the shadows too
When the moon is spare
I think of you.
I wink at you."

"It's my daddy. It's Gideon. It's my daddy. He didn't die," I screamed.

"Wait a minute, just a minute. Is that how the song goes?" called Winnie. Her voice was trembling. "No, let's not speak. Wait till he's done. Hush."

"When the night birds cry
and the swallows too
When the west winds sigh
We think of you.
We wink at you."

Then the piano solo rolled in and then it rolled back out. In and out it rolled, like the sea, until the song was done and the crowd was clapping and the announcer was introducing someone else. "Wait a minute," called Winnie again. "Hush. Is that how the song goes? It sounds different, poppet. How does it go?"

"'We think of you. We wink at you' is not part of the song," I said, crying and stuttering and shaking my head.

"It's not?" said Winnie. "'We think of you' has been added? We?"

"Yes," I cried.

"Danny's alive too. Danny too! Oh, thank goodness," Winnie cried out. She stumbled to the floor.

"Do with me what you will. I shall be forever grateful. Forever and forever," The Gram said. She was crying and she fell too to her knees next to Winnie and there on the floor Winnie and The Gram threw their arms round each other and cried.

"Dimples, where is Wink?" I called out. Dimples was at the top of the stairs. She stood there with her eyes very wide and very large in her small, pale face. She looked like a tiny disappearing spirit standing there, wavering. She seemed to be trembling as she stood on the top step with Wink dripping wet in her little arms. "Wink is all starkers so he can't be seen. And I'm sorry," she shouted. She began to cry in a loud way. It echoed in the hallway. "Is everything all right?"

"Bring Wink to me. Let me have him," I called out. "He has a message for me."

"No!" shouted Dimples. "Wink doesn't have anything."

"Yes, he does, Dimples. Let me borrow him." I climbed the stairs and I took her hand. She was still crying and I held Wink by one of his ears. He was *that* wet. We went into The Gram's room and I squeezed him until water dripped from his feet. "Help me slit open his seam. Get me the scissors from The Gram's sewing table."

"No. Don't hurt him," shouted Dimples. "Don't touch him."

"Wink won't mind. It won't hurt," I said, running for the scissors myself and snipping carefully the stitching on a small part of his front seam. When the seam was opened just a little bit, I could see there was a very small strip of paper tucked inside Wink's stuffing. I pulled it out. It was a bit damp and wrinkled. It said:

Fliss and Derek,
   My love for you both is unchanging and forever. Nothing can take it away. You asked me to promise you something, Fliss, and if you've found this, I think I can do that now. Yes, I promise you, I will be coming home.
   Love,
   Your father Gideon

   P.S. I knew you'd read The Secret Garden *one more time, Fliss. A book like that should always be read once a year, no matter how old you are! And I knew Wink would be let out of his box finally too.*

A bear like that should always be kept around
even when you're all grown up.

Later as the sun began to fade, we sat on the floor, letting the pink, glowing rim of the sky burn through our windows. The ocean sang a simple repeating song outside that sounded to me now like a kind of lullaby. My daddy-uncle, Gideon, was alive and my uncle-daddy, Danny, must be too because Gideon sang, "*We* think of you. *We* wink at you." I still had two fathers and even though it was more than most people had and a bit confusing, I was very, very glad of it. And Winnie said the war would be over soon. She said as we sat there that the world was damaged but not destroyed and that it would repair and renew itself and that light was winning over darkness. We held hands that evening on the floor, watching the last of the pink sky turn orange and red and finally a dark Mazarine blue as the sky seemed to slip away behind the sea.

Seventy-Three

I wondered how it would have been to be Ella Bathburn that spring in 1866. Did she know that soon, during the summer, much of Portland would burn because of a fire-cracker thrown into an old warehouse on the Fourth of July? Did she see the flames of Portland on the horizon? Was she wearing then the little gold ring that I now had round my neck on a chain? Did Captain Bathburn's family offer to shelter some of the people who had lost their homes? The Bathburn house seemed to have so many layers and still so many secrets. And yet that seemed to be the way it would always be. We were all to live with so many unanswered questions in our lives. Questions like, where does the sky end and how many stars are in our universe and most of all, what do all the stars mean? And why are we here on this beautiful, round ball called planet Earth? And here in such a lush and green world, why do people hurt and kill one another and why is there such a thing as war?

And so it was that things changed again at the Bathburn house. It was a sunny, bright day and when I went out to feed Sir William Percy, something came to me. It happened just as she landed on the porch railing, dropping down out of the sky with such cheer. And after the idea came to me, I wrote a letter to my father.

> *Dear Daddy,*
>
> *Thank you for your beautiful promise. I can promise you something in return. I have decided that friends may borrow and love Wink but he will always live on Bathtub Point in Bottlebay, Maine.*
>
> *And in your honor I have renamed your pet seagull, who turned out to be a girl. No longer will she be called Sir William. I have finally given her a proper girl's name. We will call her Vicky for* victory.
>
> *And about* The Secret Garden, *you are absolutely right and I've broken down and I'm reading it again. Yes, it is the most wonderful book in the whole world and I promise to read it until I am a hundred years old!*
>
> *Love,*
> *Your daughter, Fliss*

Later that day, after I had tucked the letter to my father in the box under my bed, I was in the parlor playing tick-tack-toe with Dimples. She called that game noughts and crosses. Dimples was losing because she wouldn't settle down and play correctly. She just kept dancing off with Wink and I must say, because she didn't concentrate, it cost her several games and many losses. But she said she didn't give a pig's ear about that game.

It was then that I saw the solicitor Mr. Buttons at the door. I could see his black hat through the etched-glass window. There was a shadow over his eyes and the dining room darkened suddenly in spite of the sunlight falling in patterns through the lace curtains. I went to the door. "Oh," I said, "hello. Are you here to see Derek? I am afraid he is not here."

But soon enough The Gram came out of the kitchen. "Oh no, it's fine, Flissy McBee. Let Mr. Buttons in."

I backed up and sat on the first step of the staircase. "Mr. Babbit has sent you today?" said The Gram. "Give him my regards. And do come in."

Mr. Buttons had a very large briefcase. It bulged and bothered me. There were all sorts of messy, bothersome papers sticking out of the top. The Gram asked me to bring in the coffee and toast, which I did. I didn't care for the bitter smell of the herbal coffee we now served because of coffee shortages and I set the whole thing down quickly on a small table in the parlor.

Mr. Buttons was just handing The Gram some papers. The Gram looked down at them and said, "So, we now know Derek's actual birthday. He was born May 15, 1929, in Portland."

"Yes," said Mr. Buttons, "Derek and I have been working on this for quite a while. Finding his father was the hard part. The whole case broke open when we located his aunt in northern Maine. Derek visited her for a week this spring, as you know. That's when we found out that his father had died last year. His aunt has recently signed some papers and he can now be officially adopted. It's all legal."

"And so I have changed my plans," said The Gram. "I have news too. My son Gideon is alive and did not die in the war, as we had feared. I myself do not wish to adopt Derek. Gideon has wanted to do that for a long time. Derek has expressed a great need for a father and Gideon, who already loves him dearly, will make a superb one. My son is a very special and kind man," The Gram said and when she said those words, her face radiated with a great inner light. Her whole being became a candle of brightness. "My son will be so pleased. It will be a blessing to have this official, finally, the way it should be."

I felt, as I listened to all this, like a small boat on the water being tossed this way and that. And I had so many boats now tossing in my head. Derek. Derek. Derek. Suddenly, the knowing that picked at the edge of my vision became clearer. This was what he meant. I knew it, of course. I already knew. Oh no, don't say it. Don't say it's so. Oh, but I knew Derek would love having his own real birthday, May 15. How lovely. How perfect for him. He would love finally having a real father. And of course I wanted him to have a father and his own birthday because everyone else in the world had those two simple things. And when you love somebody, you want only joy for that person.

And yet in my darkest dual citizenship self, I stewed, as if I were surrounded by blackout curtains. I simmered and sank and stewed in the deep corners of my dreadful, double-sided heart. Gideon was my father and if he became Derek's father too, then I could never marry Derek. We could never then love each other in this world of reasons and rules. Because as soon as the papers were signed, Derek and I would become brother and sister.

I fought and I struggled and twisted and I turned. The two sides of me battled and pushed and cried and stamped inside me. I took a long walk along the shore. I went way down the rocky, sandy beach to where the jetty poked out into the sea and I ran out on that jetty and I sat on the very point of it, the very closest spot I could get to England. I looked off in the distance where I knew my England was still being bombed.

I sat there and cried and I cried and I cried. Even though it had been my meddling idea in the first place, I suddenly hated Buttons, Buttons and Babbit. They had reached in their briefcases and torn my hopes apart. They had blown everything away with their dark suits and their clever searching. Didn't they know that I loved and needed Derek? Didn't they understand what all this would mean to me? Now I understood why Derek had called our kiss on the porch the last kiss.

But then another part of me popped forward as it always seemed to do. How could I, who had two fathers, begrudge Derek one? Why was everything so complicated? If I loved him, did I not want his happiness? Wasn't that the reason I had gone to Buttons, Buttons and Babbit in the first place? I remembered seeing Derek sit on the top of the ridge as the Gray Moth was arrested. I remembered seeing his face, red and windblown and desolate as his father disappeared into thin air. Soon my tears changed direction as the wind turned and I cried, remembering Derek's face that day. And in the end I felt lighter as I walked back home.

Seventy-Four

From the shore as I approached it, I looked up at the Bathburn house. How durable and strong it seemed, with its gables and chimneys and its long windows and its ornate porches and its tower room. It had weathered so many storms for so many years and I felt so very glad that I was walking towards it now, glad that I was a Bathburn and even though nothing was simple, most of me was settled with the idea that Derek would now be a real Bathburn too.

Dear Derek,

Dimples now has a baby spotted turtle living in a bowl of water and sand in our room. All night we hear him scratching about. The Gram has insisted that she release him into the wild again. But so far Dimples has refused.

And have you heard from The Gram about the recent developments concerning your adoption? The Gram will not be adopting you. It will be Gideon! Perhaps it is just as you had planned. The Gram says he wants to adopt you and told her that before he left! Oh, Derek, I know you will be so

*pleased. I understand now what you meant by a
good-bye kiss.*

With happy-sad tears,
Your sis, Fliss (It rhymes!)

*P.S. Dimples just let the turtle out in the hall
and now she can't find him.*

As soon as The Gram discovered Derek's true birthday, she began to plan a party. Derek would be home
soon and on May 15 we intended to celebrate. Dimples
and I were to make the guest list. And, oh yes, I was
happy and sad. I was happy because Gideon and Danny
were safe. And happy that my Winnie was here. But I
was sad because in the strangest of ways I was losing
Derek just as I had gained him.

By chance that week, Mr. Fitzwilliam rang us up.
"Oh, him," The Gram said, putting her hands on her
hips and frowning. "I'm surprised J. Edgar Hoover himself hasn't shown up at our door, snooping around."

"I should like to invite Mr. Fitzwilliam to the birthday," said Winnie. "Because of his atrium of butterflies
and because we have been doing some negotiating."

"Negotiating?" said The Gram, her gray eyebrows
almost curving into question marks.

Winnie just rolled her eyes and smiled and didn't
answer.

"I imagine while we are at it, we should invite Big and Little Bill," said The Gram.

Dimples, who was standing quietly nearby, stared down at her shoes. She seemed rather glum in her messy, tragic way.

"And while we are on the subject of parties, little nipper, shouldn't you and I take a trip into town to Harrison's Shoe Shop? If you promise to behave and don't throw yourself on the floor and kick the way you did last time," said The Gram. Dimples looked up sheepishly. Then she tilted her head and a happy look passed across her face. "Well, what do you say? Would you like a new pair of shoes, little nipper?"

"Oh, not half!" said Dimples, breaking into a skip.

And so we planned our happy, sad birthday party. The Gram and Dimples went off in the old Packard to Bottlebay. As they drove away, we could see Dimples bouncing about in the backseat.

Winnie and I sat on the porch together after they left and we finished gluing all the photographs of all the children into Winnie's scrapbook. After the last one was set in place, I turned the pages again and looked at the little faces in black-and-white, each child staring out at the camera in a shy way. Danny had made the passports for each of them and taken the photos. Danny got most of the children to smile. He was always good at that.

"It wasn't that I didn't love you," said Winnie. "I always longed for you. These children are safe now and I am proud of that, but many, many others never made it out. And there will be many more." She brushed my hair away from my forehead. "Poppet, darling, could you do me a favor? Do you think you could start calling me Mum, even so late as it is? I so miss being called Mum. Don't call me Winnie anymore. Call me Mummy, will you?"

"Oh, Mummy," I said, "I would have waited forever for you to come home."

"You know, Flissy," she said, looking straight at me. I was rather startled. She hadn't called me Flissy before. "Danny and you and I always lived in flats, didn't we? We never had a proper home, did we? It's a bit late and you're almost all grown up but perhaps we should have a real home after all."

"Yes," I said. "Oh yes. We should. I always wanted a real house."

"I've been thinking about something," she said.

"You have?"

"Yes, I promised to make it all up to you, didn't I, darling? Well, I meant that. I have found a house nearby. It's a bit of a wreck. It needs lots of bright colors and fresh paint and new owners. But I think perhaps Danny and I would like to buy Mr. Fitzwilliam's house. After the war is over, and it will be over soon, Danny and you and I can all live there. And then you can be my child and Danny's child and Gideon's child and The Gram's child. And you can be our all-grown-up girl too. You can belong to all of us."

"Oh, Mummy," I said and I cried a little but it was a happy cry. "It would be so lovely to have a real house." And I hugged my mother and it wasn't an awkward, uncomfortable hug. It felt just right.

A little later, I said, "I wonder what will happen to all of Mr. Fitzwilliam's butterflies when he moves away?"

"Oh, he will leave those for me," said Winnie. "You know, very often intelligence agents do not receive honors or recognition for their achievements. They work in isolation and secrecy and that is the nature of it. But Mr. Fitzwilliam and the American government are giving me a room full of butterflies for my work. And *that* is enough for me."

"Speaking of butterflies," I said, "I have a gift for you too." Then I reached in my pocket and took out a very small present I had wrapped in tissue for my mother with The Gram's approval. I gave it to Winnie and she opened it slowly. Then she held it up to the light and smiled. It was the silver hairpin that The Gram had given me earlier. It had a filigree butterfly on the top and that butterfly lilted and dipped on its little silver spring when Winnie tucked it into the braided knot of her beautiful hair.

★ Seventy-Five ★

The next day, Dimples was down on the shore walking along, singing one of her made-up songs. I could tell she was singing her lonely song today and so I went down the long steps to talk to her.

"Dimples," I said, going over to a flat rock under which I had stored a few things, "about that answer to everything that you said your friend's mother told you, I want to make a trade. I have an unusual shell here never seen before in Maine that I found on this very shore. I also have a nice ghost detector."

It was a bit of a lark and I was only curious about that answer. And I am sorry to say that the shell was a conch shell brought back by The Gram years ago from Florida and the ghost detector was a three-wheeled, twisted metal sort of thing that washed up on the rocks last week. "Will you accept these in trade for your friend's answer to everything?" I said and I wheeled the rusty contraption over to Dimples.

She took a look and walked round it. "Does it work really?" she said.

"Oh yes," I said, "when you roll it about, it starts turning in circles when a ghost is nearby."

"All right, then," said Dimples. "I accept." And she took the ghost detector and pushed it off down the shore.

"Well then, what's your answer to everything, Dimples?" I called out.

Dimples danced off, pushing her ghost detector and zigzagging along in the wind. She looked then like a little ghost herself about to lift from the ground and rise to the sky. She didn't turn round and I had to chase her all the way to the jetty. When I caught up with her, she looked rather bleak and her eyes wandered away towards the clouds. "Felicity, I am sorry to say, but I don't really have an answer to everything."

"Oh, I know, Dimples, of course you don't. There is no one answer to everything. Everyone makes mistakes and must be forgiven, even mothers and fathers," I said and I felt a little tug at those words and I decided it must be a growing pain.

"Do I have to give back the ghost detector?" said Dimples.

"Oh, Dimples, I do hope we can talk your mum into letting you stay here at Bathtub Point until the war is over. It's lovely to have you here. And, yes, you can keep the ghost detector. If anyone in the world should have one, it's you, Dimples," I said.

★ *Seventy-Six* ★

It was May 12, 1943, and Derek would be home from the government studies program in a few days. I was nervous about his return. How would I behave when I saw him? I so hoped I would be generous in my love for Derek. I so hoped I would think of *him* and what he needed and not just of *me*. Perhaps that was one way my love had changed. Perhaps.

This morning Dimples and I were moving about in our dark house, getting ready to go to school. Dimples was just saying that she wanted to be a page at the state house too. "What sort of costumes do pages wear? Aren't pages training to be knights in armor? At least they are in books. Can a girl be a page at the senate?" she asked.

"I'm not sure, Dimples, but no one wears any armor, although I imagine Derek would like that, wouldn't he?" I said.

The house was dark because we had not yet drawn back the blackout curtains. Winnie was making oatmeal in the kitchen and I opened the back door, thinking I might feed Vicky some dried bread. Outside we heard the sound of church bells ringing and it was not Sunday. They were coming from the Last Point Church, the one that sat alone amongst its old gravestones on the coast road. The bells rang and rang and rang. And then when Winnie opened the curtains in the dining room and lifted the window to let the warm morning air into the house, we noticed a foghorn sounding offshore. But there was no fog. The bells pealed and the foghorn called and called and called from the water.

Winnie and Dimples and The Gram and I went out onto the porch and looked up at the cloudless sky. Someone was running down along the rocks, coming from the White Whale Inn. He waved his arms at us and called out, "The Allies have won in North Africa. The Germans surrendered there today completely. We have won in North Africa. A lot of our boys from Bottlebay were in that campaign. The tides have changed. We're going to win this war!"

Winnie and Dimples and The Gram and I went down to the edge of the water and ran along the shore, following the person who was calling out the news. "What did you say?" we shouted, the surf pounding at our voices. "What did you say? Wait for us."

"It was on the radio," the person called. "The Germans have all surrendered there. Now we'll have control of the Mediterranean Sea. We're gonna win the war."

I thought of our Mr. Henley as soon as I heard that. He had been part of the fight for North Africa. He had helped the Allies win there and I was ever so proud that I had been his friend.

Winnie threw herself down on the ground farther along the beach, where the rocks gave way to a grassy area. She lay there with her arms flat out beside her as if she had been knocked off her feet by some invisible force. The Gram sat there too in the tall grass and the May wind roared and ripped at our clothes and our hair and the blue sky opened and spread out far above us in a great, waving expanse.

Seventy-Seven

It was May 15, breezy and sunny, and it was Derek's birthday. Our birthday party was all in order. Everyone began arriving at the Bathburn house. Mr. Stephenson and Mr. Donovan drove up in their government car. Mr. Donovan rushed towards Winnie. He threw his arms round her. "By golly, the Blue Piano did it. I didn't lose a one of you. Gideon is a wonder. And so are you." He seemed quite flustered and his hat blew off but he caught it and his necktie flapped in his face. Perhaps he too loved my Winnie just a little bit. She stood there in her new pale summer dress, shading her eyes from the sun.

Dimples and I had made a banner for the parlor that said in big letters, WELCOME HOME, PAGE DEREK! HAPPY BIRTHDAY! Dimples wasn't much help with it. She was too taken with her new shoes and couldn't stop staring at them.

Finally, it was Mr. Stephenson who drove to the train station to pick Derek up. When Derek walked across the porch, back from government studies camp, he was very tall and was wearing a light summer linen jacket with a necktie. He had only been gone a month but he suddenly looked like a young man from Eton or a true page and he had two new friends with him, one of them a girl. She had long brown hair and she was wearing a plaid jumper and bobby socks. Derek said she hoped one day to be a senator for Maine. He seemed so pleased with her. Well, I supposed it was for the best.

When I first saw him with the girl from camp, it felt as if I had been stung by a terrible wasp or bumblebee, the kind that dies after they strike, the kind that leaves you crying and jumping up and down as your arm turns red and swollen. Soon you realize it's only a bee sting and that it will pass. But then you look down and see the pitiful bee that died somehow for you or because of you and that is what hurts the most.

Derek hugged me hello and I knew it was a genuine hug, that he was so pleased to see me, that he truly loved me, that he would be for me in the future a dear brother and a true friend. I realized then that I could not ever lose Derek now. You could not lose a brother. A brother was for life.

Mr. Fitzwilliam and Mr. Stephenson all crowded into the hall to say hello to Derek and his two new friends, whose names I couldn't quite hear. Of course they had names; most people do, but somehow try as I would, I missed hearing them.

Soon The Gram roped everyone into helping carry the long table down to the shore. Gideon always said The Gram was small but mighty. Now her voice carried over the waves as they crashed against the rocks. She called out the orders, "Watch out, Little Bill. Back up, there's a large rock behind you." They set the table on the ground and I laid out the long white tablecloth with the white butterflies woven into it. Those butterflies seemed to dance across the fabric in a teasing kind of way, as if they were questions that would flit and flutter and never be answered.

And then we all sat down under the sweep of blue sky. The tide was out a little and the seagulls and terns circled and called all round us. And so it was that we had a celebration and birthday party for Derek on his true, real birthday, May 15, 1943. He was shining the way we all do on that special day that marks our entrance into the world.

In fact, he glowed sitting at the outdoor table and I knew he was happy to finally have his own day and to be rid of that assigned birthday that was really mine. Derek was free of me now in that way, though I knew in another way we would never truly be free of each other. I knew I still loved him and I was sure that he still loved me in a way. But it was a Romeo and Juliet kind of love. That is, if Romeo and Juliet had decided to obey their parents and to let each other go. If they had, then they would not have died so young and they would have had long lives and children and friends and travels and parties and books and art and all the joys of life. But there would always have been a secret passageway and a small room deep in their hearts where they still loved each other, in a way. Then so it would be for Derek and me.

And as for those nights on the road or sitting in front

of the fire or on the porch glider when we kissed, those afternoons and nights and the memory of them would carry me through the last of the war years and beyond. Then one day when I was fully grown, I would meet someone at a dance or on a walk and that person would remind me of Derek. Perhaps it would be his hair or his eyes or his stance. In that way, Derek would turn up again and again for a fleeting moment in all the faces of all the people I was to love later in my life.

Now at the party we sang loudly and clearly, as if the singing would release something that had been held back during all the time we were unsure about Gideon and Danny. It was, I suppose, a birthday song for all of us. We sang that familiar, comforting tune, "Happy birthday to you. Happy birthday to you," as we sat at the table down on the shingles and sand near the water. The white tablecloth rippled in the wind. And Winnie carried the birthday cake down the long steps to the sea. And as she walked towards us, I saw that the cake was the most beautiful blue, like the sky or the water. It was a Mazarine blue, a layered, deep blue, like the butterfly Romeo blue, the color perhaps of hope itself.

In the spring and summer of 1942, the Allies were losing the war at sea. During that time, Nazi U-boats sank many tankers, cargo ships, freighters, and other vessels along our coast. In April 1942, the American government announced that all coastal areas had to use blackout curtains. The lights from cities along the horizon were revealing the location of boats at night. The blackout helped. Cargo ships began traveling in convoys for protection. There were also various Nazi spy roundups, which I believe cut down on the information being relayed to the Nazis on ship location. Sub-watching towers and Coast Guard surveillance were put in place. By 1943, we were no longer losing large numbers of ships.

Most towns along the coast in Maine were well aware of the presence of U-boats in their waters. Recently at Bailey Island in Maine, I was able to visit the sub-watching tower there and still see its ominous eye poking out through the pine trees. Many towns in Maine also have their stories about Nazi spies and U-boats. Most of these stories are hearsay and were never proven. In Maine there is only one documented account of a Nazi spy arriving by U-boat and paddling to shore in a rubber raft. Agent 146 — a top German agent — and a helper landed one night in winter in 1944 at Frenchman Bay. They were actually spotted that night by a seventeen-year-old Boy Scout who saw them on the road and figured out by studying their footsteps where they had come from. He rushed to the police, but because he was only a kid they did not believe him. Agent 146 and his helper made it to Portland where they had breakfast in a diner. Then they took a train to Boston and finally New York City. Several months later they were arrested and the Boy Scout was honored for his insight and bravery.

I was born just a few years after the war. My family lived in England for a year and I went to school there when I was eleven. I still have my school notebooks from that year. I had to write with pen and nib dipped in a pot of ink, and I learned to add and subtract and divide British pounds, shillings, pence, and half pence all the while keeping the ink from smearing!! My love of England lives with me still and it is my pleasure to revisit it with Flissy Bathburn.

Acknowledgements

An extra special thank-you to the remarkable and likable Rachel Griffiths, my editor. Behind the scenes she orchestrates, coaxes, inspires, advises, cheers, and yes, demands (in the best sort of way)! We are most certainly a team and her editing has been crucial. Thank you also to Arthur Levine, both brilliant and supportive, and to all the adorable, charming, warm, and caring people at Scholastic. I went to meet the whole of Scholastic last spring and I think everyone there gave me a hug and there wasn't a one who didn't care deeply about children and reading. They are an amazing group! Many, many thanks to Nikki Mutch, Becky Amsel, Lizette Serrano, Sue Flynn, Kelly Ashton, John Mason, Candace Greene, Whitney Stellar, Whitney Lyle, Bess Braswell, Jana Haussmann, and Anne Marie Wong. Thank you to my kindly friends Yvette Feig and Bob Murray, who bravely read an early and rough manuscript, typos and all, and to Marian Campbell for helping to spark my imagination about the coast of Maine during World War II. Thank you to Linda Smith who lit up my path at the end with her encouragement. Thank you to my mother, Ruth Stone. Three days before she died I sat on her bed and read the first half of this book aloud to her. The second half had not been written yet. We had a lovely day together. She was always my best listener and reader, and I will miss her forever. Thank you finally to my husband and dearest friend, David. Not only did he read this book early on, he also, on a daily basis, keeps me from walking into walls and getting run over in Boston, among other things!